Advance Praise for *Heart of Lies*

"A deeply compelling and extraordinary debut novel. It has everything you want: suspense, adventure, and romance across several continents."

—Dorothea Benton Frank, *New York Times* bestselling author of *Return to Sullivans Island*

"*Heart of Lies* takes the reader on a thrill ride that spans continents and decades, but at heart it's an enduring love story."

—Melanie Benjamin, author of *Alice I Have Been*

"A sweeping saga reminiscent of Jeffrey Archer and Susan Howatch, *Heart of Lies* is brilliantly researched and beautifully written. I could not put this book down."

—Karen White, *New York Times* bestselling author of *The Girl on Legare Street*

Lauren Nguyen

ABOUT THE AUTHOR

M. L. MALCOLM is a Harvard Law graduate, journalist, recovering attorney, and public speaker. She has won several awards for her writing, including recognition in the Lorian Hemingway International Short Story Competition, and a silver medal from *ForeWord* magazine for Historical Fiction Book of the Year. She has lived in Florida, Boston, Washington, D.C., France, New York, and Atlanta, and currently resides in Los Angeles. Her Web site is www.MLMalcolm.com.

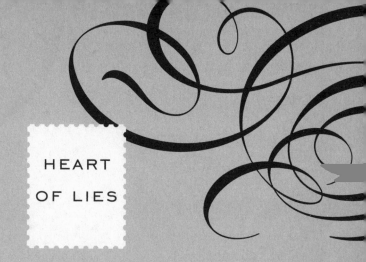

HEART
OF LIES

HEART
OF LIES

M.L.
MALCOLM

Previously published as *Silent Lies*

HARPER

NEW YORK · LONDON · TORONTO · SYDNEY

HARPER

A hardcover edition of this book was previously published in 2005 by Longstreet Press, and in paperback in 2008 by A Good Read Publishing, under the title *Silent Lies*.

FIRST HARPER PAPERBACK PUBLISHED 2010.

Designed by Justin Dodd

Library of Congress Cataloging-in-Publication data is available upon request.

ISBN 978-0-06-196218-9 (2010)

10 11 12 13 14   ov/rrd   10 9 8 7 6 5 4 3 2 1

For John, my counselor in perplexity and the love of my life

ACKNOWLEDGMENTS

To Tom and Vickie Warner, the owners of Litchfield Books in Pawleys Island, South Carolina, for serving as my literary fairy godparents and getting *Heart of Lies* into the hands of the amazing Carl Lennertz at HarperCollins; to Carl for believing in my books; to my wonderful agent, Helen Zimmerman, who held my hand every step of the way and made everything so easy; and to my editor at Harper, Wendy Lee, for her many insightful suggestions.

To my wonderful in-laws, Daniel and Marian Malcolm, to whom I eternally and joyfully owe an enormous, unpayable debt of gratitude; and to my two children, Andy and Amanda, who often put up with a busy and distracted mother as I worked to bring my "third baby" into the world.

To my mother, Lea Wolfe, who always told me I could accomplish anything I wanted to do; and most of all, to my husband John, who made me believe it.

Heartfelt thanks to all of you.

HEART

OF LIES

PROLOGUE
BUDAPEST, 1919

He had not spoken to Julia since the day he ended their affair. Now he watched as her dark eyes scanned the hotel lobby, and he had the odd feeling that she was looking for him. Why would she want to see him, now, after nearly three years?

The war had been kinder to her than to most; she was smartly dressed, wrapped in sable, and didn't have the gaunt look of someone who'd been waiting in line for food. That didn't surprise him. Countess Julia Katiana Podmaniczky was the type of woman who got what she wanted: one of her many desires had been the surrender of his virginity when he was barely sixteen. Of course the Countess would find a way to thrive during the war.

She caught his eye and approached his desk. He stood and came around it to greet her. Only then did he notice the lines around her eyes and the shadows under her neck, all conspiring to betray her loveliness.

"Good evening, Leo," she said, with that familiar, mocking smile. "Are you surprised to see me?"

He took her hand and bowed over it, pressing his lips to her slim fingers. "No, Countess, not surprised. Enchanted."

Her smile was replaced by one of genuine pleasure, and then, just as swiftly, by a look of apprehension. "Leo, we must find a place to talk. Immediately."

"Certainly." He could not be rude. She and his foster mother, Erzsebet, were close friends, although he was sure that his endearingly naïve guardian was unaware of Julia's penchant for illicit sexual adventure. He could not explain to Erzsebet that he did not find it necessary to be polite to his seductress. Escorting the Countess by the arm, Leo led her across the lobby to an office he knew would be vacant at this time of the evening.

Julia waited until they were both seated before she spoke again, and Leo could tell by the look on her face that something truly horrendous was behind her unexpected visit.

"Leo, you must not go back to the villa tonight. Something terrible has happened, and it's too late to do anything except save yourself."

"What are you talking about?"

"Erzsebet and József have been shot."

"What?" He was standing now, towering over her, his blazing blue eyes demanding a retraction.

"Leo, I wish I could say that it were not true—" Julia's voice rose in astonishment as he lifted her by her shoulders, out of the chair and off the ground.

"When? Are they alive?"

"Put me down," Julia demanded, keeping her voice low. If someone heard them and came in, if he created a scene, they could both be lost.

He looked at her as if he did not realize that he held her dangling in the air. Then he lowered her back down and took a deep breath, trying to regain his composure.

"Are they alive?" he repeated, his voice a toneless staccato.

Julia shook her head.

"Who did it?"

"Counterrevolutionary forces," Julia spat out, her voice drenched in sarcasm. "Our 'secret' police. The men who are allegedly protecting us from the Rumanians." Then her tone softened.

"Leo, I'm sorry. I came as soon as I found out. My husband has connections. Sometimes we find out about these things more quickly than others would. I had to be the one to tell you because . . ." She faltered, and reached up to touch his tormented face. "I want to protect you, if I can, from the same fate."

He shoved her hand away. "Protect me? Why didn't you protect Erzsebet? If you have these *connections*, why didn't you use them to protect your friend?"

"Because I couldn't. Your brilliant József was a communist. Erzsebet was a collaborator, whether she realized it or not. She was too delighted playing hostess to members of parliament to care about what politics it involved. She didn't know that her dinner parties were her death warrant. I tried to warn her. I'm sure you did, too. But Erzsebet was always too willing to believe what she wanted to believe. And she believed in József."

Leo looked away. Julia was right. Hungary had been mired in political and economic mayhem since the Emperor abdicated his throne at the end of the war. Erzsebet Derkovits and her brother, József, had used their influence and what was left of their family fortune to help form a communist government out of the chaos, but Leo did not get involved;

in fact, he'd deliberately absented himself from the house whenever meetings took place there. He was not a political person, he said; he felt lucky to have survived two years on the Italian front, and to have found a job as a concierge in a posh hotel when most of the population was starving.

He and Erzsebet should have fled months ago, when the Rumanians invaded and the communist government collapsed. He should have made her leave.

But József would not hear of it. "Only cowards flee," he'd said. So they stayed, and now József and Erzsebet had paid the price.

Leo pictured Erzsebet as she had looked this morning, sitting happily at her desk as she made her list of errands for the day. His rage ebbed away. She'd loved him the way his own mother never had. His heart felt like an anvil in his chest.

Julia sensed that his anger was dissipating. "Leo, the villa is being watched. In a few days it will be confiscated as government property, the forfeited property of traitors. If you go back you'll be implicated. There's nothing you can do now. Nothing except save yourself."

He looked at her dully, not wanting to think about self-preservation, not wanting to accept his loss. She went on.

"If you need money—"

"No, thank you. I'm entitled to rooms at the hotel. Where are . . . what have they done with the bodies?"

"I don't know," Julia lied coolly. She would not let him risk his life for the sake of visiting a corpse. There was one more thing she had to say.

"Leo, does anyone here at the hotel know that you're Jewish? Hoffman is not necessarily a Jewish name."

He seemed surprised by the question. "Jewish? I don't really know. I don't suppose so. I've never had any reason to mention it. Why? What does that matter now?"

"I hope you'll understand why I'm telling you this. You must not, under any circumstances, tell anyone that you're Jewish."

The anger returned to his eyes. "Why? What are you saying?"

"You don't understand the extent to which these men are motivated by jealousy, by bigotry, by hatred. József and Erzsebet were not killed just because they were communists. They were killed because they were Jews. In all this madness, there's a chance no one important will make a connection between you and the Derkovits family."

"So I'm to hide my heritage to stay alive, is that it?"

"Is it so wrong to try and stay alive when you're being persecuted without a reason?"

"What about honor?"

"Honor? Honor won't warm your gravestone, Leo. I know how much Erzsebet loved you, how much you've meant to her ever since the day that József brought you home from that pit of a village where you were born. You owe it to her to stay alive."

"I owed it to her to keep her from dying."

There was nothing more that Julia could say. He would heed her advice, or not. After a silent moment she made a move to leave, pausing only to murmur, "Leo, darling, if you need anything, please—"

She watched as a range of emotions flickered across his handsome face: grief, outrage, and, perhaps, a touch of gratitude. Then he was once again all business, holding his hand out to her as if she were a departing hotel guest. "Thank you for having the courage to tell me this. Thank you for the warning."

Ignoring his proffered handshake, Julia moved a step closer and closed her hand around his wrist. "You won't go back to the villa?"

He shook his head. She breathed a sigh of relief and let go of him. That, at least, was something. Pulling her wrap tightly around her shoulders, she left the office without another word.

Weeks later Leo walked by the magnificent villa on Andrassy Avenue that had been his home for seven years. A brass plate on the door declared it the future offices of the Ministry of the Treasury. So this was another joke that life had played on him; he'd escaped the dismal world of his childhood, only to have a life full of promise depleted of every source of hope. He'd survived the war, only to lose the two people who meant the most to him. He was not yet twenty years old.

ONE
BUDAPEST, 1925

It was said that in Vienna one could spend hours in a coffee house and no one would notice, but that in Budapest, you could live there, and no one would notice. By the time he was twenty-five, Leo Hoffman's regular table at his favorite coffee house was the closest thing he had to a home.

He first came to the New York Café with Erzsebet, when he was twelve years old and still new to the city: awed by electricity, terrified of riding the subway, and overwhelmed by the ornate majesty of the many magnificent buildings constantly under construction as the newly minted, wealthy Hungarian *bourgeoisie* worked to turn Budapest into an architectural marvel that would rival the other capitals of Europe. But none of these modern wonders had impressed Leo more than the gilded columns, crystal chandeliers, flashing mirrors, and flawlessly poised waiters of the New York.

Erzsebet had adored the New York, and Leo was delighted whenever she invited him to accompany her there, mostly because the café was such a wonderful place to watch, and to listen. It was the perfect place for conversation, inspiration, and infatuation. Old lovers went there for the express purpose of publically ignoring each other, while at any given moment a dozen new love affairs began to bloom. Arguments in innumerable accents would roll through the expansive room, thicker than the heavy cigarette smoke, as art, politics, and popular fashion were all rigorously critiqued. Discussions begun before lunch merged and mutated throughout the early evening, until the affluent exited and those for whom the coffee house was the night's entertainment reclaimed their usual tables; then everyone who could afford it returned for a late night supper and a hearty serving of gossip. It was true that there were many, many coffee houses in Budapest (Erzsebet frequently and needlessly explained) but there was only one New York.

When Leo finally returned, a year after Erzsebet's death, the Grande Dame of Budapest had become an aged, impoverished widow. The linens were worn, the china chipped, the floor in need of repairs. Gone was the vivacity that once filled the air with a charismatic sense of hope; the city's optimism lay buried in the trenches with the bones of a million men.

He'd been surprised that the head waiter showed him to one of the best tables, close to the front windows with a full view of the formerly elegant room. Perhaps he remembered Leo from the days when he'd show up with Erzsebet for a pre-theater dinner, or perhaps the old man was just pleased to have someone reasonably well-dressed and youthful to show off to anyone passing by, hoping that the sight would remind potential customers of what the New York had once been and entice them to come in, if for no other reason than to share a drink and a memory.

Since then Leo found time to stop by almost every evening. On this night, as he walked in, a familiar figure waved him over.

"Leo, wonderful to see you again. Please join me," said Janos Bacso, president of the Magyar Commercial Bank. Leo had met Bacso while courting the man's daughter two years earlier. He'd expected Maya's father to object, given that the wealthy banker knew nothing about Leo's background, about which Leo shared only vague details, not all of them accurate. But the war had changed everything, so much so that a self-made man like Bacso now put more stock in potential than in pedigree when evaluating a prospective son-in-law. He'd seemed comfortable with the match.

But Leo ultimately stopped short of proposing, even though it would have meant a change of career from hotel concierge to bank officer. A door had closed inside him that Maya could not open. Although he was tempted, he vowed that he would not dishonor her by entering into a marriage based primarily on ambition.

When he heard that Maya was engaged to a young bank officer, Leo reintroduced himself to her father at a regular, late-night card game at the New York. Aloof at first, Bacso's affability returned after Leo discreetly let him win a significant amount of money. Leo considered it a good investment.

"I don't usually see you here this early," he said as he took the chair Bacso offered him. "Are you meeting someone?"

"After a while. Back at my house."

Leo had to smile; for Bacso to describe his home as a "house" was quite an understatement. The man had purchased the city home of an aristocrat bankrupted by the war, for a fraction of what it was worth. Leo wondered how Bacso had managed to hang on to his money.

Probably diverted it overseas before the real fighting started.

"Well I'm lucky to have caught you, then," Leo commented as he signaled for the waiter.

"Actually, this might be a lucky break for me, running into you like this. Our fourth cancelled."

"Oh?"

"I'm going to be playing bridge with a couple of visitors this evening. Any chance you could join us? Nothing formal. We'll be wagering, but the stakes won't be higher than our usual game. Do you think you could get free?"

"Are you sure you want to inflict me on people who actually know how to play?"

"No false modesty, Leo. You'll hold your own quite well."

"I'm flattered you think so. What time should I be there?"

"Around ten."

"I suppose that's possible."

"Excellent. You remember the address?"

"Of course."

Bacso reached for his wallet, but Leo motioned for him to stop. "Allow me," he said. "After such a generous invitation, the least I can do is treat you to a coffee."

"Thank you." Bacso stood up. "So, we'll be expecting you."

Leo arrived at precisely ten o'clock. As the butler showed him into the foyer, he was struck again by how very different Bacso's mansion was from the flamboyant and colorful Beaux-Arts villas of Andrassy Avenue, where he'd lived with Erzsebet and József. These dark stone walls spoke of wealth: old, immense wealth, wealth far removed from its origin and the merit of its masters. The place was luxurious but mirthless. Even the paintings in the entry hall were somber; Leo faced a grave Madonna and child, a gloomy Dutch landscape, and a bloody battle scene featuring the heroic St. Stephen, founder of the kingdom of Hungary, ruthlessly beating back some invading horde nine hundred years ago.

The butler returned to show him into the library. Bacso and two other men whom Leo did not recognize all stood as he entered the room.

"So glad you could make it, Leo. Please come in and meet my other guests. James Mitchell, Leo Hoffman."

Bacso was speaking English; Leo assumed that Mitchell was British. When Leo first started at the Hotel Bristol, English had not been his best language. Now he was head concierge, and five years of contact with a constant influx of well-to-do British visitors, none of whom seemed willing to venture out of their native tongue, had greatly improved his fluency.

"The pleasure is mine, I assure you," he said as he shook hands with the white-haired gentleman. The man laughed, not a pleasant sound.

"If your card game is as good as your English, the pleasure will be mine. You sound exactly like a Brit."

Leo realized at once that Mitchell was an American. The other man, whom Bacso introduced as Lajos Graetz, was clearly not. Leo was struck by the firmness of his grip, and his crisp, military bearing. His hair was the only part of him that seemed to be wearing out as he aged. A soldier, no doubt: most likely a former officer in the Emperor's army.

Mitchell and Graetz could not have been more different, thought Leo. The former was overfed and a bit coarse, the latter a study in the manners of a bygone era. A very odd pairing.

Neither Graetz nor Bacso spoke English well, but it seemed that they all spoke passable German, so they settled on that as the language of the evening. As Mitchell had implied, Leo was to be the American's partner, to help smooth over any translation problems. *So that explains the sudden invitation.* Few people in Budapest spoke passable English.

"So, Mr. Mitchell, where are you from?" asked Leo as they took their seats at the card table.

"Shanghai."

"I beg your pardon. Shanghai is in China, is it not? Your accent sounds very American for someone born in China."

"I wasn't born there. I'm most recently from there. From the American Concession, now known as part of the International Settlement."

"And what brought you there?"

Mitchell sat back in his chair, obviously embarking on a favorite topic of conversation. "If you knew anything about Shanghai, you wouldn't have asked that question. No one goes to Shanghai if he has anywhere else to go. You'd ask, instead, how I managed to leave."

"Would you care to explain?" Leo inquired, as Bacso began to deal the cards.

"Shanghai is a great port city. It's also the only place in the world one can enter without a passport or a visa, no questions asked, and set up shop, whether you're a con artist, gun runner, opium dealer, or disgraced industrialist."

"Surely there are some legitimate business enterprises?"

"Well, yes. A lot of factories. Buckets of money to be made in the China trade. Entrepreneurs import goods to the teeming yellow millions and export Chinese goods to the rest of the world. But the law-abiding types have lost out on the most lucrative import, that being the opium that comes from India. It's been declared illegal to bring it into China. Which makes it all the more profitable, of course."

"I see. And in which category do you place yourself? Robber baron? Opium dealer? Entrepreneur?"

Mitchell tilted his head back and poured a glass of champagne down his throat. "Capitalist, Mr. Hoffman, venture capitalist. I venture where there is money to be made. I made plenty in Shanghai. I hope to have a few years left to make a little more in Hungary."

"And I hope to help you make a little for us tonight," Leo remarked, raising his glass to his partner. The cold December wind howled against the windows. The play began.

They were at least an hour into the game, with Leo and Mitchell well ahead, when Graetz commented, "So, Mr. Hoffman, Janos tells me that you have a gift for languages."

"He's too kind."

"There's no need for humility. Five languages fluently, is that correct?"

"At the moment, yes."

"At the moment, you say. How long does it take you to learn a new language?"

"Not long."

"Extraordinary. And do you translate?"

"Do you mean written, or simultaneous verbal translation?"

"Either."

"I'm afraid my verbal skills exceed my ability to reproduce languages on paper."

"Meaning?"

"I'm proficient at verbal translation, much slower at written transcription."

"So it's the ear you were born with."

"Yes, as you put it, 'the ear' is what I was born with." Leo had the awkward sensation that he was being put through his paces. He looked at Bacso, whose face revealed nothing. He was concentrating on his cards.

Graetz did not stop. "To be able to learn a new language so quickly, now that is a valuable talent. There are many opportunities for a man of your ability."

"There weren't after the war."

"But it's been five years. Things are improving. We're back in the League of Nations. The currency has stabilized. You're wasting your time working in a hotel."

"I have no complaints. It's a good enough job, and I'll have the opportunity to move into upper-level management eventually."

"Come come, Mr. Hoffman. Is that all the ambition you have? To be the manager of a hotel?"

No one had played a card in several minutes. Leo was beginning to feel like a mouse caught in a trap when Bacso finally joined the conversation.

"Leo, you're here on my recommendation. I know you to be an intelligent young man and a loyal Hungarian, who served our country honorably in the Great War."

"Honorably maybe, but not voluntarily."

Bacso made a dismissive gesture. "No Hungarian fought voluntarily. But the Hapsburgs have drawn us into war for the last time. The last conflict finally freed us from our Austrian yoke, and it's time for us to take advantage of our freedom. At the moment our country is weak, but we can make it strong again. We'd like to offer you an opportunity, a business opportunity, to help us do so."

"Are we discussing patriotism or capitalism?"

"Both," said Mitchell, chortling. Bacso shot him a curt look before continuing.

"You are familiar, I'm sure, with the terms of the Treaty of Trianon?"

"No more so than the average person."

"You must know the cursed pact cost Hungary seventy percent of her territory, and limited our country's armed forces to thirty-five thousand men," Graetz interjected, his thin face quivering with agitation.

"That much I did know."

"Which leaves us unable to defend ourselves in the event we face another threat from Rumania or Yugoslavia," Bacso explained.

"But do we face such a threat?" Leo's question, innocently posed, set off a chain reaction around the table.

"Always."

"The French will not rest until they see us under Serbian rule."

"The Rumanians are salivating over the agricultural capacity of our heartland."

"Do you really think you can rely on that asinine League of Nations to protect you?"

"The point is this," Bacso said at last, "readiness is the best deterrent. The resources we need are the new, automatic weapons being developed in the United States and Soviet Russia. There are, of course, strict controls on the shipments of such armaments. But there is the possibility—I can tell you no more—the possibility that our soldiers could obtain a supply of these advanced weapons through, shall we say, unofficial channels."

Leo looked back at him, puzzled. "What does this have to do with me? Shouldn't this be done through the government?"

Graetz leapt in again. "That's just the problem. The government is powerless to act. We must rely on private individuals to accomplish what our hamstrung politicians cannot."

"I have no interest in becoming an arms dealer." Leo rose from the table. Bacso reached out and grasped his arm.

"What have you done lately of which you've been proud, Leo?" the older man asked. "Arranged a picnic? Hired a driver? Do you not think that the gift God gave you should be used for a nobler purpose? Does the future of your country mean nothing to you?"

The words stung. Leo sat back down.

"What would you expect me to do?"

The other men exchanged glances. Graetz answered. "Simply this. We will have a meeting, very soon, of the people who could, in theory, supply the weapons, those who could, conceivably, transport them, and the men who are willing to pay for them. They come from different countries, including Switzerland, Soviet Russia, Germany, and America. Having you at that meeting will enable us to communicate effectively. Of course, you'll be sworn to secrecy."

"So you need me to translate? That's all? Surely there's someone else who can do this."

"No one with your proficiency. Without you we would have to have several interpreters present. The more people who know about this, the more dangerous it becomes for all of us."

"But couldn't you merely agree to speak the same language, as we've been doing all evening?"

Again, the men exchanged glances. This time it was Bacso who spoke.

"You see, Leo, we need you to do more than just be at the meeting. We need for you to eavesdrop, telephonically, on the other participants, after the actual meeting, to make sure that we aren't being betrayed."

"Telephonically? Is that really possible?"

Graetz nodded. "The technology exists."

"And," Mitchell added, "You'll be very, very well compensated for your services. In fact, if you perform well in this capacity, it could lead to great things for you. Yes indeed, great things."

Leo thought for a moment. Was it such a terrible crime to disobey unjust laws that had been forced down Hungarian throats? If they were caught, they'd go to jail. But wasn't his current life a prison of sorts, anyway? Five years ago he'd abandoned the idea that he could use his talents to create a dazzling life, and settled instead for the limited satisfaction he could achieve by mastering the details of an unimportant one. He spent his days fulfilling the shallow whims of the wealthy. Maybe it was time to take a chance on something. He felt a flash of excitement, a feeling he'd not had in a long time. It felt good.

And Bacso's words had touched his pride. He'd told these men the truth; he picked up new languages very quickly. But in fact his ability to make sense of new sounds and turn them into words was just one aspect of his talent. Leo paid attention not only to the words a man used, but also to the motion of his hands, the posture of his body, and the way he held his eyes. He was captivated by the smallest nuance of expression. He might look in the mirror and still see a boy raised in a stable, but the people around him did not. His methods of imitation were so subtle—a stance, a gesture, a slight inflection of speech—that he was able to make people feel comfortable, without them noticing that their comfort was grounded in the seductive power of familiarity. Perhaps it was time to exhibit his skills on a wider stage.

"Where is the meeting to be held?"

Bacso smiled. "Ah, there, you are in luck. We're to meet in four days, in Paris. Our affairs should take no more than three or four days. You can take a long holiday and stay in Paris for Christmas."

TWO
PARIS

The Orient Express arrived precisely on schedule, early in the morning on the 18th of December. It had been ten years since Leo had traveled in such luxury, and he'd missed it. He missed being the object of another's solicitous attentions, of eating a meal cooked to perfection, of having his bed linens readied by a careful hand. And now he was in Paris: to be able to spend a few days in Paris was worth risking a little time in jail.

None of the other participants in the negotiations were traveling on the same train. They were to meet tomorrow morning, in a suite at the Ritz, on the Place Vendôme, where Bacso and the people with whom they would be negotiating were staying. Bacso instructed Leo to check into a small but perfectly acceptable hotel on the Rue de Rivoli, near the Louvre. They were to register under assumed names, except for Bacso. The banker explained that although he'd never before stayed at the Ritz, he was so frequently in Paris on business that an alias would be ineffective; indeed, rather than protect him, use of a false name could prove needlessly embarrassing.

After a leisurely lunch in a café bordering the Jardin des Tuileries, Leo walked up Rue Castiglione in search of the Ritz; he wanted to make sure he knew exactly how to get there the next day. The shops along the way displayed luxuries of every conceivable description, from furs worthy of a Czarina, to jewels capable of tempting the crowned heads of Europe, to antiques worth more than most men would make in a lifetime.

At the Place Vendôme he confirmed the location of the Ritz and then headed north again, where the street name changed to Rue de la Paix. Destination: the Paris Opera. Leo wanted to compare this building with the elaborate opera house on Andrassy Avenue. He found the Paris house impressive, but dull by Hungarian standards. Too few flourishes, not enough gilt.

Leaving the Place de l'Opera behind him, Leo once again headed west, determined to get at least a glimpse of the famous restaurant, Maxim's. Many of his well-traveled clientele at the Bristol maintained that people-watching at Maxim's provided better entertainment than any performance hall. On his way toward Rue Royal he passed by the Olympia music hall, world-renowned for its spectacular entertainment. The sight of it made him think of Erzsebet, telling him in her entertainingly silly way about a show she and József had once seen there. She always got the name of the performer wrong. He walked quickly past the theater.

The street broke into another wide-open space, and Leo stopped short. He was gazing at an enormous Greek temple. A bronze plaque informed him that it was in fact the Church of Mary Magdalene. The classic refinement of the building created an oasis of perfect harmony amid the pandemonium of cosmopolitan Paris.

At the edge of the square, across from the church itself, Leo spotted a lively café and went to investigate. Upon entering, he was struck by how similar the interior of this establishment was to that of the New York in its prime. Tall, gilt-edged mirrors covered the walls. Angels and nymphs created a Belle Époque pageant along the edge of the ceiling, the center of which was covered with a mural depicting an idyllic day in a rural Roman paradise. Ornate wrought iron chairs partnered dainty marble-topped tables. At the front of the shop was a small counter displaying the delicacies of the day.

Leo chose a seat near the huge front window and ordered a hot chocolate. At four-thirty the winter sun was already fading. Matrons passed by with long, crusty baguettes tucked under their arms, making their way home to prepare the evening meal. Businessmen walked in pairs, their long black coats flapping behind them, buried deep in conversation about currency trades and the price of sugar beets. Children pranced along in cheerful clusters, full of plans for Christmas.

Leo liked Paris. He liked the fervent, free rhythms of the city. *This is what Budapest should have been, what it could have become, if our side had not lost the war.*

A young woman approached the window. Leo sat up straight. He caught her eye briefly but she immediately, modestly, looked away.

Leo was used to seeing beautiful women, and he was used to having beautiful women look back at him, but the sight of this particular young woman sent little pulses of pleasurable excitement radiating through his whole body. Like a good tourist, she was reading the menu posted outside before coming in. Leo was fumbling for pocket change, to pay his bill quickly in case he had to follow her down the street in order to meet her, when she passed through the café's double glass door. She moved with unconscious grace over to the front counter and studied the temptations spread out under the glass.

Leo left his table and walked toward the counter until he stood just behind her. Her head barely cleared his chin. Amber-gold hair peeked out from under her cloche hat and curled against the base of her neck. He fought an impulse to kiss her right where the escaped ringlets rested.

The young woman sensed someone close behind her. Without turning she pointed to a plate of small, golden, rectangular tea cakes, which Leo had already learned were named in honor of the church that adorned the square in front of the café.

"What are these?" she asked politely. The words were French, but the accent was distinctly German. As she finished her sentence she looked back over her left shoulder to catch Leo's response, and jumped slightly when she saw he was not a waiter.

"Those are called 'Madeleines.' Very tasty," Leo answered in French. "Would you care for one? Just come this way."

She smiled. It was a smile that began gradually, like the morning sun peeking over the horizon. By the time its full brilliance hit Leo he was mesmerized. Grasping her hand as if he were escorting her to the dance floor, he led her back to his table.

"But you've already finished your chocolate," she said with dismay as Leo pulled out a chair for her to sit down.

"Oh, no, I haven't finished anything. Won't you please join me?"

She hesitated. Sensing her unease, Leo came around to stand behind her and placed his hands on her delicate shoulders. He bent down and whispered to her, his mouth nearly touching her ear. "Please, won't you join me?"

She sat down.

Leo took the seat across from her, trying not to stare. Her face was truly, splendidly heart-shaped. Her emerald green eyes, greener than spring, were punctuated with flecks of gold. Her amber hair glowed.

He extended his hand across the small table. "Leo Hoffman."

"Martha. Martha Levy," she replied, touching his hand for a fraction of a second.

He noticed the green guidebook she put down on the table as she removed her gloves. "So, are you visiting Paris for the first time?"

"Yes." Her German accent once again betrayed her origins.

"What do you like best so far?"

"The people."

Leo laughed. "That's unusual. The French don't have a good reputation for making visitors feel welcome."

"Aren't you French?"

"No, I'm Hungarian."

"Hungarian? But you speak with no accent."

"No, I speak French with a French accent, as opposed to a Hungarian one. And you are German, correct?"

"Is it that obvious? Don't answer that."

"So where are you from in Germany?"

"Munich."

"And what brought you to Paris?"

"I'm here for a short vacation. I've been going to the university in Munich, but next semester I want to take some time off from school to work for a while. I thought I should come to see Paris now, before I find a job, because otherwise it might be a long time before I can travel. I'm sorry, I really am prattling on."

"No, it's perfect. I want to know. I want to know everything about you. Do you have any brothers and sisters? How many pairs of shoes do you own? Do you take sugar in your coffee? What's your favorite color? How long are you staying in Paris? Are you here with your family?"

Now it was Martha's turn to laugh. "Do you always interrogate your new acquaintances this way?" she asked, randomly flipping through the guidebook to give her fingers something to do. She heard herself talking, but it was like listening to someone else, someone far away, whose voice did not matter. How could this happen? What was there about meeting this man that instantly reduced the eighteen years of her life to a meaningless period of waiting, of waiting for this moment, the moment when she came alive?

"Oh, look," she said, attempting to steer the conversation to safe ground. "Here's a description of the beautiful church across the street. The Madeleine. Why, that's the same—"

"—Name as the little tea cakes. I assure you it's not a coincidence. Shall we order some?"

"If you wish." She put her nose back in the book and began to read aloud.

"A magnificent example of neoclassical architecture, the Church of Mary Magdalene was begun in 1812 by the Emperor Napoleon as a monument to the victories of his Grand Army. After Napoleon was overthrown, the building was consecrated as a church."

She looked up. "Ironic, isn't it, how war and arrogance can give birth to such beauty?"

For the first time in his life, Leo gazed into the face of an attractive woman without seeing a reflection of how she saw him, or a suggestion of what she wanted him to be. He saw only Martha, exuding a blend of confidence and innocence that struck him as the perfect expression of femininity. He thought suddenly of the Rigo Jancsi torte, the irresistible confection served at Budapest's most elegant bakeries. The famous pastry had been inspired by the true story of a Belgian princess who'd run off with a gypsy violinist, leaving her husband, family, and fortune behind without a word of explanation. Now that story made sense. What the French called the *coup de foudre*: the lightning bolt. Something more than love at first sight. Surely she felt it, too. She had to. He saw the flush on her cheeks and the way she looked at him while trying not to look at him. She was his. She was his already. He knew it.

He asked her question after question. She was staying with an old school friend of her father's, and his wife, in their apartment on the Rue de Babylon. She had an older sister who went to graduate school in Graz, in Austria, and would remain at school over the winter break, to study for her comprehensive exams. Her father was a professor. Martha planned to be back in Munich in time for Christmas.

"Perhaps we should go?" he proposed, as she finished her last sip of coffee.

"Of course," she stammered, deliberately misunderstanding him, "I should go."

Wordlessly Leo stood up, came around the small table, and pulled Martha's chair out for her. She rose quickly, accepting his help with her coat, preparing to bolt. She had to flee, to run back out into the street, to escape this man with his astonishing blue eyes and his hypnotic smile.

"Well, it was a pleasure meeting you," she said lightly. "Thank you for the coffee. If you're ever in Munich—"

But she could not finish. He was looking at her with those eyes. She instructed her feet to back away, but her body would not listen.

"Surely you're not going to abandon me so abruptly?"

She could not speak. Leo touched the tip of her nose with his finger. "What time are you expected back this evening?"

Martha found her voice. "For dinner. Around eight."

"Excellent. I don't have to give you up for three hours. Have you been to the Champs-Élysées yet?"

She shook her head. "I thought I would go tomorrow."

"Might I accompany you now? I don't believe it's very far from here. There we'll be able to admire another one of Napoleon's monuments to himself, and perhaps I can even persuade you to let me treat you to an apéritif."

"That sounds delightful." Everything about him was delightful, Martha thought as they left the café: from the carefree way a few of his black curls had escaped their pomade prison, to the poised confidence of his long stride. When he took her arm she fought the urge to reach up and touch his face. Touching him would be her undoing. She hid her free hand in her coat pocket.

"How long are you in Paris?" she asked.

"Just a few days. I have to be back at work the day after Christmas."

"In Budapest?"

"Yes, indeed, mademoiselle. You are looking at the head concierge of the Hotel Bristol, the most elegant establishment on the Corso."

"Corso?"

"The most fashionable street in the city. It runs along the Danube."

"Sounds beautiful. I would love to see it someday."

"I would love to show it to you."

She blushed. This sudden intimacy was not . . . normal. But then what was normal? For her to feel out of place and restless? In her mind's eye Martha saw a picture of herself, standing in the center of a stage, surrounded by all the people she knew in Munich. Everyone was prepared for the curtain to rise. Everyone knew their cues and their lines. But she did not. She was in the wrong play. Was that normal?

Leo stopped short and looked down at her. "Don't worry," he said. "I feel the same way." Martha did not ask him to explain.

They strolled leisurely down to the Place de la Concord and then up the grandest boulevard in the city, stopping periodically to admire an interesting architectural detail, to comment on the luxurious goods laid out in the brightly lit store windows, or to make a quip about a patron in one of the many cafés lining the street. When they reached the Arc de Triomphe at the end of the avenue, Martha pulled out her guidebook and added to Leo's knowledge of that famous landmark, then they settled into a small bistro for a snack and a pre-dinner cocktail.

"To you, Martha Levy, and the fates that brought us together today," Leo said as he raised his glass. She laughed. *I could spend my life listening to her laugh,* he thought. *Maybe I'll be able to do just that.*

"So tell me more about yourself," she said after taking a sip of her drink. "I think the inquisition has been a little one-sided so far."

"Ask me anything."

"Well, does your family come from Budapest?"

He pondered all the imprecise answers he usually gave that question, and thought at first that he would resort to one again, but then found himself telling her the truth. "No. I was born in a very insignificant village not far from what used to the Austrian border. My father was the blacksmith on the local baron's estate. When I was twelve, a student from the university came to start a small school. I impressed him and he brought me to Budapest, where I lived with him and his sister until . . . until after the war."

"And your parents just let you go?"

He shrugged. "I was a very different sort of child, and my parents made it very clear that being different was dangerous. In fact I've sometimes wondered if I was actually my father's son. Good God, I've never mentioned that to anyone."

She reached for his hand and gave it a quick squeeze. "I know what it's like to be different. My father and my sister are so very . . . German."

He smiled at her. "And you're not?"

"Not like them." She glanced at her watch. "Oh, no! I didn't realize it was so late. I have to leave now to get back by eight."

"May I escort you?"

"I don't think so. The family I'm staying with would be a bit surprised to see me return accompanied by a man. But, thank you."

"When will I see you again?"

"Do you want to?"

"Do you have any doubt about that?"

She looked down at the table. "No," she whispered.

"Good." He came around the table and pulled back her chair, but when she stood up he did not move away. She turned to face him. They gazed at each other, the strength of their desire enveloping them like a shared baptism. Then his hands were cupping both of her cheeks, tilting her face upward as he brought his lips closer to hers.

Leo wanted to devour her then and there, but they were surrounded by far too many amused French eyes pretending not to watch them. All he could do was briefly touch her lips with his own.

"Can you meet me at the Madeleine tomorrow? Around five o'clock?" he asked, still just inches from her face.

"Nothing could keep me away."

He fell asleep thinking of Martha, hoping he would dream about her, but the war came back to him that night. He was huddled at the bottom of a frozen trench, surrounded by faces that were no longer human, their features distorted by the ravages of toxic gas. Other men scuttled like rats among the dead bodies of their own comrades-at-arms, risking execution for the chance they might find something of value they could use to obtain cigarettes or extra rations on the black market. And he saw again the real rats, fat and defiant, waiting for men to die, or brazenly feasting on men not yet dead, no longer afraid of their screams.

He awoke bathed in sweat despite the cold December air. Gradually, the cacophonous symphony of an urban morning replaced the sound of mortar fire. He blinked. He was lost. Then he remembered. He was in Paris. He'd met Martha. And today he'd finally have a chance to impress some very important men. It was shaping up to be the best day he'd had in a very, very long time.

At eleven o'clock he entered the modest front door of the grandest hotel in Paris. He could not remember the last time he'd felt so full of purpose.

Leo was not the first to arrive. Janos Bacso was already engaged in conversation with a man whom Leo did not recognize.

The newcomer was short. His face was round, his mouth thin, and his eyes slightly almond-shaped. He had black hair and a dark olive complexion. His badly cut suit was made from a fabric with a loud stripe that might have looked decent on someone taller, but looked comical on him as he sat with casual arrogance in an armchair made for a finer class of person. At first Leo thought he was a gypsy, but immediately disregarded that possibility. Janos Bacso would never do business with a gypsy.

Bacso made the introductions. "Allow me to present Imre Károly, the chief of police of Budapest. He'll be participating in our meeting tomorrow evening." Károly rose from his seat. Leo automatically extended his arm to shake the man's hand, then resisted the urge to wipe his own hand off on his pants. He'd never seen Károly, but he'd certainly heard of him. Few people in Budapest had not. He was one of Gyula Gombos' chief henchmen. Gombos was the head of Hungary's small but noisy Fascist party. Although the Fascists had not garnered much popular support among the Hungarian voters, through sheer ruthlessness and the maximization of their few political connections they'd managed to place some people, like Károly, in positions of power. Leo wondered why Bacso was involved with this man.

It was not the first time that he'd been forced to be gracious to an avowed anti-Semite. His post as concierge required that he ignore the political opinions of the hotel guests, but this was testing the limit. On the other hand, he couldn't back out just because he didn't like the company. There might be valid security reasons for including the chief of police. He would have to wait and see how the game played itself out.

Soon five men were in the room: Leo, Bacso, Graetz, Mitchell, and Károly. Despite his burning curiosity about how to accomplish his electronic surveillance, Leo didn't feel comfortable broaching the issue when everyone else seemed content to make small talk. Graetz and Károly debated the relative merits of two types of machine guns. Mitchell told several bawdy tales about what services one could buy from a Chinese whore in a seedy quarter of Shanghai known as Hong-kew. After forty-five minutes Bacso dismissed the group, reminding them that the time and place for tomorrow's all-important negotiations would be communicated via a message delivered to their respective hotels. He asked Leo and Károly to stay for a few moments, to discuss "logistics."

"Leo," Bacso began, "each of us is going to spend the day preparing for certain aspects of tomorrow's meeting. Imre is here as our electronics expert. He has valuable experience in this area, and will assist you in learning how to use the telephone wiretaps we will be utilizing. I'll leave you two alone to get acquainted."

So that's it, thought Leo. *He's the espionage expert. Must come in handy in his business.*

"So how about some lunch before we get to work?" Károly offered, proceeding to pinch his bottom lip between his thumb and forefinger in an absent-minded gesture Leo found particularly repugnant. This was going to be a long day after all; at least until he could escape and meet Martha.

They decided to eat in a restaurant overlooking the Place de la Concorde. After relieving them of their overcoats, a disenchanted waiter led them to a poorly positioned table. Károly sat down and immediately ordered cocktails for them both. Some of the hostility Leo was feeling toward the offensive little man must have spilled out from under his normally composed demeanor, for Károly gave him a suspicious look.

"Do you have something on your mind?" he asked.

Leo came up with an excuse for his scowl. "Just reacting to the look that waiter gave us, a special face I'm sure he reserves for his old war buddies. As if they could have beaten the Kaiser and the Emperor without the Americans to haul their constipated little asses out of trouble." He threw a dirty look in the direction of the perfectly innocuous waiter, who, somewhat startled at the depth of animosity he saw in Leo's face, immediately approached the maître d'hôtel about assigning Leo and his companion to another server.

Evidently placated by this response, Károly looked around to confirm that no one was within earshot. "Listen, Leo," he began, looking around once more. "That brings me to something I want to discuss with you. I have a bit of personal business to attend to while I'm here in Paris. I'd like to buy a present for a lady friend."

A carnivorous grin replaced the scheming look he'd worn the moment before. "She's a sweet one. I'd tell you who she is, but she belongs to someone who would take my nuts home in a little glass jar and feed them to his cat if he found out I even knew what his girlfriend's tits look like. So, until I can arrange to have him eliminated from the competition, I need to be uncharacteristically discreet. The problem is, I want to get her something that will knock her right off her little high-class ass."

"So, are you looking for suggestions?" Leo asked, hoping to avoid a lengthy description of exactly what services this man expected to get in exchange for his token of affection. He then signaled for the waiter to replenish their drinks. He'd need a bit more liquid fortification to make it through this lunch. *In less than four hours I'll see Martha again.* That thought cheered him up considerably.

"Christ, no," Károly was saying, "I know what I want. I saw it yesterday. Trouble is these goddamn French bastards. I could tell from the moment I walked into the store that no one was taking me seriously. So I thought, 'They'll listen to the sound of my money.' But then I said to myself, 'To hell with it. Why should I give them the satisfaction after they pissed on me?' Besides, it's better if I don't buy the thing myself. Even though we're in Paris, I do have a certain notoriety. Besides which, I'm a married man, and this present is not going to end up around the neck of the current Mrs. Károly."

"Are you saying that you want me to buy a certain necklace for you?" Leo asked, relieved to be at what seemed like the end of a long and distasteful tale.

"Exactly. I like that in a man. Get right to the point. Look, Bacso tells me you speak French as well as a damn French poodle, and you have the look, the carriage, whatever the hell you want to call it. I've seen you in action at the Bristol. You'll have those little French pricks kissing your ass the moment you walk in the door."

Leo was too disgusted to be flattered. "Where do you need me to go?"

"Cartier."

It took a supreme amount of self-control for Leo not to spit out his drink. What kind of money did this man make? And for what? Extortion? Murder for hire? No wonder he felt out of place walking into one of the most prestigious jewelry houses on the whole continent. Leo stifled a laugh as he imagined the faces on the distinguished Cartier salespeople when the police chief sauntered in. Károly must have looked like a pig in church.

"Why Cartier?" he asked with a smile, hoping the real subject of his mirth remained hidden.

"Because this," replied Károly, stabbing his finger into the air too close to Leo's face, "is a Cartier-quality cunt. Do this favor for me. You won't regret it. We'll have plenty of time to play with the telephonic toys this afternoon, or tomorrow, even."

"Look," said Leo, trying to find a way out, "I'm not sure that we should be taking care of personal business at a time like this, and I have another appointment at five—"

He stopped talking. Károly's cold stare made clear that his hesitancy was not appreciated. *That's all he needed, to offend the chief of police. Damn. What could it hurt?* Tucking his doubts into a dark, quiet corner of his conscience, Leo agreed to make the purchase after lunch.

It was a short walk back to the Place Vendôme and the Cartier showroom at No. 13, Rue de la Paix. A block before they reached it, Károly pulled Leo aside and handed him a long rectangular wallet. "There should be enough cash in here to pay for the thing. It's a sort of diamond collar, in the center display case, straight ahead of you as you walk in the door. I'll meet you back at your hotel at three o'clock. You're at the Hotel du Louvre, right?"

"Wouldn't you rather just wait here? I could just hand it to you."

Károly shook his head. "I want to inventory the equipment we'll be using. And I trust you, on account of you'll never get out of Paris alive with the money or the necklace if you try anything stupid."

What a way to win friends. Leo slipped the fat wallet into the breast pocket of his suit and the two men parted. Well, now he was in it: may as well finish the nasty business. As concierge at the Bristol he'd brokered many purchases for wealthy guests, some of which he knew were not destined for lawful spouses. His commissions on these purchases paid for his few luxuries, such as the elegantly tailored suit he wore today. But he'd met few people as distasteful as Imre Károly.

He walked the short distance to the twin marble columns that adorned the entrance to Cartier's and rang the buzzer that signaled a request to enter. An answering buzzer advised him that the door was now unlocked. He entered the oak-paneled splendor of the showroom and removed his hat. A guard to the inside right of the doorway gave him a stoic greeting.

Leo walked straight to the velvet-lined display case in the center of the room. The attractive sales associate standing behind it favored him with a smile that was anything but stoic.

"Good afternoon, sir. May we show you something special this afternoon?"

Leo smiled at her as he removed his hat. "You already have." The woman blushed.

He looked down into the display case. There it was: a truly spectacular necklace fashioned out of emerald-cut diamonds, each one at least four carats. Three rows of them were set end to end, side by side, in barely visible bezels of pure platinum. The stones seized and dissected the light, glimmering with unspeakable brilliance.

The necklace was displayed on a small, truncated sculpture of white marble, resembling a woman's neck and shoulders. Leo understood why Károly was so taken with this piece. It formed a tight collar, reaching high around the neck. The wearer would possess the diamonds, and yet be possessed by them. Men, seeing that necklace around the neck of a beautiful woman, would instantly wish to see her wearing just the diamonds, and nothing else. He would love to see it on Martha.

He indicated his interest with a small nod of his head. "This also intrigues me."

"Of course, sir. One moment, please."

In a few moments a middle-aged gentleman emerged from the doorway that led to the private office where important clients were invited to examine prospective purchases at their leisure. "Bonjour, Monsieur," he greeted Leo, in a crisp but amiable manner. "Henri Xavier at your service. And whom do I have the pleasure of addressing?"

"Jean Pierre Printemps," Leo answered, using the French equivalent of "John Smith."

Xavier took the name for what it was: a request for privacy. "Marie-Therese informs me that you are interested in examining one of our latest pieces, the diamond collar. A most extraordinary piece, as you can see, made of flawless, five-carat emerald-cut stones. It signals a complete break from the Art Nouveau style, reflecting Monsieur Cartier's expanding interest in geometric forms. Unfortunately, Monsieur Cartier is in London at the moment, but I shall be happy to retrieve it for you." With a few deft moves he unlocked the display case and removed the necklace, then placed it in a box lined with black silk velvet.

With a slight bow Xavier invited his client to his private office, where Leo settled comfortably into a low-backed chair. Xavier displayed the necklace in front of him. The diamonds sparkled like liquid fire.

"Some champagne, sir?"

"No, thank you. A loupe, if you please."

Xavier removed a jeweler's loupe from his pocket and handed it to Leo. "They are all colorless, and perfect."

Leo gave him a look of polite dismissal, clearly communicating, "*That, I will have to judge for myself.*" He had only a general idea of what to look for *in* a diamond, but he knew precisely how one should look when looking *at* a diamond. After a few moments of seemingly careful study, he handed the loupe back to Xavier. Both he and Xavier seemed satisfied.

"Beautiful. And the price?"

"Fifty thousand francs."

Leo steeled himself against any reaction. Was he carrying that kind of money?

"I'll take it."

"Ah, an excellent choice, Monsieur Printemps. Will you carry it with you, or shall I have it sent?"

"I'll take it with me."

"And, the financial arrangements?"

Leo reached into his breast pocket and pulled out the wallet Károly had given him. He opened it. It contained a stunning quantity of crisp 1,000 franc notes. He began to count them. He reached fifty. To his amazement, there were still several left. Leo nonchalantly redeposited them into the wallet and tucked it back into his breast pocket.

"Merci, monsieur," said Louis Xavier as he handed Leo a velvet box containing the necklace. "I hope that it gives the wearer enormous pleasure."

Leo could not resist. "So do I," he said in a deadpan manner as he collected his hat and coat. "It's for my mother." He allowed himself a small smile at the startled look on Xavier's face.

Back on the street, he tried to decide what to do. It was now just past two-thirty. He would never have agreed to be the guardian of the necklace had he known its value, not when the owner was someone like Imre Károly. Now he understood the significance of Károly's warning.

Seeing a potential pickpocket on every corner, Leo nervously made his way back to his hotel. He was a bit concerned that Károly was not already in the lobby when he walked in. After waiting a few moments he approached the young man behind the front desk.

"Good afternoon. Are there any messages for room 415?"

"Just a moment, please, I'll check your box." He returned with two envelopes, one embossed with the crest of the Ritz, the other plain, white, and inexpensive.

Leo stepped away from the desk and opened the plain one. Scrawled in a sloppy hand was a message from Károly. He read the short note:

Leo,
Hope it went well. Seems we have some extra time on our hands. Put my present in the hotel safe. I'll come by tomor-row morning at nine.

Imre Károly

What was going on? He tore open the second envelope. It was an equally cryptic message from Bacso:

Dear Leo,
Some complications have arisen. Our meeting is to be post-poned by one day. Wait for contact from Károly.

Janos

Now what? Leo was becoming increasingly suspicious. Something had gone awry, and he was not a party to the details. Well, he was just a peon, albeit a valuable one. Still, the whole situation smelled sour, and Imre Károly's stench was the foulest of them all. Leo realized that he did not know how to get in touch with anyone other than Janos Bacso at the Ritz. Surely Janos would enlighten him. No, his note clearly said to wait to be contacted by Károly. Well, at least he would get rid of the necklace.

He took a step toward the desk then stopped himself. How could he hand over an item of such tremendous value to the desk clerk at a second-rate hotel? He knew how easily a small bribe could open the safe of an unscrupulous establishment. Well, what of it? Károly had told him to put the necklace there. It would serve him right if the thing were stolen. But no, if the hotel clerk couldn't come up with that necklace tomorrow, he, Leo, would be a dead man, no matter what the story of its disappearance.

Another idea sprang into his head. He could put the necklace in the safe at the Ritz. The Ritz was a hotel used to safekeeping important jewelry, and the concierge would give him a receipt. Then he could just walk over with Károly tomorrow and retrieve it. The police chief might be angry at first, but he would certainly calm down once the necklace was safely in his hands.

Leo congratulated himself on his plan. With the necklace safely stored at the Ritz, he could enjoy his evening in Paris with Martha. Then tomorrow he would see what was going on with the rest of this business, and decline to participate if he found anything not to his liking.

An hour later he was once again headed away from the Place Vendôme, with the Ritz and the necklace behind him. Tucked into his shoe, to frustrate the notorious Parisian pickpockets, was a receipt for one diamond necklace, valued at fifty thousand francs. Leo had given Janos' room number (plus a generous tip out of his own pocket) to the junior concierge and asked the young man to deposit the necklace in the hotel safe. He assured Leo that, as a guest of the hotel, no one else would be able to collect the necklace, and that even he must present the receipt to do so. The concierge might somehow discover that Leo was not who he'd claimed to be, but he would have no reason keep Leo from retrieving the necklace.

Feeling confident that he'd put his troubles of the moment behind him, Leo sauntered back up the Rue de la Paix and headed toward the Madeleine. He was almost an hour early, but had no desire to go anywhere else.

Martha was already there waiting for him.

"How wonderful to see you again," he said as he approached.

"No sneaking up behind me this time?"

"I will scale the walls from whatever direction necessary, in order to conquer the pathway to your heart."

"My goodness. Do all Hungarians talk that way?"

"Only when properly inspired."

"So why don't I know of any great Hungarian poets?"

"Probably because they all write in Hungarian."

"That would make sense."

"Nothing about love makes sense."

"Oh? Have you been in love so often?"

"Only once. I fell in love with a beautiful German girl I met in a café. Yesterday."

She blushed, but did not respond. Leo took her hand, kissed her gloved fingertips, and then put his arm through hers. "Where to, mademoiselle?"

She was about to say, "It doesn't matter, as long as you are holding my arm," but she wasn't sure she could carry it off with Leo's casual sincerity, and didn't want to sound flippant.

"Have you been to Notre Dame?" she asked instead.

"Not yet. Is that where you'd like to go?"

"If you don't mind."

"It doesn't matter where we go, as long as I'm with you."

"I was just . . . I was just thinking the same thing."

He smiled down at her. "Good."

They meandered down the grand thoroughfares of Paris, neither really interested in anything but each other. At last they came to the cathedral of Notre Dame. When they entered it Martha looked up at the soaring vaulted ceiling and gasped.

"Think of it," she whispered, just loudly enough for him to hear her, "the wonder of this place, all those hundreds of years ago. How could you walk in here and then doubt the existence of God?"

Leo did not answer. The events of the past seven years had taken their toll on his faith, but even before the war he'd felt the religion of his childhood slip away; from the very first day he'd moved into the Derkovits' modern household, where there were no visits to the synagogue, no prayers said, and no Hebrew spoken: a place where one's wealth and the wealth of one's friends was openly discussed, but God was never a topic of conversation.

"It's more like a tribute to the creative ability of mankind, I think," he finally said.

"Maybe."

When they emerged it was almost dark. Martha stopped outside the elaborate doorway and looked up at him. "I can't just go home to Munich thinking that I will never see you again."

His gaze locked onto hers. "You'll see me again."

Martha felt her mouth go dry, and another part of her become inexplicably damp. She must have him. She could not lose him. "I told the couple I'm staying with that I would be spending the night with a girlfriend tonight," she said, "a friend from Munich who has family here." It was a lie, but she had to be with him. She had a key. There was always the chance that her hosts would not wait up for her. If they did, well, she'd face the consequences tomorrow.

Leo's eyes widened. To hell with the tourists, priests, and pigeons watching them. He had to kiss her, now. This was Paris, after all.

As he bent over her she tiptoed up to meet his lips. Then his arms were around her and she relaxed into him, opening her mouth slightly and letting out a delicate sound that was half sigh, half moan. Their embrace felt painfully brief, and left them both aching with the taste of unquenched passion.

"Are you sure?" he asked her. She nodded, too overwhelmed by their kiss to speak. He put one arm around her shoulders and pulled her close to him as they began to walk across the square in front of the cathedral. *Where could they go?* His hotel room was out of the question; he did not want to risk running into any of the men he was with. He thought of the thousand-franc notes still in his pocket. The price of the necklace had just gone up by one thousand francs. After all, he'd rendered Károly a service; he was entitled to a commission. If that cretin challenged him, Leo would explain that the extra thousand was a special luxury tax. He could not think of consequences beyond this moment, beyond his tremendous need to be with Martha, *now.*

A welcoming fire flickered in the lobby of the small, elegant hotel where Leo signed them in under a false name as Mr. and Mrs. Hoffman, swearing to himself that he would make the title genuine as quickly as possible. The matron working the desk listened sympathetically to Leo's sad tale of luggage lost by an idiotic porter who stupidly loaded their bags onto the wrong train.

"And on your honeymoon, too," she clucked, carefully making change for the large note Leo had given her and then handing him a key.

"How did you know it was our honeymoon?" Leo asked, genuinely taken aback.

"*Chéri*, if it is not, it should be. In all my years behind this desk, I have learned to recognize love. You two are positively glowing with it."

Given the education he'd received during his brief affair with the hedonistic Countess Podmaniczky, there was little that Leo did not know about the mechanics of physical intimacy; but nothing about that relationship or his subsequent, less complicated experiences with women had prepared him for the rapture of making love to a woman with whom he was in love. Martha's passionate eagerness, even given the pain she felt initially, both fueled his desire and filled him with incredible tenderness.

Consummation, he thought hours later as she lay lightly sleeping, their bodies intertwined. *In any language, this is exactly what the word "consummation" is supposed to mean.*

Leo awoke before Martha, and marveled again at the exquisite curves of her body. Then he ran his fingers lightly down her back to waken her. Her stunning green eyes opened, and she smiled.

"Hello, Mrs. Hoffman."

"Mrs. Hoffman? Is that a proposal?"

Leo laughed, a warm, rippling sound, full of contentment. "Martha, I adore you. Will you marry me?"

"Leo, you're speaking German."

"Do you have an objection to being proposed to in your native language?"

"Darling, you could propose to me in Swahili and I would still say yes."

"Do you speak Swahili?"

She giggled. "Wouldn't you be surprised if I said yes? But, sadly, no. I am limited to the more practical European tongues of German, French, and a little English."

"Excellent. Then in which language shall I ask, 'Are you hungry?' "

Martha extricated her limbs from Leo's with exaggerated slowness. This completed, she arranged their bedraggled bed sheets around her primly and replied, "I am indeed, very hungry, in any language, and will permit you to escort me to dinner."

"With pleasure, my treasure. Luckily we're near the Latin Quarter and ten o'clock is still a perfectly acceptable time to go searching for a meal."

They dressed like playful children, snatching each other's clothes and chasing each other around the room. Leo had trouble getting Martha to stifle her laughter long enough to make a quiet exit from the hotel under the knowing eyes of the patroness behind the desk.

Hand in hand, they strolled across the bridge connecting the Isle de la Cité with the famous Left Bank, the River Seine glistening beneath them like liquid silk. Once in the Latin Quarter they took their time exploring the narrow streets, tempted by the jazz in this restaurant, the smell of potatoes frying in that one, and finally settling on a small café that offered "rabbits stewed until midnight."

"What if the rabbit can't stay awake that long?" Martha asked with affected innocence as they took their seats.

"My tender-hearted one, worry a little less about *le pauvre lapin* and a little more about what wine you'd like to drink," Leo suggested, tapping her lightly on the hand with the wine list.

"No violence, if you please, honorable sir, or I shall reconsider my response to your proposal."

He turned serious. "Martha, please don't say that. Don't even tease me about that."

The expression on Leo's face made Martha regret her glib comment. She picked up his hand, brought it to her lips, tenderly kissed his knuckles, then nestled his palm against her cheek. After a moment he withdrew his hand and brushed a strand of hair away from her face.

"When can we get married?"

"Well, I suppose you ought to meet my father."

"Then I'll come home with you."

"Now?"

"In a few days."

"Now that's what I call a special souvenir from Paris."

"If you like, I'll tattoo a tiny Eiffel tower on my chest. Just a small one, though."

"Will we live in Budapest when we get married?"

"We can live wherever you like."

"That's rather daring."

"I'm feeling rather daring right now. Here comes the rabbit stew. *Bon appétit.*"

They ate in silence for a few moments, each contemplating the enormity of the change that had just swept through their lives.

"All because I went to investigate a plate of Madeleines," murmured Martha.

"I have news for you, my dear. I was prepared to chase you down the street if necessary. I could tell through the window that you were the one for me."

"Really?"

"Absolutely. Must have had something to do with the way you wrinkled up your nose when you were reading the menu. Much like what you're doing right now."

"Hmm. Now it's the cheese tray I am considering."

"The glorious cheeses of France. I tell you, we Hungarians eat well, very well, but I believe the French have superior cheese."

"And wine."

Leo adopted a wounded look. "That could only be said by a person who does not know Hungarian wine. We can rectify that. Why, with the exception of champagne—"

"Isn't that the exception that swallows the rule?"

"Now that you mention it, that's the one thing this evening is lacking. Waiter? Champagne, please. The best you have."

Glasses filled, Leo raised his to Martha. "My darling, this is the best I can give you now, but I promise better things in the future. No, don't interrupt. I promise to love, honor, and cherish you, and to create a wonderful life for you. Just believe in me."

She tapped her glass against his. "I do believe in you."

Leo watched two thin, parallel lines of bubbles dance from the bottom of his glass to the surface. He had so much to tell Martha, so much to share with her, so many things he wanted to do for her. He would need a lifetime.

Hours later the morning burst upon them, cold and clear, for in their haste to get back to bed they had forgotten to close the heavy interior curtains in their room. They made love one more time before rising, with the slow rhythm of lovers willing to explore each other without reservation.

This time they dressed wordlessly, communing in the shared privacy of their last moments together before they faced the outside world.

"May I bring you back to where you're staying?" Leo asked as they left the hotel.

"No, I think not. But when will I see you again?"

Leo pondered this for a moment. He didn't know what his day would be like, or how much time his activities would take.

"Martha, I'm desperately sorry to say that I have another business meeting. It concerns a new career opportunity for me. I'm sure, though, that I can get free by tonight. Can you meet me at five o'clock at Angeline's?"

"Of course." She tried not to pout. Five o'clock seemed like several lifetimes away.

They walked to the taxi stand in the square across from the Notre Dame cathedral, where he kissed her, and kissed her again, unable to make himself let go. She finally pushed him away and jumped into a taxi, blowing him kisses as the driver sped away.

He watched until the cab lost itself in the mass of early morning traffic, then started back to his own hotel. *Damn*. He'd forgotten to ask her if there was a telephone number he could use to call her. No matter. Nothing could keep him from being at Angeline's this afternoon.

He was passing a newsstand on the corner of Rue de Rivoli when a headline caught his eye. Leo fished in his pocket for a franc and tossed the coin to the proprietor, snatching up a copy of *Le Monde* and folding it under his arm without waiting for his change. He stumbled into the closest café, ordered an espresso, and opened the paper. In bold letters he saw spread across the front page:

FRAUD AT THE HAGUE
HUNGARIAN OFFICER CAUGHT
PASSING FALSE FRANCS

A Hungarian army officer, Ion Kovacs, was arrested yesterday after attempting to cash a counterfeit 1,000 franc note at the central bank of The Hague. The clerk who accepted it noticed subtle differences between the counterfeit note and the other, genuine notes in his currency stack as he closed out his drawer a few moments later. The astute clerk notified the guards immediately, and they were able to intercept Kovacs before he left the building.

The quality of the forgery has given rise to fears that this scheme is being perpetrated on an international scale. Police in Belgium, France, England, Liechtenstein, and Switzerland are already cooperating in an intensive investigation. Merchants and money changers accepting French francs are warned to verify the authenticity of all large bills. Any discrepancy should be immediately reported to the police.

Leo dropped the paper. How could he have been so stupid? Now he knew where Károly had obtained his money: from a printing press.

He checked his watch. It was not quite eight o'clock. Cartier's would not open for another two hours, but they might already know they'd been duped. Were they looking for him already?

Panic rose like bile in his throat. He could give the necklace back. He could explain. He would turn Károly in. No, the French distrusted the entire Hungarian nation. They would thank him for his information, call him a liar, and he would still go to jail for a very long time.

His disoriented brain tried to think of other alternatives. He could try to negotiate a deal with Károly. He would give the bastard the necklace in exchange for his own freedom. Now his life mattered. His continued existence was no longer a cosmic joke. He had found Martha.

Martha. He had no way of getting in touch with her. He would have to find somewhere to hide until five o'clock. Good God, were Janos and the others in on this scheme, too? Had he been the patsy from the outset?

He threw some change on the table to pay for his untouched coffee and went back into the street, pulling his hat low over his forehead. There was no reason for anyone at the hotel to connect him with Jean Pierre Printemps. Unless, of course, a physical description of him was already being circulated to the public. He would have to risk that much.

Within a few minutes he was back at his hotel, relieved to see that the police chief was not already waiting for him in the lobby. He needed time to collect his thoughts, to come up with a plan. Ignoring the elevator he sprinted up the four flights of stairs to his room, his adrenaline pumping full force.

Leo burst into the room and sat down on the small single bed, head in his hands. *Now think. Think about how to save yourself.*

Károly's voice interrupted the silence. "Well, you little Jewish bastard, where have you been all night?"

Leo stood and turned to face Károly, who was stepping out from behind the door, which Leo had not even bothered to close. Károly did so now, and locked it. It was then that Leo noticed the gun in his hand.

Károly came closer, until he was standing just on the opposite side of the bed from Leo. His face wore the sneer of a coward in complete possession of unearned power.

"So, tried my lovely necklace on the neck of a little French whore, did you? You'd better answer me, pretty little Jew boy. It isn't in the hotel safe. Where is it?"

"You set me up."

"So you've heard the news. Well, we managed to change thousands of francs before Kovacs got himself caught. Of course I set you up, you cocksucking fool. You executed the biggest single trade we accomplished.

"Imagine Janos Bacso's surprise when I showed up yesterday and told him that his brilliant interpreter, the man who was nearly his son-in-law, is in reality a vile, untrustworthy Jew. You can see how embarrassing it was for him to have recruited *your* assistance in the purchase of arms for our organization. Luckily I brought a suitable re-placement.

"Janos was only too pleased to allow me to persuade you to help us in other ways. The cash we're raising, the guns we're buying, they're not going to aid the spineless military who allowed the dogs of Europe to rape our country. We're fortifying the future rulers of Hungary, the men who have the strength of will to reclaim the Empire."

Gombos. It all made sense now. Appalling sense. Károly and Bacso were working for Gyula Gombos, head of the Hungarian Fascist party. They wanted weapons to take by force what they could not achieve through democratic means: complete control of Hungary.

Károly's expression shifted from triumphant to threatening. "Where's the necklace?"

Leo felt the receipt for the necklace burning a hole into his foot. "It's not here."

"You expect me to believe that? Take off your coat and toss it to me. Slowly."

Leo did as he was told.

"Now your jacket." Again, Leo complied.

"Now turn your pockets inside out." Without pointing the gun away from Leo's chest, Károly spread Leo's clothes on the bed and searched them with one hand. He found nothing but the wallet he'd given to Leo, Leo's wallet, and Leo's passport. He tossed the clothes onto the floor.

Leo could tell that the man was losing control. *Good. Get angry. An angry man doesn't think clearly.* He must goad Károly into making a mistake.

"You can't just shoot me here in broad daylight."

"You're wrong about that, you stupid shit. Bystanders don't react that quickly. By the time anyone realizes a shot has been fired, I'll be gone. In fact, I'll enjoy shooting you. I'll get nearly as much pleasure out of shooting you as I did out of putting a bullet in the mouth of that brainless communist bitch you lived with on Andrassy."

Erzsebet. The villa. It was now the property of the Ministry of the Treasury. A horrifying numbness overcame Leo as the full implication of Károly's words hit him.

Then the reaction set in.

Black rage poured out from behind the closed door in his soul, filling his muscles with violent power. He stood motionless, poised to kill. He knew how to kill a man with his bare hands. The war had taught him that much.

Károly was still talking. "Tell me where the necklace is, or I'll start breaking pieces of you off until I find it, starting with your well-used testicles."

"It's in a safe place," Leo muttered through clenched teeth. As he spoke he shifted his gaze a fraction, almost imperceptibly, down toward the bed and then back to Károly's. *Look away, bastard. Look away for just one second*

Erzsebet's killer stepped into the trap. Keeping the gun pointed at Leo, he leaned over and tried to pull up the side of the mattress with one hand.

Using the bed as a springboard Leo came at him, lunging across the small bed with the speed and strength of a creature from hell. His raised forearm caught Károly full in the throat, pinning him to the wall. The man had no time to cry out, for the force of Leo's blow crushed his larynx. His stunned reflexes were unable to fire a shot. Leo went for the gun, snapping two of Károly's fingers as he twisted the weapon out of his hand.

Leo saw the pain and terror in the man's eyes, and exulted in it. With one push he shoved Károly face first onto the bed, then, lifting the gun high in the air, smashed the metal butt into his skull. Again. And again, until the sight of blood oozing from the back of the dead man's head brought him to his senses.

He became aware, first, of the heavy quickness of his own breath, as if he'd just awakened from a nightmare. Looking at Károly's lifeless body, he felt no remorse, only a vague sense of having finished an exhausting task. He leaned against the wall to steady himself, and looked down. His pants and shirt were spattered with blood. Quickly he removed his shoes, took out the receipt from the Ritz, then stripped off the rest of his clothes. He then used a corner of his shirt sleeve to wipe his fingerprints from the gun. He left the gun, and the wallet with the counterfeit notes, on the bed beside the corpse.

Someone knocked. Leo reeled toward the door. The chamber maid's worried voice floated in from the hallway.

"Sir? Are you all right? Is everything all right?"

Leo snatched a towel from the wash basin and wrapped it around his waist. He composed his features and unlocked the door, opening it a fraction wider than was decent given his nakedness, using his body to block the woman's view into the room.

"Yes?" He gave her a devastating smile, designed to make her think that the sight of her at his door brought a special joy to his day.

"I thought . . . there was a noise. You're in no trouble?" she stammered.

"I'm so sorry. This is so embarrassing. I fell out of bed. Can you imagine?" His smile invited her to imagine other things as well. "I guess I'm just too big for a small bed. I hope the noise of my hitting the floor didn't disturb you."

"No, sir, it was the man in the room downstairs."

"Please give him my most sincere apology, will you? I'll be checking out today so it certainly won't happen again." Another smile, this one requesting her assistance, telling her she was the only one in the world who could help him with so important a matter.

"Of course, sir. I will explain, sir."

"Thank you." He smiled once more. She melted. He closed the door.

How much time did he have? He couldn't leave the hotel in a way that would arouse suspicion. He whipped a razor across his face, put on a fresh suit, and threw the remainder of his things in his suitcase. Then he wrapped his blood-stained clothes in a towel and tossed that in, too. He would have to get rid of them later. He took a few more seconds to wipe down the gun, then the wash basin, the desk, the doorknobs, and anything else he might have touched during the one night he had stayed there.

Before leaving he took an extra blanket from the closet, covered Károly's body, and tossed two pillows over his head, so that anyone glancing in might not be tempted to investigate the rumpled bed linen immediately. He retrieved his coat, wallet, and passport from the floor, put the Ritz receipt in his wallet, and left the room, pulling on his gloves and then carefully locking the door behind him. Now, at least, the police would have to rely on eyewitness descriptions of him. Thank God he'd registered under an alias.

The hopelessness of his situation struck him as he made his way downstairs. Any moment the police could be after him, for counterfeiting, for murder. He took out his wallet and examined its contents. He had enough money to get out of Paris, for he still had the better part of the thousand francs from the note he'd changed yesterday at the hotel where he'd stayed with Martha. *Martha.* He could not think of her now. It would break him.

But where could he go? Not back to Budapest. Gombos' men would kill him as soon as he returned to Hungary. Within hours, within minutes, he would be a hunted criminal throughout Europe. Where could he go, without proper papers, that would be far enough away for him to create a future that could still include Martha?

And then, the solution came to him. But it meant retrieving the necklace.

Moving as if in a trance, willing himself to walk forward, he made it to the Ritz. If word was out, if the concierge at the Ritz had connected his necklace with the one purchased with counterfeit notes at Cartier, the police would already be there waiting for him.

Taking a deep breath, he strolled into the Ritz lobby, displaying a calmness he did not feel. He could not believe it that was just now nine o'clock. Luckily, the same concierge who had helped him yesterday was on duty this morning.

"Ah, good morning Monsieur Bacso," said the young man affably, gesturing to Leo's luggage, "checking out, I see?"

Leo nodded. He handed the receipt to the concierge, who politely excused himself. An eternity passed. The young man returned. He handed the velvet case back to Leo.

"It's an exquisite piece. Even around here, one is not privileged to see jewelry of such magnificence very often." Leo nodded again. Speech was beyond him. He left the hotel.

At three o'clock that afternoon, a junior detective from the French Ministry of the Treasury was engaged in the monotonous chore of reviewing the concierge's records at the Ritz to see whether, by chance, any of the establishment's guests had stored a particular diamond necklace in the hotel vault. It was a tedious, dead-end task, but his supervisor had ordered him not to leave a single stone unturned, and Claude Boulanger was a man who obeyed orders.

His heart began to race when he found an entry made the previous afternoon, checking in a diamond collar valued at fifty thousand francs. After quickly confirming with the front desk that the guest in question was still registered at the hotel, he placed a call to his supervising officer. By God, this would make his career.

"Hello, Captain Bossard? Lieutenant Boulanger here. I've found something very interesting. I suggest you order the immediate arrest of Mr. Janos Bacso, a Hungarian national currently staying at the Ritz."

At five o'clock, a waiter at Angeline's glanced repeatedly at the door, waiting for a particular girl to enter. He would normally have refused the role of courier, but the size of the tip pressed upon him by the distraught, dark-haired gentleman, and the description of the girl to whom he was to deliver the note made him change his mind. Ah, that must be the one. He waited for the beautiful woman to be seated, then with all the elegance he could muster from his short, stocky frame, he handed the letter to her.

A minute later he regretted it, regretted it with every ounce of his romantic Gallic blood. What bastard would make a woman cry like that? What dirty bastard would do that to such a beautiful woman? Why, the bastard should be taken out and shot.

Late that night, Leo Hoffman left the train station in Marseille, hired a cab to take him to a dock at the bustling port, and boarded a ship bound for Shanghai.

THREE

Martha leaned her head back against the firm, worn leather of her seat, and tried not to think.

The words that he'd written found a rhythm in the cadence of the train's steady movement as it rolled along the tracks. "Please trust me," the steel wheels murmured. Martha lifted her head slightly and shook it, trying to dislodge the unbidden words from her brain. Still, they haunted her. *Please trust me. Please trust me. Please trust me.*

The Great War had given Martha's entire generation an early introduction to sorrow, and she was no exception. Martha lost her mother during the winter of 1919. Although it was influenza and not a soldier's bullet that had killed Ruth Levy, Martha would never shake her conviction that the war had contributed to her Mother's death. By the winter of 1919 the residents of Munich had insufficient coal to warm their houses, insufficient food to warm their bellies, and insufficient faith to warm their spirits. Martha believed that her mother had died from the cold that the war brought to them all.

She had mourned her mother long and deeply. But nothing had ever prepared her for the pain she felt rip through her as she read Leo's letter. She had anchored her soul in his, only to have the promise of a lifetime of fulfillment jeopardized by a few hastily written words.

She'd promised herself not to read the note again until she arrived in Munich. Now she broke that promise, digging the crumpled and tear-stained piece of paper out from the bottom of her purse. Looking at the page served no real purpose, however, for every word was burned into her brain:

My Darling Martha,

I don't expect you to understand this. All I can ask is that you trust me. Please trust me. I cannot meet you. I've already left Paris. I betrayed some powerful people who were doing something illegal, and am now in great danger. You would be threatened, too, if you were with me, and I cannot allow that.

I think I know of a place where we can live the life that we tasted last night. It may take me a while to get there, and it may be some time before I can send for you. But I swear that I will. Please trust me. Please wait for me. I cannot live without you.

I know that this note will bring you tremendous pain, and for that I am profoundly sorry. I dare not ask your forgiveness. I can only tell you that I adore you. Please hold on to that.

Forever yours,
Leo

What could have happened? Whom could he have betrayed? Was he really, this moment, fleeing for his life? Who was this man she had fallen in love with?

Martha tried to think about all this in a practical, realistic way, the way her sister Bernice would, the way her father would want her to do. This was an untenable situation. When he contacted her, why, she could decide what to do after hearing his explanation. If he did not, well, then she would go on with her life. They were together for only two days, after all. Only one night, really.

The self-imposed lecture did not help. She could not think the way her father and Bernice did, with their ability to apply logic to every situation. She could not square, with logic, her abandonment by Leo with the love she had seen in his eyes, and the love she had felt in his arms. The words he'd written must be true; otherwise the truth of the words he'd spoken to her during their night together were false.

One night. A volcano erupts and destroys an entire countryside in one night. A hurricane rushes ashore and destroys an entire island in one night. An earthquake hits and destroys an entire city in one night. Her love for Leo had the power of a volcano, a hurricane, an earthquake. She could not just go on with her life as if she had not met him. She had to believe that he'd meant what he said. She had to believe that he would find her.

She had to trust him, or her life would not be worth living.

On the morning she and Leo parted, Martha had been able to let herself into her hosts' apartment without being discovered. This had, at least, spared her the embarrassment of a confrontation that would have eventually involved her father. After buzzing through the morning like an intoxicated bee, Martha collapsed for a long nap in the afternoon. When she awoke she explained to her puzzled hostess, Madame Bernard, that she'd come in late the previous night because she'd run into a college classmate. Martha told the skeptical Parisian matron that she planned to go out with her friend again that night, for dinner, and would probably be out late again; in fact, Martha added, she might even spend the night with her friend and her parents at their hotel in the Latin Quarter. Normally uncomfortable with deception, Martha found it easier to lie in a foreign tongue. One could blame one's awkwardness on the language.

The friendly old couple was surprised to see their lovely guest return a scant two hours after her sunny departure. She shuffled through their front door, face puffy and eyes swollen, complaining that she did not feel well. Madame Bernard, always worried about the flu in December, hustled her off to bed, where the exhausted girl stayed the entire next day. Martha then announced that she wanted to go home.

Madame Bernard immediately sent a cable to Martha's father, explaining that his daughter did not feel well. "No fever, no vomiting; but wants to come home. Will arrive tomorrow midmorning," she wrote. Fortunately, it was not a difficult trip: one overnight express from Paris, and a change of trains in Stuttgart. She could sleep most of the way.

The astute little Frenchwoman thought the girl looked heartsick, but she dared not share *that* diagnosis with Martha's father, or with her own husband, who'd known Martha's father since they were in school together many years ago. The possibility was both plausible and perplexing. When could she have . . . ? Well, this was Paris. She only hoped that Martha's tender young heart had not been too badly damaged. And she hoped that Martha would get home before the young man showed up on their doorstep to apologize. The lady of the house did not want to witness any romantic upheavals. She'd lost both of her sons in the war, and had faced more than enough trauma in her own life. She did not wish to share anyone else's. She no longer had the energy for it. She would help Martha pack her bags, and keep her theories to herself.

Martha's train arrived in Munich only slightly delayed by the copious quantities of snow that poured from the sky. As she descended the stairs to the platform, Martha was touched by the worried look she saw on her father's normally impassive face.

David Levy's heritage was Jewish, but his family had lived for ten generations in Frankfurt, and he was as German as any Prussian. A teaching post at the university brought him to Munich when he was in his early twenties, and he'd met and married his wife in the refreshing atmosphere of the Alpine air. Yet he'd remained essentially unaffected by the more open Bavarian way of life. David Levy had never felt comfortable with emotions of any kind. The greater the crisis, the calmer his approach. But today he was clearly relieved to see his youngest daughter, and Martha appreciated the fact that his concern, for once, was transparent.

If anyone had ever been bold enough to ask Professor Levy which of his two daughters was his favorite, he would have said he loved them both equally, although in his heart he knew this was not true. Bernice was his eldest. He was often startled by how closely her thoughts tracked his own, and reassured by how easily they understood each other. She lacked the flighty nature of most women, and knew that coolheaded reasoning was the key to handling any problem. Even her plain features resembled his own, too much so for her to ever be called pretty. Professor Levy knew that Bernice was his favorite, for she had been the perfect child for him to raise. She had been so easy.

Yet it was Martha to whom he felt the greater responsibility, precisely because she always seemed balanced on the edge of some harrowing danger, from climbing up on tables as a toddler, to escaping from the house to watch the Palm Sunday riots in the spring of 1919, during the short-lived reign of the Bavarian Soviet Republic. One could never be sure what the child would try next.

His wife's love had filled him with awe, and yet always made him feel inadequate, for he had never known how to return it. When Ruth died, David knew the only way he could thank her for all the love she had given him was to take care of her Martha. For Ruth understood that Martha was born with a more restless spirit than she, or her husband, or their brilliant daughter Bernice, possessed.

He knew that to protect her he had to teach his impetuous and unruly daughter to rein in her dangerous emotions; he had to persuade her that only cool heads and clear minds would succeed in these turbulent times. To educate her in this manner was the only way he knew how to express the love he felt. He could only hope that it was enough.

Now he was chiding himself for having let her go alone to Paris. Yet she'd wanted to go so badly, and seemed so grown up, so practical, in suggesting that she take the trip as soon as her exams were finished so that she could look for a job right after Christmas. She was determined to take at least one semester off and work, to see if that helped her become more motivated to succeed at her studies. Given this admirably rational plan and the new potential for self-discipline it revealed, Professor Levy had agreed that a short trip to Paris was not such a bad idea. What had gone wrong?

He watched Martha descend from the train, then walked up to her, put one arm around her shoulder, and gave her a light squeeze. Martha looked up at him in grateful surprise. A public hug was profound, coming from Professor Levy.

"So, you don't feel well?" he asked her as they headed toward the station exit.

"No, Papa, I'm fine, really. Just too much rich food and not enough sleep. I tried to see too many things in too short a period of time. No self-restraint, isn't that what you always accuse me of?" Her question could have been provoking, but it was not. Delivered with a tired smile, her words contained an element of resignation that Professor Levy found disconcerting. A change had come over Martha. He could not quite put his finger on it. She looked at him with eyes that seemed . . . different.

He hired a cab to take them home, an unusual luxury for the frugal professor, for one could generally walk wherever one needed to go in Munich. As they passed by the snow-covered rooftops of the town, Martha could not help but compare the massive twin towers of Munich's cathedral to the ornate architecture of Notre Dame. The two towers of the Frauenkirche were each adorned with a clock and topped with a low, round, copper cupola. The townspeople had run out of money before finishing the steeples in 1488, so they decided to add the Gothic spires later. But by the time more funds became available, the people of Munich decided not to make any additions to the church. They liked it just the way it was. For all of their fun-loving ways, Bavarians hated change. For the most part they were as immoveable as the mountains that surrounded them.

Martha and her father lived on the northern outskirts of Munich, near the university and just south of the village of Schwabing. This little hamlet had grown through the years into a bustling artist's colony. The cultural menagerie of Schwabing attracted an eclectic mix of painters, sculptors, composers, writers, and mere admirers of the arts. Some, who came to soak up the creative energies of the place, like Vasili Kandinsky, Franz Marc, and Bertolt Brecht, exploded like comets into international view. Most remained obscure.

The older townspeople of Munich regarded the Bohemian community to the north as something of a mildly bothersome, occasionally entertaining nuisance. The students and younger residents of the city found Schwabing an essential part of life. To Martha, Schwabing was a haven that made her continued existence in Munich possible. An ironic smile briefly touched her lips as the taxi passed a sign giving motorists directions to the main street that cut through the heart of Schwabing. The street's name: Leopoldstrasse. Leopold Road. If only it could lead her to Leo.

Martha and her father said little during the short ride to the house. He wanted to ask her about her trip, what she had seen, and what she thought of Paris, but her reticence made it clear that she did not feel like talking. Once inside their small but comfortable home, he broke the silence.

"Well, Harry will be happy that you are home. He has been moping around like a lonely puppy. You should call him up. Perhaps he will come over and read the latest popular poetry from Berlin. Or bring his violin. You can sing, with that pretty voice of yours. Harry loves to hear you sing, and I would not mind a private concert, myself." He pantomimed the playing of a fiddle as he moved around the room in a rough parody of a waltz. This was so out of character for him that Martha had to laugh in spite of how she felt.

"Maybe I will call him," she said as her laughter subsided. Funny, she'd not thought about Harry for three days. Leo had swept him completely from her mind.

Henrich Jacobson, known to all of his friends and relatives as "Harry," was originally from Leipzig. He'd come to the university at Munich to study engineering, and everyone agreed that Harry would be a brilliant engineer. Everyone also agreed that it was a shame. It was a shame to be so very talented at something that was so irresistibly practical, when Harry's first love was, and always would be, music. But no one, at least no true German, could ignore a gift like the kind that God had given Harry—the ability to divine the complexities necessary to hold a bridge together, or simplify the intricacies of raising a skyscraper—just to indulge oneself in the tranquility of a sonata for the violin. Music was not a "real" career, unless one was extraordinarily gifted; and, although Harry was good on the violin, indeed, *very good*, he could not wield a bow with the same virtuosity with which he could wield his mechanical pencil.

Harry himself realized this. So he resolutely pursued his degree in engineering, winning prize after prize in student competitions, all the while entertaining himself and his closest friends with his musical gift. He kept his fantasy of playing with a symphony orchestra tucked away in a solitary corner of his imagination.

Harry had another fantasy as well. He wanted to marry Martha Levy.

At first he'd worshiped her from afar, the way one would admire a rare object of art. He saw her regularly on the campus, for even before she enrolled as a student, she often came to hear special lectures or to have lunch with her father. Sometimes he could sense her presence before he could actually see her; he would feel a glow in his stomach, and a quickness to his heartbeat, and then there she would be, honey-spun auburn hair dancing around her face, green eyes trapping the sunlight like a pair of emeralds.

Occasionally she would smile at him, a frank, matter-of-fact invitation to friendship, but Harry could only blush and look away. He was too shy and too in love to just start talking.

Then Harry realized that this enchanting princess, whose visage floated through his bittersweet daydreams as he played lovesick tunes on his violin, was none other than Bernice Levy's younger sister. Bernice, unlike Martha, was eminently approachable. She was not an intimidating beauty, and she was a fellow engineering student. He could certainly talk to Bernice. He would just have to work up the courage to talk to Bernice about Martha.

He rehearsed his speech for weeks. On a bright April morning, he caught up with Bernice after a lecture and asked her if she would like to go with him for a hike in the foothills now that the weather had warmed up. He would bring a picnic. She could bring her sister.

Bernice was not really offended. It was, after all, a predictable and sensible strategy. Bernice had long ago accepted the fact that Martha was the pretty one, and she was too busy with her engineering studies to devote any time to romance. But David Levy was exceedingly protective of his pretty, high-spirited younger daughter, and Bernice knew better than to acquiesce in Harry's plot without her father's permission.

"Harry Jacobson," she said in a stern voice, "my little sister is only seventeen. If you would like to court her, you had best ask my father, not connive with me." She had to squelch the urge to laugh as a look of utter mortification filled Harry's soft brown eyes. Harry would make an excellent engineer, but Bernice suspected he would never be very good at wooing women.

"I couldn't. I didn't mean—"

"Of course you did. You're not the first. But it's a dead-end."

The wretchedness smothering Harry's features made Bernice take pity on him. He was so earnest. And decent looking, too: trim but not a weakling. Nice height, with wiry brown hair and an intelligent, warm look to his eyes. Martha would start dating eventually. They couldn't keep the floodgates closed forever. Harry might be a good choice. She thought it over for a moment while Harry stammered more apologies.

"Oh, stop. I'll help you. Come to my house for dinner next Thursday night. Afterward, we can study for our physics test together. It will give my father a chance to look you over, and give you a chance to meet Martha." Dazed with joy, Harry pumped Bernice's hand until her shoulder shook. She tolerated this for a moment, then sent him off with, "Get out of here before I change my mind. I'm already late for my next class."

So began the special friendship of Martha and Harry, under the watchful but eventually trusting eye of Professor Levy. Five months later Bernice was away at graduate school in Graz, Austria; Harry was beginning his last year at the university; and Martha, who was by then eighteen, had enrolled for her first semester in college.

She had always been a reasonably good student, but studies at the university required a drive for a particular discipline. To her family's dismay, Martha did not feel driven. She did her best, trying to keep up with her work, but fell behind as soon as she was tempted by any sort of distraction.

And Schwabing provided all sorts of distractions. Luckily, she experienced most of them under Harry's careful protection. He never pressured her; never expected anything more than a hug and a swift good-night kiss. Martha felt completely safe with him. Not having a mother to talk to, and not feeling close enough to Bernice to discuss anything more personal than a grocery list, she was left with a vague sense that there must be something more to romance than the shared joy of an evening in a literary cabaret, something more intense than the pleasant contentment she felt when she saw Harry's face light up at the sight of her. But she did not feel compelled to explore the issue too closely. She'd spent too long mourning the loss of her mother's love, and trying to earn her father's, to be concerned about capturing anyone else's.

Near the end of her first semester Martha tried to confront the nagging restlessness invading her life. She decided that her general sense of dissatisfaction stemmed from boredom with school, and boredom with Munich as well. By December she concluded that a vacation and a job were the twin solutions to her ennui. A vacation to Paris, on her own, and a new career: surely that would cure her.

Then she met Leo. Then she understood what she'd been missing. And now that she'd made that discovery, her whole existence seemed wrong without him.

No, she would not see Harry today. She did not know what she would do today. Or tomorrow. Or the day after that, or the day after that. Except wait.

Time crept forward. Martha refused to leave the house, and refused to see anyone. She said she wanted to take advantage of some time alone to relax and read. After making her see a doctor, who confirmed that there was nothing physically wrong with his normally gregarious daughter, her anxious father had no choice but to chase Harry and the rest of her worried friends away.

Christmas Eve arrived. Like many others German Jewish families who, over time, had become fully assimilated into the German way of life, the Levys practiced neither Judaism nor Christianity. Many retained their faith in God, but, instead of following an established religion, they created an informal household liturgy grounded in a deep respect for the Ten Commandments, while blending some of the traditions of their heritage with secular celebrations of certain Christian holidays. It was therefore not unusual to find an old German Jewish family that celebrated Christmas, but not Hanukkah, or Passover, but not Easter.

Christmas had been Ruth Levy's favorite time of year, and after her death Martha carried on the tradition. She decorated the house, cajoled Bernice into helping her prepare mulled wine and treats for the carolers who strolled through the neighborhood, and bought small presents for her sister and her father. They reciprocated, although they did so only to please Martha. Neither cared very much about what was, in their opinion, a pagan celebration of the winter solstice co-opted by the Christians to celebrate the birth of their savior. Neither of them possessed the romantic spirit that allowed for the creation of Christmas magic. Martha, on the other hand, believed.

This year Martha once again performed her annual rituals. She decorated the tree, put fir branches and candles in the windows, and cooked a lovely Christmas goose. But she did so with no magic in her heart. Her mind was focused on one single thought. *Leo is due back at the Hotel Bristol the day after Christmas. The day after Christmas.*

Martha did not really think that Leo would be back at work on December 26th. If he were really in danger, how could he just go back to his regular job? But the people at the hotel might know something.

To make an international call from Munich, one had to go to the post office. That is where Martha went, precisely at two o'clock in the afternoon the day after Christmas. One hour later, the operator put her call through.

A bland, "Go ahead, miss," signaled that the connection had been made. She took a deep breath.

"May I speak to the manager?" she queried in German. She already knew from Leo that most businesses in Budapest used German as a second language because so few outsiders spoke Hungarian. "It's a matter of some urgency," she added.

"One moment, please." The silence stretched across the miles. At last a male voice responded.

"Laslo Orgovany at your service. Whom do I have the honor of addressing?"

"My name is Maria Schwartz. I'm looking for Mr. Leopold Hoffman. I'm a cousin of his. I understand he works there?"

"He did. If you will forgive me, this is, frankly, a strange day for a cousin to be calling from out of the blue. The police have already been here asking about him. Is he in trouble?"

Martha could not hide her disappointment. "You don't know where he is? You haven't heard from him?"

"No, and frankly, I wouldn't tell you anything that I have not already told the police. He went on vacation; to Vienna, I think. He was supposed to report to work this morning, and he did not. Do you know what all this is about, Miss, ah, Schwartz?"

"No. That is, I don't know why the police would want to talk to him." A sudden wave of fear hit her, and uttering a hasty "thank you," she hung up.

At least now she knew that some of what Leo had told her had been true. He was from Budapest. He had worked at the Bristol. He was in trouble. Confirmation of that much was something. But that was all she had.

She would give him six months. Six months. Six months and then what?

"Then who knows?" she said aloud as she trudged home through the snow, fighting back the tears that threatened to overwhelm her again. "Who knows?"

The knowledge she gained from her telephone call to the Bristol and her self-imposed deadline of six months gave Martha the strength to come out of hiding. The following morning she asked her much relieved father to tell Harry that she would speak to him the next time he called.

The eager young man was at her door a few hours later. "Martha, how are you feeling? We've all been so worried about you."

"I'm fine. Just tired from my trip, that's all."

She looked at his apprehensive face and felt a rush of tenderness mixed with pity. *Please*, she thought. *Please don't let Harry love me the way I love Leo. I don't want to hurt him that much.*

To her father's surprise, after a short search for a job Martha took a position as a librarian's assistant at the university. He thought that her desire to pursue a career would have led her to sell clothes in a ladies' shop, or to work as a photographer's assistant, something at least mildly glamorous. Instead, Martha threw herself into the world of books, the world that was her father's home, a world from which only a month ago she'd wanted to escape.

But Martha found the library a comfortable place. Her days full of catalogue numbers and retrieval requests, she did not have to establish any new relationships with the people inhabiting a place to which she no longer felt connected. The cerebral quiet helped her recover some measure of tranquility. She worked. She thought about Leo. And she waited.

The head librarian noticed a distinct increase in the number of young men studying in the library during the hours that Martha was on duty. Martha's supervisor was happy to note that Martha seemed oblivious to this phenomenon, and, rather than encourage any disruption on the part of her admirers, concentrated quite satisfactorily on her duties. Of course, there was invariably someone who offered to help her with the heavy books she had to carry. Martha politely declined each offer with a smile that made her rebuff seem like a gift, unaffected by both the attention she received and the sensation she created.

Harry Jacobson was ecstatic. He spent the better portion of each weekday at a table in the library reading room, where he could catch frequent glimpses of Martha as she made her way around the stacks, reshelving books with a delicate hand. He could barely keep his mind on his studies.

Every day when Martha got off work, Harry would greet her and offer to walk her home. Carefully staking out his claim in full view of the other hopeful admirers, he helped her on with her coat, and took her hand with gallant firmness. Implausible as it seemed to the other young men surrounding her, Martha Levy did not seem interested in spending time with anyone other than Harry Jacobson. The herd of hopefuls vibrated with envy every time Martha left the library under Harry's courteous escort. How could a nondescript guy like Harry capture a firebird? Where was the fairness in that?

Always grateful for Harry's company, Martha started to worry that she was, in some way, leading Harry on. She knew, now, that she was not in love with him. At times Martha felt compelled to straighten out any misunderstanding that might be building between them, but she never found a way to broach the subject without sounding presumptuous, for Harry had never formally declared his love to her. And until she heard from Leo, she was reluctant to say anything that would jeopardize her relationship with her friend, for Harry was, in his kind, mild way, very precious to her. So she let things be, aware of the faintly selfish undercurrents that kept their little boat rocking along, unwilling to say anything that might capsize it.

Ultimately it was Harry who forced the issue, in a manner that took Martha completely by surprise. "Would you like to go for a picnic tomorrow, now that the weather has finally gotten warmer?" he asked one April evening as he walked her home.

"Why yes," Martha responded warmly. "What a lovely way to spend my day off." She loved hiking through the countryside in April. It was such an optimistic time of year.

Martha was totally unaware of the fact that Harry had just reissued the exact invitation he had given her sister Bernice one year earlier. He repeated the words as a good luck omen. She had to come with him. His dreams depended on it.

The next afternoon found Martha and Harry seated on a woolen blanket, savoring soft bread, sausages, and dried fruit while they admired the formidable peaks of the Alps carving white shadows into a crystal blue spring sky. They'd chatted amiably about everything and nothing as they made their way into the foothills of mountains. Now a comfortable silence descended, as they enjoyed the view and their lunch.

Harry had rehearsed this scene in his head dozens of times over the past few weeks. Yet somehow, all of his eloquent speeches deserted him as he contemplated the beauty of the scenery and the promise of his future, a future that could, that must, include Martha.

"Martha, this will be my last term at the university."

"Well, I know that. Have you decided where to go for your graduate degree? Is it to be Berlin after all?"

"Yes. I mean, no. That is, I have decided, and it's not Berlin."

"No? Where then?"

He looked into her eyes with ominous intensity. "Martha, I am going to America."

Martha's eyebrows shot up into two perfect arches. She wanted to say something congratulatory: all that came out was an echoing question.

"Going to America?"

"Yes, America." Harry's words poured out ever faster as he found the courage to say what he wanted to tell her.

"I've been accepted by the graduate program of mechanical engineering at the Massachusetts Institute of Technology. Well, it's not Harvard, but it's better than Harvard if you're an engineer. And Boston is a city alive with music. I'm going to the United States of America. I'll be there at least four years for my doctorate, and then, perhaps, I can stay. For if one is building the cities of the future, isn't America the country with the brightest future? The place where there is space and democracy and opportunity? Isn't that where I need to be? Isn't that where *we* should be?"

The import of his last question escaped Martha as she tried to contemplate the image of Harry busily building skyscrapers in New

York. "When will you leave?" she asked, hoping it would not be too soon.

Harry looked stunned by her question. "When will *I* leave? Martha, I want you to come with me. As my wife. I want to marry you. My beautiful friend, please, will you marry me? Marry me and come to America?"

Now the surprise on Martha's face turned to alarm. Could he be serious? Of course he was. She should have realized that this moment would come. And she knew that she loved Harry as a dear friend, but that to him, she meant more. Much more. Her heart ached for him. She did not know how to make her answer any easier for him to hear.

"Harry, I—"

"Don't." He raised a finger to her lips. Her face told him everything. *She needs more time*, thought Harry, wildly. It was a jolt, after all. Not just a proposal, but a request for her to leave her home, her country, her family. He mentally kicked himself. It was too much to expect, a positive answer to all that at once. He must give her time.

"Martha, please don't say no. Not yet. I know that this is all very sudden; my scholarship, and wanting to go to America. But surely my love comes as no surprise to you. Would you at least tell me that you will think about it? Please?"

Martha knew what her response ought to be. *No. My answer is no. I don't love you the way you love me. I love someone else.* But how could she hurt Harry that way? Ashamed of her cowardice, she hedged her answer as best she could.

"I don't know what to say. I haven't really thought about marriage yet." *Except to Leo.*

To her relief the answer seemed to help. "Fine," he said. "Wonderful. Now you can start to think about it. Take all the time you need." Martha could see the bright tears of relief in his eyes.

Later that night Martha lay in her bed, unable to sleep. She stared at the ceiling, and thought about Harry's proposal.

She knew her father would approve. He was so pleased that Martha was keeping company with such a stable, trustworthy fellow. Did everyone expect them to wed?

She rolled over, inadvertently twisted her legs up in her sheets, and then kicked violently in an effort to untangle herself. The source of her irritation was not the offending bed linen. She was angry at herself. Angry at herself for holding onto a fantasy, and angry at herself for being tempted to let go of it.

Harry would leave at the end of May, he said, right after his graduation. Seven weeks. In seven weeks she could be a married woman, on her way to live in a prosperous country with an adoring husband; a husband who would undoubtedly be respected and successful; a husband who would never get in trouble with the police, never hide things from her. A husband who would never make her heart sing. A husband who could never make her forget Leo.

Martha put her pillow over her head and let out a muffled cry of frustration. Why hadn't he gotten in touch with her? Where was he? How long could she go on waiting and hoping, unable to make any decisions about her life? She'd already spent four months being tortured by her memories and her desire.

She rolled over on her back again, pulled her pillow out from under her head, and hugged it to her chest. How long could she make Harry wait? Could she be honest, and tell him that if she married him, she would enter their marriage in friendship, hoping that love would grow?

Would he have her on those terms? Could she live by them? Could she make love to Harry?

Burning tears crept out of the corners of her eyes. She could feel Leo wrapped around her, pushed deep inside her, his fingers lost in her hair, his warm face buried in her neck. Was that one night all she was to know of intimacy and passion? Was he safe? Didn't he know how much she needed him?

But the night held no answers. And once again, as on so many nights since Christmas, Martha cried herself to sleep.

Two weeks before Harry was to leave, he asked Martha to join him on a walk through the English Garden, the public park in the center of Munich that often served as the scene for romantic rendezvous. He stopped when they reached a peaceful spot in the center of the park, on the edge of the tranquil lake, where an ancient willow tree's arching limbs provided a touch of shade from the glare of the late afternoon sun, and a bit of shelter from curious eyes.

"Martha," he began, as they both settled down in the long grass. "I know that if you'd made up your mind about marrying me, you would have told me yes or no before now. And I know that I've continued to say that you should take more time, as much time as you need, to keep the answer from being no."

She started to say something, but he cut her off, not willing to let her speak until he had finished.

"Please listen to me. I think it would be best if I were to go to Boston by myself. Then, after a few months, you can come visit me, and see how you like it, and see how you like being with me, in another place. Then, you can decide." He gave her a wry smile. "Who knows? You might even miss me a little."

"Oh, Harry." Martha threw her arms around his neck and started to cry. She cried because she *would* miss him. She cried because she felt lucky to be loved by someone so kind and patient. She cried because she was so wretchedly guilty that she could not return his love. She cried because she was in love with the wrong man.

"What's this, what's this, my sweet darling?" Harry murmured. His own heart was gloriously light. She *would* miss him. There *was* still a chance.

"Please, Martha, don't cry." He stroked her back until he felt her sobs subside, and then pulled away from her slightly. "Look, I have a present for you. Will that cheer you up?"

With a loud sniff she accepted his offer of a handkerchief, wiped her eyes and blew her nose. "You shouldn't be giving me a present," she protested. "You're the one graduating. I should be giving you a present."

"If you will accept this gift, and agree to think a little while longer about my proposal, that would be a perfect graduation present." He pulled a long, slim case from the pocket of his jacket.

"I wanted to get you an engagement ring, but I didn't want you to feel pressured to accept it. So I had this made for you, instead, my beautiful songbird, to remember me by when I'm living across the ocean, always thinking of you." As he finished his sentence, he opened the box.

Martha gasped. Inside was a golden medallion on a long chain. Carved into the surface of the gold was the image of a nightingale, sitting in a rose bush, wings spread and breast held high as it exploded into song.

"I can't possibly accept this. It's much too valuable. It's the most beautiful thing I've ever seen."

"You must accept it. It was made for you, Martha, for you are the most beautiful woman that I've ever seen. Whatever happens between us, whatever the future holds for us, this is yours, because you've made this past year the happiest time of my whole life."

Martha let Harry put the chain around her neck, and then let him kiss her; not the usual, light wisp of a kiss that signaled the end of an evening, but an ardent, if somewhat clumsy, embrace.

"You could do worse than Harry," her father told her.

"You could do worse than Harry," her sister told her.

You could do worse than Harry, Martha whispered to herself as she stared at the ceiling, faced with yet another restless night.

But her heart would not listen. *Six months. You promised me you would give him six months.* She would try to ignore her heart. She would try to be practical. She would try to stop hoping. And, maybe, she would go to America.

"Martha, I have a letter for you," Professor Levy called out to his daughter.

Martha looked up from the mass of flowers she was arranging. It was now mid-July, and the summer blossoms were at their peak. She tried to keep a fresh arrangement on the dining room table. Fresh flowers always lifted her spirits.

"Really Papa? Again? From Harry?" During the two months that Harry had been gone, she'd received ten letters, two mailed before he even left Germany.

"I do not believe so," came the somber response as her father entered the room. "I went by my office this afternoon to catch up on a few things, and, of course, to pick up any correspondence. There was one letter in my box that seemed a little strange. No first name, just 'Herr

Professor Levy,' care of the university in Munich. It must have taken a long time to find me. But when I opened the letter, it contained another sealed envelope, with your name on it."

"For me?" Martha said weakly. Her hands began to tremble. She buried them in the flowers.

"I did not open this letter out of respect for your privacy, but I find this a very curious situation. Who do you know in Shanghai?"

"Where?" She could barely get the word out.

"Shanghai. In China. The postmark shows the outside envelope was mailed from Shanghai."

"I . . . I don't know," she faltered, then leapt forward with the first outright lie she'd ever told her father.

"It must be that girl I met in Paris. She was going to Shanghai to do missionary work. I'd forgotten I'd given her my address. I thought it would be fun to get a letter from China, to hear about her adventures as a missionary. I guess she lost my address, but remembered you were with the university here." She busied herself with the flowers, pulling one after another out of the vase and then putting it back in a new position, endeavoring to convey the impression that she was concentrating on achieving perfection with her artistic composition.

Professor Levy gave her a puzzled look. "You never mentioned that you met a girl in Paris."

"Yes. Just another student. An American girl. We met in front of a church, and had coffee together." She was amazed at how smoothly the lie grew once it had emerged.

For a moment Professor Levy said nothing. Then he drew the letter out of his pocket. Wordlessly, he offered it to Martha from across the table.

Martha could not take it from him. She was sure that if she stopped her compulsive motion with the flowers he would notice that her hands were shaking. She tried to feign disinterest.

"Could you please just leave it there on the table for me? I haven't time to read it now."

"Very well." Professor Levy tossed the letter on the table and turned to leave the room. He paused at the doorway and peered over his shoulder at Martha, still busy with her flowers. "I will be in my study if you need me for anything."

Martha smiled at him. The setting sun shimmered through the window, bathing Martha and her flowers in a golden halo. It was a beautiful sight.

He had no way of knowing that he would never see her again.

Martha kept her hands clenched around the stems of the flowers until she heard the door of her father's office close. Her hands were bleeding from where she'd grabbed the thorns on the roses. She did not notice. She lunged for the envelope. There it was: her name neatly printed in block letters. Underneath, in smaller script, she saw the word, "personal."

Holding the envelope to her face as he scrambled to her room, she tried to detect some trace of Leo's presence from the paper that had traveled across the world. She locked the door, sat down on her bed, tore open the envelope, and began to read:

My Darling,
I'm not a religious man, but if there is a God, I pray that he guides this letter into your hands. I know of no other way to reach you.

I'm in Shanghai. My first few months here were not easy. I didn't contact you sooner because I was afraid that, if I did, someone might use you to try and find me, and I couldn't put you in jeopardy.

I hope you can forgive me for what I put you through. I hope to have the rest of our lives to make it up to you. All I can tell you is that I betrayed some members of the Hungarian Fascist Party, who would like to see me killed for what I did. If you remember Hitler, and what he stood for when he tried to take over Bavaria in 1921, then you will understand the kind of people that I'm dealing with.

It's not safe for me in Hungary, or Germany, or France. Perhaps nowhere in Europe. So, I came to Shanghai.

I'm doing well now, and have not stopped thinking about you for a moment. I want to keep the promises I made to you.

Enclosed is a bank draft to cover your passage to Shanghai. It's a long journey, and will take several weeks. Please cable me at the address below with your decision. I love you so very much. Please come. Please come right away.

Forever yours,

Leo

Martha thought she would stop breathing. She thought her heart would stop beating. What could she say to her father? How could she explain this to Harry? How could she leave her home and her country to go to a terrifyingly foreign place like Shanghai?

But even as she listened to the chorus of doubts rising within her, she knew she had to leave. Now that she knew where to find him, she could not take any steps that did not lead to a life with Leo. And she knew that she must leave immediately, without hesitating, so that the qualms taking shape in her mind did not grow into an insurmountable barrier.

How could she face her father? He would talk her out of going. He would look at her with those dark, serious eyes and convince her that she was being ridiculous. She dare not confront him.

She sat down at the small desk in her room, picked up a pen, and started to write:

Dear Papa,

I know this will come as a shock to you, but I've fallen in love, and I'm leaving Bavaria to join the man I will marry, in Shanghai. I'm sorry that I haven't been honest with you. I know that this will hurt you, and for that, also, I'm truly sorry.

    Please don't worry. I know I'm doing the right thing. You've always tried to teach me to be sensible, but I think our hearts speak a different language. I must listen to mine. I will keep in touch.

Your loving

Martha

She reread the note quickly, realizing how inadequate it was, yet unwilling to risk writing anything more. She must go, now.

She packed a small suitcase, retrieved her small savings from under her mattress, pinned Leo's bank draft to the inside of her coat, and, without a word or a backward glance, walked out the door of her father's house.

It was not until she was seated in the train, miles outside Munich, that her brain started to function again, and she realized that she still wore Harry's medallion around her neck.

FOUR
SHANGHAI

For the fifth time in as many days, Leo Hoffman paced up and down the wide sweep of Waterfront Boulevard, known in Shanghai as the Bund. Although the brutal humidity of late August hindered all movement, every limb of Leo's frame radiated impatience as he made his way along the riverfront. Periodically his anxious body froze, and his eyes swept the opaque water of the Whangpoo River.

It was not a scenic river, like the Danube; or a romantic one, like the Seine. The Whangpoo was ugly and slow-moving. It stank of sludge, decay, and multiple forms of human abuse. Even now, after living in Shanghai for eight months, the overpowering stench of the river sometimes startled Leo when he opened a window or stepped out onto the street. It lay waiting for him, like a lethargic old beggar, too complacent to try and attract his attention with any ruse more energetic than an assault on his olfactory organ. The Shanghailanders said one got used to the smell, in time.

But for all of its natural indolence, the Whangpoo was a frenetic waterway. It had been seized, dredged, and made useful by foreign hands eager to exploit the enormous Chinese market. For the British, the Americans, the French, and the Japanese, the Whangpoo was now the carotid artery of the China trade. Manufactured and imported goods were piled onto barges in Shanghai harbor, then transported twelve miles on the lazy, smelly river to the mighty Yangtze. From there, the valuable cargos dispersed into the vast Chinese countryside via a network of waterways that flowed through the interior for thirty thousand miles. Down the Whangpoo to Shanghai came rice, cotton, silk, tea, and tobacco; peanuts, rosewood, leather, and tung oil. And silver. Vast quantities of silver. Yes, the Whangpoo might smell of refuse, but it also smelled of money. It was, as the Shanghailanders claimed, a stench one could get used to.

Leo stopped his compulsive pacing and scanned the busy river traffic. Boats of every shape and description jostled and dodged each other in the gray-yellow light of early evening, covering the harbor with a floating quilt of tramp steamers, passenger ships, sampans, and junks. This menagerie of vessels brought cargo to and from the massive freighters anchored close to the mouth of the Yangtze, as only smaller craft could navigate the shallow port. The squat sampans served as water taxis, and also as houseboats for thousands of Chinese. From the shore Leo saw charcoal stoves belching out black smoke, and blue cotton laundry hanging out to dry. Here and there a Chinese toddler played in split pants, attached to a mast by a short leash.

But this evening Leo's eyes swept over the exotic Chinese vessels without interest. The one boat he ached to see was not yet there. No steam launch from the Peninsular and Oriental Steam Navigation Company cut through the foamy yellow water toward the sturdy piers that lined the foreshore of the Bund. It was now seven o'clock. Martha would not arrive tonight.

With a short sigh of frustration, Leo turned on his heel and headed toward Nanking Road, back to the cool shelter of the Palace Hotel bar and the ephemeral comfort of a brandy. He cut a path through the mass of humanity crowding the walkway. The last vestiges of daylight would soon disappear, but the Chinese entrepreneurs who worked the Bund with territorial possessiveness were still active. He passed a wizened old coolie selling hot, succulent pork dumplings, and a round-faced, smiling grandmother peddling bamboo trinkets and jade earrings. A tired pregnant woman dressed in pink silk squatted behind a pile of embroidered slippers for sale. They and dozens like them filled the air with a steady din of enticements, encouragements, boasts, and insults. They called out in Chinese, in Pidgin English, and in broken, bastardized French. Leo ignored them all as they shouted to be heard above the engines, whistles, and horns of the harbor. The noise one had to get used to, or go deaf or crazy. Incessant noise, like the stench of the river, was part of life in Shanghai.

The collapse of the Manchu Dynasty in 1911 left the Chinese empire at the mercy of competing warlords. These ruthless land pirates divided the once mighty kingdom into private fiefdoms, slaughtering those who resisted. But Shanghai remained an island of productivity amid the anarchy. There, under the tender protection of warships flying the flags of the United States, Japan, and half a dozen European countries, the invisible hand of capitalism guided the lives of a million Chinese and fifty thousand foreigners with relentless economic discipline.

Since the 1840s, treaties guaranteeing "extraterritoriality" to the foreign residents living within two geographic districts, the French

Concession and the International Settlement, rendered the Shanghailanders subject only to the jurisdiction and laws of their respective countries, as interpreted and executed by the local Shanghai Municipal Council. If an American committed murder in Shanghai, he might be punished. For an economic crime he was virtually untouchable. Most European residents enjoyed the same liberty. Greed and vice were the mainstays of Shanghai commerce, and Shanghai justice was as shallow and corrupt as the waters of the Whangpoo.

Never had there been such a boisterous blend of east and west; never had there been such a clamorous coexistence of the devout and the deviate, the prosperous and the penurious, the opulent and the oppressed. Staggering wealth and stunning poverty existed side by side, each a tribute to the unique world that was Shanghai. It was, as Leo had been told by the crude American James Mitchell, a perfect place to begin one's life anew.

The best asset a fugitive could bring to Shanghai to aid him in the metamorphosis from hunted and haunted to secure and wealthy was a sizeable bankroll. The second was a good supply of raw luck. Leo had arrived in Shanghai with both.

Six months earlier the Shanghai weather had been in the throes of its opposite but equally uncomfortable extreme. Shanghai's winters brought with them a damp, insidious cold that bore no resemblance to the invigorating briskness of a Hungarian winter. Dozens of beggars froze to death every night, their stiff bodies stretched alongside automobiles equipped with sable lap rugs to keep their affluent occupants cozy. The only decent thing about winter in Shanghai was that it did not last long.

Despite the uninviting temperature, on the day of his arrival in Shanghai Leo had abandoned his small cabin just after sunrise. He found a little-used corner of the deck and waited, wanting to catch a glimpse of the land that might mean his salvation.

For the five long weeks of the voyage, he'd kept to himself, engaging in civil conversation when necessary, but unwilling to risk making the acquaintance of any of his fellow passengers. He did not disembark at any of the ship's ports of call, so that he did not have to show his passport to anyone other than the ship's bursar. He wanted to make sure that no one would remember him, or be able to identify him: that no one could connect him with a murder in Paris. For the time being, he needed to be left alone.

Given his desire for privacy, Leo was not pleased when he saw a cashmere-clad passenger saunter out into the cold air of early dawn. Before Leo could withdraw, the new arrival spotted him and headed his way, ready for a conversation.

"Good morning, Cosgrove is the name. Lawrence Cosgrove." The trim, middle-aged Englishman offered Leo his gloved hand. Leo shook it, barely meeting Cosgrove's eyes as he did so.

The Englishman paused, puzzling over the lack of a reaction on Leo's part. "I say," he said, with some hesitation, "you do speak English, don't you?"

Leo reconsidered his cool response. He did not want to insult anyone; he just wanted to be ignored. This man would not forget him if he behaved too rudely. A small smile of resignation skirted Leo's mouth as he replied politely, but without enthusiasm.

"Yes, I do."

"Ah, good. I thought so." Cosgrove looked relieved. He went on.

"I don't speak anything but my mother tongue. Well, I can manage in a French restaurant, you know, but I'm not what you would call conversational. In French, that is. First time to Shanghai?"

"Yes, it is." This man Cosgrove seemed determined to chat. Leo would have to let him blather on for a bit before excusing himself.

"Well, you're about to get your first peek at Chinese soil," the garrulous gentleman continued, inclining his head toward the blue-gray waves rocking the ship. "The sea water will change color soon."

This piqued Leo's curiosity. "Really? Does the water become that shallow so far from shore?" He colored his normally perfect English accent with a trace of French, and a touch of German. He did not want to give away his origins.

"No, my lad. It's the mud of the Yangtze delta. Seeps out from the river and stains the ocean a sort of yellowy brown for miles out. Lets you know what you're up against, in a way. Mud from the river stains the sea, stains the soul. Shanghai is that kind of place."

Leo smiled despite himself. "Are you a missionary, then?"

"Good God, no. Although Shanghai attracts a veritable army of them, and for good reason. As one busy man of the cloth said, 'If God lets Shanghai survive, then he owes an apology to Sodom and Gomorrah.'"

Leo did not find this comforting. "Is it really that bad?"

Cosgrove nodded. "Oh, yes. But it's also an excellent place to make money. I'm an architectural engineer, actually. We've had several commissions in Shanghai over the past few years, though I haven't been back since '21. This time out I'll be working on the engineering plans for the new Customs House on the Bund. That's the main street lining the harbor. Sort of a financial district, only with cargo ships unloading right out front. But you'd think you were sailing up to the heart of any European capital, with all the stonework and marble columns. Our new building will be the crowning glory of the Bund. Should be about a year before I head back to England." Cosgrove waited a moment, as if giving Leo a chance to comment. Then, apparently unbothered by Leo's lack of participation in the conversation, he kept talking.

"First time here, did you say? Not such a bad decision, really. The whole city is booming again. Things were off a bit right after the Chinese outlawed the importation of opium, but now the Shanghailanders—that's what the white residents call themselves—are making money faster than they can think of ways to spend it. Of course, once the big merchants began making money, that is, *real money*, everything else just followed along, you know, doctors, lawyers, the telegraph, tramways. Why, there are suburbs full of Tudor homes and Mediterranean villas; you can even import roses and magnolias for your garden, if you like. Buy anything you want in the department stores. It's downright civilized, Shanghai is, except, of course, for the fact that one is in China." He finished his soliloquy with a snort of amusement.

Leo digested all of this information without comment. He was beginning to reconsider his strategy. Perhaps a chat with this Cosgrove fellow would prove useful, after all. He knew nothing about Shanghai, except for two, equally important facts: he could enter without a visa, and there was money to be made there.

"You sound like an old China hand," he remarked, encouraging Cosgrove to go on. The older man seemed flattered.

"No, not really. Not like some of the chaps out here. Taipans, they're called: the real industrialists. The men in charge. It's an odd society. Classless, in a way. Money is the only calling card you need. The only thing a well-placed silver dollar cannot obtain for you is a seat on the short end of the Long Bar at the Shanghai Club. The club is the one place that caters to a more traditional British crowd. But the rest of the city . . ." He spread his hands, palms up. "Few rules, no limits."

"So, most of the foreign residents are British?"

"No, actually, though the King's subjects probably control the biggest slice of the pie. My friends there tell me that the problem now is the White Russians, who started pouring in after I left in '21. Poor bastards. They're the only whites actually subject to Chinese law. Ghastly business. Stateless, helpless, fleeing for their lives from the Soviet Reds. Lots of pretty Russian women, though, if you're interested in paying for that sort of thing. But without changing the city's entire immigration policy, there was no way to keep the poor Russian bastards out. Some of them claim to be royalty, of course, which is hogwash. Anyone with a shilling to their name would have gone to England, or France, or, well, anywhere, other than Shanghai."

Leo tried to ignore the flutter of apprehension that brushed against his ribs. "Why? If it's a place of such opportunity?"

Cosgrove chuckled. "Well, let me put it like this. I am only a periodic visitor, but from what I've seen, Shanghai is a damn fine place to get rich, and not a bad place to be rich, but it's a wretched place to be poor."

"In my experience, there's no good place to be poor."

"No, I guess not. But there must be better than Shanghai." The Englishman grew pensive and stared out at the ocean for a moment. Leo, thinking that their discussion had ended, was about to take his leave when Cosgrove pulled out of his somber reverie.

"So, are you heading to Shanghai at the behest of your company?"

"No." Leo looked down at the ship's rail with a small twist of a grin. "I'm on a more independent venture."

"I see." He did not press further. Leo remembered Mitchell's words: *If you knew anything about Shanghai, you wouldn't have asked that question, for no one goes to Shanghai if he has anywhere else to go.*

"Look, there," he then heard Cosgrove saying. "See the water? It's gone brown." Leo looked. So it had. They were approaching the land of his future.

The two men continued their conversation for the better part of two hours as the ship cruised across the few remaining miles of the East China Sea and into the placid mouth of the Yangtze. Leo easily elicited a wealth of information from the loquacious Englishman, including a recommendation on where to stay. "I'll be staying in an apartment that our company maintains for part-timers like myself," Cosgrove explained, "but I'm sure you'll be quite comfortable at the Palace Hotel, until you find your own place."

Torn between his desire to cling to the safety of anonymity and his hunch that Cosgrove could prove a useful acquaintance, Leo decided that he could not pass up the opportunity to gain a potential entrée into Shanghai's upper crust. By the time the ship lowered its anchor, they had arranged to meet in two day's time, for what Cosgrove called "a rousing Shanghai evening."

"I'll just leave a message for you at the Palace. It's been a pleasure," Cosgrove said as the two parted, and Leo felt comfortable with his decision to pursue the man's acquaintance. Information translated into confidence, confidence into security, and security into sending for Martha.

Hours later, settled into a comfortable suite at the Palace Hotel, he tried to come up with a feasible plan. With a small pocketknife he removed the Cartier necklace from its hiding place in the lining of his vest and laid it out on the bed. The stones shimmered, cold and beautiful, unaffected by bloodshed, by heartache, by flight. He lifted the heavy necklace to eye level, dangling it gingerly from the clasp. The diamonds caught a stray sunbeam and fractured it into hundreds of tiny rainbows, scattering them around the room.

Now he understood the true reason that Károly had been interested in this particular necklace. He saw the logic of buying a necklace made up of smaller, but perfect, stones. A single large gem would have been easier to trace. While the individual stones would never fetch the same price as the original Cartier necklace, their simplicity rendered them fungible. Marketed discretely, they would never be traced back to the original piece. And there were over forty of them.

Leo was no longer interested in working for a paycheck. For Martha, he needed security. He needed money. He needed a lot of money, money that could be used to build an impregnable wall between his new life and his past. But to obtain that kind of wealth, he would have to take risks. Leo studied the necklace. It was his ticket to freedom, or his writ of execution. He had to use it correctly.

"Well," he said to the stones, "until I discover the best way to use you, my little friends, I had best take care of you." He carefully stitched the necklace back into the lining of his vest. It was very cold. Wearing a wool vest all the time would not appear unusual.

After bathing and changing, Leo ventured into the hotel lobby. He had long since learned that the best way to attract money was to convey the impression that you did not need it, hence his decision to stay at a fine hotel, rather than economize. The pennies he would save by staying at a lesser establishment would not matter, in the long run. If he went broke, they would not matter; if he succeeded in converting the necklace into significant wealth, they would not matter. What mattered were the opportunities he seized upon right now.

Leo could see that the Palace was an establishment worthy of the name. It sat on the corner of the Bund and Nanking Road, where the financial world and the shopping district converged. The proud hotel catered to the well-to-do, itinerant population of Shanghai. Japanese, French, British, American, and Chinese businessmen lounged at the bar. Busy wives and mistresses flitted through the lobby, where impressive piles of hat boxes, suitcases, and steamer trunks testified to the financial success of their mates. High heels clicked on the marble floor. Telephones rang. Ice clinked musically inside the crystal glasses served by slim Chinese waiters clad in white. To Leo, it was an engagingly familiar scene.

He approached the concierge's desk. According to Cosgrove, the Brits seemed to carry the most clout. He launched into a breezy, upper-class British accent.

"Hello, good man. I'm a new arrival here. Need some advice. Any ideas on where to buy a rather nice piece of jewelry? Something a bit out of the ordinary?"

"May I suggest Katiana's? Her shop is about a mile down the way, near the big department stores, on Nanking Road. She has an unusual collection of quality items, including quite a few pieces of Russian and Chinese imperial jewelry. Just give her my card and she will be sure to show you her best."

"Wonderful. Actually, come to think of it, I suppose I need to pick up some of the local currency first."

"The cashier will be happy to oblige."

"Very good. Thanks much."

Once outside, Leo turned left to head up Nanking Road, and was immediately engulfed by the crowd. Herds of people, mostly Chinese, crowded the sidewalks, the street, and the storefronts. There were quite literally people everywhere, along with dozens of different ways of transporting them, their wares, and their purchases; there were rickshaws, wheelbarrows, ox-carts, pony-carts, handcarts, pedicabs, scooters, and bicycles. Human beasts of burden trotted along with bamboo poles slung across their shoulders, bent double by the weight of the baskets full of fish, firewood, or bricks that dangled from each end of the pole. The tram clicked and hummed its way up the avenue. A few automobiles chugged arrogantly through the maze of wheels and faces. A turbaned Sikh directed vehicular and pedestrian traffic at each major intersection, making no real distinction between the two.

And then there were the stores. Cosgrove had been right. You could buy anything on Nanking Road. Leo passed the American Book Shop, the Chocolate Shop (advertising its "famous American ice cream sodas"), and the Lao K'ai Fook silk shop, bursting with bolts of shantung, pongee, and iridescent silk. He walked by jewelry shops and optometrists, shoe stores and a store that sold nothing but baby carriages. Exactly one mile from the Bund were the department stores, Sincere, Sun Sun, and Wing-On, where one could buy German cameras, French perfume, English leather goods, and Japanese pearls; or play ping pong, billiards, or roller skate; listen to music; or just have a drink and watch the sea of faces roll by. It was bedlam. But, at least for the immediate future, it was home.

Later that day Leo was back in his hotel room, necklace in hand, prying the first of the stones free with a pair of pliers he'd picked up at a hardware store. By studying Madame Katiana's inventory and inquiring rather directly about prices, he now knew, roughly, what one of his own stones was worth. Now he would sell one. Selling more than one might be dangerous, for he had no idea what type of information, if any, would be available about the theft. One transaction would test the waters.

He also knew where to go to sell his diamond. He'd go straight to the place Madame Katiana had warned him to stay away from: Avenue Joffre, the heart of the "White Russian" district in the French Concession. Leo had no doubt that she found some of her own pieces there, or she wouldn't have tried so vigorously to steer him away from the "crooks and cheats on Avenue Joffre" when he inquired about other dealers in estate jewelry.

The following morning he hired a rickshaw to take him there. Skirting the boundary of the old Chinese walled city, the even trot of the sinewy coolie brought Leo, with surprising speed, to the heart of the French Concession and the lengthy boulevard that had earned the nickname, "Little Russia." The road was lined with dress shops, fur salons, Russian restaurants, and questionable nightclubs. Here and there a small knot of shabby men clustered around two compatriots playing chess. Banners advertised instruction in mathematics, Russian, French, and tutoring for musical instruments of all kinds. Leo was surrounded by Russian music, Russian writing, Russian voices, and Russian faces. He felt like he'd turned a corner and crossed the border.

He elected to investigate the neighborhood on foot. Stepping down from the rickshaw, Leo tossed the driver a tip he did not yet realize was far too generous. Rather than express gratitude, the cunning Chinese leveled several loud curses at Leo, decrying his stinginess, hoping that he could embarrass the uninformed foreigner into giving him even more; but Leo, intent on his mission, was already walking away. When the driver could see that no more coins were forthcoming, he picked up his poles, added a few more curses for emphasis, and retreated.

Leo's frosty breath created a mist half a foot above the heads of most of the men and women he passed. He walked down alleys and side streets, looking for the Cyrillic characters indicating a jeweler. He needed a man of talent, and a man who could be trusted.

At last he saw a sign that intrigued him. The Russian word for jeweler decorated a small silk banner, hung over the door to the basement entry of a nondescript two-story building. Leo descended the uneven stairs and knocked on the plain wooden door.

"Da," a voice called out from behind the door. Leo walked in.

It took a moment for his eyes to adjust to the dark, for the small half window let in little light. Leo could make out an armchair, a small Franklin stove, and a workbench displaying the delicate tools of the jeweler's trade. For an instant he thought he saw a large, long-haired animal crouched on the stool at the bench. Then the creature turned toward him, and Leo could see the face of an old man peering out of what appeared to be a fur cape. *Muskrat*, thought Leo.

"May I help you in some way?"

Something in the old man's voice put Leo at ease. It was not the voice of a shopkeeper waiting to pounce upon a prospective client, but the welcome of a humble artist, looking to be of service.

"I hope so," Leo replied, the Russian words flowing effortlessly from his lips. "I have an item I would like to sell. It will, I think, interest you." He removed a silk handkerchief from his breast pocket.

With a patient expression the old man extended a pale, wrinkled hand from underneath the mound of fur engulfing him, and beckoned for Leo to come closer. He did so, and placed the handkerchief on the table. He unfolded it to reveal the diamond.

Wordlessly, the jeweler lit a candle, then put on a bizarre pair of glasses; two cone-shaped magnifying loupes were positioned where ordinary lenses should have been, giving him the visage of a monstrous insect. Holding the diamond close to the flame, the jeweler inspected it. A sharp intake of breath caused the candle to flicker, letting Leo know that he was impressed.

"If it is what it appears to be . . ." Putting the stone back on his table, he removed his glasses and picked up a small brown bottle from which he extracted liquid with a dropper. The acid splashed harmlessly off the diamond, then hissed softly as it ate into the varnished wood of the workbench.

"A marvelous stone. A beauty. Emerald cut, five carats, colorless, and perfect. I am afraid that I do not have the resources to pay you what it is worth."

"What could you give me for it?" Leo was ready to counter any offer.

"What I could give you is irrelevant, unless you are desperate, and you do not strike me as a desperate man. Not yet, at any rate. Believe me, my son, I have given many desperate people the help that they needed. But I cannot help you. I could cheat you, but I cannot help you."

Startled, Leo realized that the man was not adopting an artful bargaining strategy; he was speaking the truth. His frustration quickly crowded out any sense of gratitude. "Do you know of anyone who would be interested in such a stone, and willing to pay a fair price for it?"

For a moment there was no reply, and Leo was about to repeat the question, when the old man spoke.

"There is a man, a Chinese, who comes here to my shop, for he knows I occasionally acquire worthy pieces. His name is Lee Wusong. He works for an influential man. A rich man. This man, for whom he works, is very difficult to impress. But even Liu Tue-Sheng is impressed by perfection, and he has three wives to satisfy. Do you have three such diamonds?" The old man smiled, revealing teeth that Leo wished had remained unseen.

"Perhaps."

"Even better. I will give you Mr. Lee's address. You may tell him that Olanavich sent you. He will speak to you. When he finds the time." The wrinkled hands appeared again to scribble a name and address on the back of a calling card, which the jeweler then courteously offered to Leo.

"Thank you."

"It is of no consequence. Thank you for sharing with me an object of such rare beauty." The old Russian carefully wrapped the diamond back into its temporary home and handed the handkerchief back to Leo, who thanked him again, and turned to leave. Just before opening the door, he stopped short.

"This gentleman, Liu Tue-Sheng, is he discreet?"

Another brief silence. Then, a nonanswer.

"You are new to Shanghai."

Leo stepped back into the center of the tiny room. "Yes. Is there something I should know?"

The old man shrugged. "If you do not yet know of Liu Tue-Sheng, you soon will. They say he is the head of the Green Gang, an ancient and secret organized crime society. They say he is responsible for gambling, prostitution, kidnapping, and most of the illegal opium trade. They say that he has compromised the integrity of the entire police force of the French Concession, and the French ambassador as well. They say that he has a private army. I know that he serves on the board of two banks and several charities; I know that he keeps his word and pays his debts. I would say that you can trust him to be discreet about where he acquires his diamonds."

This time Leo did more than thank Olanavich. He took a handful of silver coins out of his pocket and laid them on the table. Then he went back out into the cold.

Leo decided to delay his call on Mr. Lee until after his meeting with Cosgrove. He wanted to run Liu's name past the Englishman to see if he could confirm any of the information the Russian jeweler had given him. He was not disappointed.

For their night on the town, Cosgrove took Leo to Mina's, a club that, judging from the crowd, seemed to appeal to affluent British bachelors. The Russian hostesses were eager to please; the food was good, and the drinks only slightly watered down. A raucous floor show consisting of scantily clad, long-legged women provided intermittent entertainment. Cosgrove was thoroughly enjoying himself.

After giving his companion a brief, fictional account of his own life (he admitted to being "in the hotel business," and said he was from Vienna), Leo spent a long evening listening to Cosgrove recount the history of Shanghai, and elaborating in excruciating detail the engineering challenges encountered by the intrepid settlers willing to build a European city on the muddy swampland bordering the Whangpoo.

Leo congratulated Cosgrove on his brilliant architectural achievements, and then brought up Liu Tue-Sheng

"Tell me, what do you know about a man by the name of Liu Tue-Sheng?"

Cosgrove raised his eyebrows. The cigar he was savoring tilted up at a forty-five degree angle. He removed it to speak.

"Good Lord, you haven't gotten mixed up with him already, have you?"

Smiling, Leo shook his head. "I've just heard some interesting things about him, and wondered how much of it was true."

"Well, chances are it's all true and then some. What have you heard?"

"That he's obscenely rich, has three wives, and has the French police in his pocket; that he's involved in prostitution and opium smuggling, but seems to have carved out a respectable niche for himself, at least in some circles."

"Well, that's all true enough, except I don't agree with the 'respectable niche' part. Liu is a character all right, and a damn dangerous one. Why, I heard that he once sent a coffin 'round to someone he thought had cheated him. Had it delivered to the front door, just like a telegram. Chap had the good sense to leave the country, too, chop chop. Liu doesn't make empty threats."

Cosgrove paused for a moment to check his cigar. It had gone out. He signaled for one of the hostesses to come over and relight it for him. A tall brunette did so, suggestively striking a match without taking her luminous eyes off Leo. Cosgrove did not appear to notice. He took another puff of his cigar, briefly watched the resultant circle of smoke hover over the table, then resumed his speech.

"And as for the French police, why, the Frogs on this side of the Pacific don't know the meaning of the word integrity. I've no doubt he has the whole force sewn up. Good thing he hasn't yet wormed his way onto the Municipal Council."

"I hear he owns a bank, and is on the boards of several important charities, including a hospital."

Cosgrove gave Leo a curious look. "Listen here. I don't know what kind of deal you may be cooking up, but Liu is a bad character. Rather than fight corruption, he profits from it. He covers his evil tracks with a veneer of respectability, but the polish can't hide the dirt underneath. I've heard that nonsense about him being a man of his word, but I wouldn't put it past him to sell his children if the price were right. They just don't have the same conscience, these Chinese. Even if they seem trustworthy, doesn't mean they won't do you in. And you won't see the knife coming, either."

"I'll keep my eyes open." The reappearance of the dancing girls curtailed their conversation, and gave Leo a moment to think. It sounded like Liu might be just what Olanavich had suggested: a criminal, but also wealthy and discreet. Just the man to approach with some black market diamonds. Three of them. One for each wife.

The next day he tracked down the address Olanavich had given him. It led him to a handsome villa on Bubbling Well Road, in the British residential section. Mr. Lee was not at home. Leo left a message, neatly written on the back of his own freshly printed calling card, displaying his new address at the Palace.

Mr. Lee,
A mutual friend, Mr. Olanavich, suggested

that I contact you regarding the purchase
of some precious gems. Please feel free
to get in touch with me at your leisure.

Then he waited.

For a week he heard nothing from the mysterious Mr. Lee. To pass
the time he tried to busy himself by learning more about life in Shanghai. He started by chatting up the workers in his hotel. Cloaked with
the invisibility of servitude, they learned a lot about the wealthy and
the powerful. He engaged the hotel pianist, the flower shop girl, and
the bartender in cozy conversations. Reticent at first, they all eventually talked freely. It was impossible not to talk to Leo.

He also hired a real estate agent to show him houses, pretending
that he was quite ready to buy one. He picked a man who was as gossipy
as Cosgrove. Leo soaked up details about his new home as quickly and
intensely as he had when he was a young boy new to Budapest.

Then, just as he was about to try and find another way to sell his first
few diamonds, he received a telephone call.

"Mr. Hoffman?" The voice sounded raspy but cordial, and definitely Chinese.

"Speaking."

"This is Mr. Lee. Our mutual acquaintance, Mr. Olanavich, tells
me that you are new to Shanghai, and suggests you have something of
value in which my employer may be interested. He thought you may
have three such items."

"He did?"

"Yes. I must confirm such things."

"Of course. I understand."

"Mr. Olanavich indicated that you are Russian. Yet, you speak English with no accent. Very difficult. My compliments."

"Thank you." Leo offered no explanation. His origins were irrelevant.

Mr. Lee continued. "Could you possibly bring these items to a meeting this evening?"

"This evening? What did you have in mind?"

"Do you know the Willow Lake Tea House?"

"I've seen it, but I've not yet been inside."

"You will find it most charming, I am sure. Shall we say four o'clock?"

"That would be convenient."

"Very well. I will arrange for a private room. Ask for me when you enter."

"Of course."

"Then, until this evening."

"Yes."

"Goodbye."

The Willow Lake Tea House was in Nantao, the old Chinese section of the city. It sat in the center of a small lake. One reached the decorative oriental villa via a zigzagging foot bridge, a path designed to confuse evil spirits, which, according to Chinese lore, could only cross water in a straight line.

Leo arrived on time. He was immediately shown to a small, private room. A full English tea had been laid out on the low table. Mr. Lee was waiting.

He was a small, dumpling-shaped man, dressed in a comfortably cut, crisp wool suit. Mr. Lee gave no indication that theirs was anything other than a purely social visit, making small talk for the better part of an hour. Leo knew better than to push. He knew he was being evaluated.

Just when Leo thought his meeting would prove fruitless, Mr. Lee asked to see the stones.

He pulled a loupe out of his pocket and examined them for several minutes, saying nothing. Then he looked up. A sparkle of intrigue glinted from within his dark brown eyes.

"I will communicate with my employer. If he is interested, I will contact you."

Leo received a note from Mr. Lee two days later. Something about the obsequious air with which the hotel clerk delivered it made Leo curious about the size of the tip that had been passed to ensure that it reached his hands unopened. He ripped into the envelope.

My employer would like to meet with you regarding the transaction you proposed. A driver will be sent to escort you. Please be prepared to leave the Palace at 3:00 p.m. tomorrow.

Mr. Lee

The invitation did not provide the opportunity to respond negatively. This confirmed another fact regarding Liu Tue-Sheng: he was accustomed to power. Leo would not tempt the man's patience. The next afternoon, at precisely two fifty-five, Leo took a seat in a comfortable leather chair in the lobby of the Palace.

He did not have long to wait. A bearlike Asian man, his barrel chest crammed into a western-style suit, strode into the lobby at a moment before three. Glancing around the crowded lobby, he zeroed in on Leo and marched over to his chair. He spoke in the hissing, deeply accented speech of a coolie who has just moved beyond Pidgin English.

"Meesta 'Offmann?"

Leo did not stand. He had to establish his authority over Liu's subordinates.

"Yes?"

"The cah await."

"And for whom is the car waiting?"

This confused the driver. "You not espec a cah?"

"I'm not in the habit of climbing into strange limousines. If you have instructions suggesting that I should accompany you, you must first tell me who issued the invitation, and where we are going."

Leo could tell he'd stumped the man. He could see consternation building across his face as he weighed his alternatives.

"We go to Meesta Liu Tue-Sheng house, sir," he finally said.

"Very good." Thus informed, Leo stood up. "I will retrieve my coat."

Settling into the back seat of Liu's Rolls Royce, Leo felt for the three diamonds nestled in his breast pocket. Now, finally, something was happening. This was his first chance to turn disaster into triumph. His first chance to create a future that could include Martha.

With many aggressive maneuvers and much blowing of the horn, Liu's driver pushed through the chaos of Nanking Road. Once clear of the commercial district they sped past the gracious lawn of the municipal racecourse, then turned left at Mohawk Road, which took them into the residential heart of the French Concession. Within twenty minutes the car stood outside the gates of Liu's estate.

Leo was immediately struck by the fortifications. The compound was surrounded by an eight foot brick wall crowned with vicious looking slabs of broken glass. The guard at the gate house peeked into the back seat to confirm Leo's presence, then looked in the trunk as well. Once granted admission, the car meandered up the long, winding driveway. Small guard posts dotted the landscape at regular intervals. Despite the intense security, the grounds were serene and beautifully landscaped, a pleasure for the senses even in the middle of winter.

The vehicle reached the main house and pulled up under the stone porte-cochere. The mansion was built in the manner of an Edwardian villa. Arches, balustrades, and Palladian windows endowed the facade with an airy symmetry. The gigantic building looked like it had been imported stone by stone from Europe.

A young Chinese servant dressed in a floor-length gown of starched white cotton greeted Leo at the door. Once inside, the resemblance to a European residence diminished. The entrance hall was lined with glass cases, displaying not antiques or bibelots, but an impressive arsenal of rifles. Beyond the entrance hall the decor was unmistakably Chinese. Elaborately carved, high-backed chairs, silk settees, exquisite screens, and numerous plants and porcelain pots filled the rooms. Here and there Leo spotted a costly European piece: a Louis XIV clock, a Chippendale chair. Either Liu had an excellent eye, or he knew enough to take the advice of someone who had one.

His guide stopped in front of what appeared to be the entrance to a private study. Before showing him in, the boy executed a delicate but professional frisk of Leo's person. Leo acquiesced without comment, then was shown into the room.

Lustrous rosewood paneling glimmered on the walls. The room's grand windows offered a view of a small Buddhist temple, tucked under the branches of an ancient willow tree. The study contained two writing tables, with several matching mandarin-style chairs. The carved wood was inlaid with mother-of-pearl. Rolls of parchment, which Leo took to be correspondence, covered the desktops. A few feet from the desk, a mahogany dragon rose four feet into the air to form the base of a pedestal. Balanced upon the dragon's curved tail was a crystal bowl containing a large, fan-tailed goldfish.

Leo had only a moment to admire the view before he heard footsteps. As he turned to face the door, Liu Tue-Sheng entered the room.

He was thin, terribly thin, but tall for a Chinese; his gaze met Leo's directly. The long, traditional Chinese robes he wore were made of heavy, cream-colored silk. The high mandarin collar and wide sleeves were embroidered with red and gold thread. The hem stopped just short of the floor, revealing pointed, western-style boots.

Liu's face was long and narrow; his cheekbones high and gaunt. What remained of his hair was gray and cut short. His nose added no character to his features. There was nothing particularly intimidating about this man, except for the fact that his black eyes conveyed absolutely no emotion. He had the eyes of a shark.

"Mister Hoffman. I am Liu . . . Tue-Sheng. Thank you for accepting my . . . invitation." He delivered the words in precise, near-flawless English, but the cadence of his speech was stilted. Leo suspected that his awkwardness resulted from the concentration required to avoid the pitfalls of an oriental accent. It seemed that Liu would rather speak slowly than sound like a coolie. Again, Leo was impressed.

"Thank you for inviting me to your beautiful home. It is an honor."

Liu acknowledged this compliment with a slight motion of his head. Swinging a wide sleeve away from his slim frame, he gestured toward one of the chairs.

"Please be seated. I regret that we have not much time today to conduct our business. You have brought the stones with you, I assume?"

"Of course."

Liu took a seat behind one of the desks and cleared several scrolls out of the way.

"Would you be so kind as to let me examine them?"

"It would be my pleasure." Leo placed the handkerchief containing the diamonds on the desk, then reclaimed his seat.

Liu unrolled the handkerchief carefully, allowing each stone to roll onto the wooden surface. He then picked them up one by one, and held each up to the light for a fraction of a moment before setting it back down on the desk.

"Exquisite."

With this comment, Liu rose, and drifted over to the fish bowl. The crystal orb's graceful resident detected the presence of its master and swam to the surface, its greedy mouth already searching for goods. Liu removed a pinch of a flaky brown substance from a small porcelain container. With meticulous care, he sprinkled the fish's repast across the water, and then spoke again, the motionless brocade of his silk-covered back still facing Leo.

"I have been assured that the three diamonds you offer are spectacular. I assume that you could, if necessary, locate others of a similar caliber?"

Liu knew. Why else would he think there were more diamonds? This was a trap. With every ounce of self-control he possessed, Leo remained outwardly unperturbed. He must find out whether he was in any real danger.

"Why? Would you be interested in more?"

"There is that possibility." Now Liu turned, moving with the unhurried air of a man used to setting the pace of a conversation. The expressionless eyes once again focused on Leo.

"If we could reach an appropriate arrangement, I have an acquaintance who might find your diamonds useful. He is involved in, shall we say, a certain project, which requires that he distribute reasonably large amounts of capital to various interested persons—"

"Payoffs?" A pause was the only confirmation Leo received.

"These people, with whom he is dealing, are peasants. They do not trust paper money, and silver *taels* are quite cumbersome to move around the country. Gold, is, of course, an alternative, but it would seem that a quantity of stones, such as these, could also prove to be a convenient way of transferring funds from my friend's hands to the greedy hands he must placate."

"What do you mean by a quantity?"

"As many as you can obtain."

"I see." Leo's mind was racing. Liu's story sounded plausible, but it had been his own gullibility with respect to Károly's scheme that had landed him in this predicament in the first place. On the other hand, what did he have to lose? If Liu intended to see him arrested in order to collect some kind of reward, then he already had enough evidence to connect Leo to the stolen stones. Maybe his best alternative was to dump all of the damn things now and hope Liu did not turn him in.

A lull of awkward proportions was starting to develop when Liu asked, "Are you a gambler, Mr. Hoffman?"

The nonsequitur took Leo off guard. He answered with some hesitation, wondering where the question would lead.

"I've been known to play an occasional game of chance."

"Good. I, also, enjoy a game of chance from time to time. All Chinese do. It is in the blood: the desire to take risks. To seek a shorter path. For most Chinese, the long path leads only to suffering. Most of the Europeans who come to Shanghai are also seeking a shorter path. Or running away from something. Or both."

Leo interpreted this as an opportunity for him to explain the reason for his own presence in Shanghai, but Liu did not seem inclined to wait for an answer.

"There are times when one's path crosses another's at a mutually convenient time. Perhaps this is such a time for the two of us. Perhaps we should take a chance, together. What do you think?"

"I'd like to know the terms of the wager."

"Of course." Liu brought the tips of his fingertips together and rested them under his chin for a moment before continuing. "Your diamonds are lovely. And very valuable. But I have found that there is nothing as valuable as information. I will give you a choice; you may receive, for your diamonds, the full value of what one could buy them for from a jeweler on Nanking Road . . . what do you call it . . ."

"Retail value."

"Yes, retail," continued Liu with a small nod, "or, I will pay half of that amount. In the latter case, I will also give you a piece of advice on how to invest the proceeds. This information could prove much more valuable than the diamonds themselves, but that success is not guaranteed."

Leo tried to consider all the possibilities. The man must at least suspect that the diamonds were stolen. But in that case, why would he bother to offer anything more than street value for them? Where was the catch?

"I can obtain no more than forty diamonds," he said crisply. "Does that affect the terms of your offer?"

"No. I had hoped for more, but forty diamonds could prove very useful."

"And what is the nature of this 'investment advice,' that you mentioned?"

"One cannot, as you Europeans say, expose too much of one's hand, Mr. Hoffman. I will say only that I genuinely believe the information to be of tremendous value, if handled . . . properly. Does the possibility of multiplying your investment in your diamonds intrigue you?"

"Did I ever say that they were my diamonds?"

"Ah, my mistake. I did not take you for a broker. Perhaps it is the owner of the diamonds with whom I should speak." Liu issued this suggestion matter-of-factly as he rose from his chair. Startled, Leo raised his hand.

"There is no one with any greater negotiating power than I."

The words had the desired effect. Liu resumed his seat.

"So, now it is time for a decision. Will you take what you and I know the diamonds to be worth, or will you take a chance?"

The eyes did not flicker. Leo had never met anyone so unreadable. But there was something about Liu that seemed trustworthy. Not because he seemed morally upright; it was as if lies were simply not worth his time. *Honor among thieves.* "I will take the information, and two-thirds of what the diamonds are worth."

This time Liu did smile, conveying satisfaction at a bargain well made, rather than pleasure. "A brave choice, and an intelligent one. I did not misjudge you. Tomorrow evening at eight o'clock my associate, Mr. Lee, will meet you in the lobby of the Palace hotel. He will accompany you to a place where the authenticity of the diamonds can be verified. You will then receive your money, and a letter containing the information of which I spoke. And now, forgive me, but I have other affairs to which I must attend."

Liu rose, extending a hand to Leo. The tough, thin fingers felt like the claw of a bird.

A moment later he was back in Liu's limousine, oblivious of the driver, ignoring the scenery that had fascinated him only a short time ago. He wondered why Liu agreed so readily to the higher price. He wondered if the diamonds were the real reason that Liu had wanted to meet with him; after all, Liu could have ordered Mr. Lee to handle the entire transaction. He wondered if Mr. Lee was going to lead him straight into the welcoming arms of the French police. What sort of investment opportunity had he bargained for? And when, and how, would he be able to see Martha again?

Two days later Leo received another letter on Mr. Lee's stationery. He was to bring his "merchandise," that night, to an address located in the old Chinese section of the city.

An hour before their scheduled appointment, Leo emerged from the warmth of the Palace Hotel into a brutally cold, damp night. For this trip he preferred to be responsible for his own transportation. It was difficult to escape from a moving automobile. Wary even of the miserable rickshaw drivers huddled outside the hotel's entrance, Leo made his way on foot into the contorted maze that was the original city of Shanghai.

The neighborhood did not inspire confidence. Unlike the welcoming European face of the Bund, this part of Shanghai retained a hostile countenance that made all but the most seasoned China hands feel ill-at-ease. The layers of ancient buildings, crouched along their narrow, winding streets, provided the perfect setting for an ambush. Leo moved cautiously, senses alert, trying to discern whether he was being watched or followed. The bent and shrouded figures shuffling quickly along the twisted, windswept streets revealed nothing. The only apprehension he could detect was his own.

The address led him to what appeared to be a money changer's shop. The sparsely furnished store looked deserted, but the ever-punctual Mr. Lee responded instantly to Leo's light tap on the heavy wooden door.

Once inside, Leo handed the man a small leather case containing forty diamonds from the Cartier necklace. Nodding and smiling politely, Mr. Lee pulled a bell cord, and, within seconds, invisible hands lowered a small wire basket through a circular hole in the low-slung ceiling. Lee then placed the unopened satchel in the basket, which promptly disappeared in the same fashion. During the day, unseen clerks in the upstairs room would normally count currency, convert it, and extract a commission. Tonight, in the tiny room above their heads, an expert was carefully examining each diamond to make sure that Liu Tue-Sheng was not cheated.

Leo managed to make polite responses to Mr. Lee's chatter. His nerves were stretched to the limit. The minutes ticked by, and he waited. It was worse than waiting for a screaming mortar shell to find its point of impact.

After what seemed like an eternity, the basket came back through the hole in the ceiling. The satchel was still there. Smiling once more, Mr. Lee retrieved it and handed it back to Leo.

"Please examine contents, to note that all is satisfactory."

Leo did as he was asked. The diamonds were gone. In their place was what seemed to be an enormous quantity of cash in pounds sterling, and a small white envelope.

"Everything looks in order." He wondered if he should count the money.

"Please, count," Mr. Lee said.

Leo did so, examining each note for signs of genuineness. He did not intend to be paid in counterfeit notes after what he'd been through.

"There does not seem to be a problem with the money."

"And, the envelope? Please?"

Again, Leo followed Mr. Lee's suggestion. The envelope contained a small white card. Printed on it, in English, were the words:

Rubber makes a nice birthday gift.
Buy some today.

He stared at the message. "What does this bloody riddle mean?"

Mr. Lee's polite expression did not change. "The information is there."

"Information? What information? I was supposed to receive some information I could use to enhance my profits. This is just—"

"The information is there," Mr. Lee said again, his face still bland.

Leo stared at the sparse words. Rubber. Birthday. It clicked. Leo knew what he was supposed to do. He'd gambled. Now he must act on this tip, and see if the gamble would pay off.

On a balmy evening in early June, Leo accepted an invitation from Lawrence Cosgrove to dine at the Shanghai Club. As a non-English person of ambiguous origin, Leo could never become a member of the stolid British institution, but the mere invitation to dine as the guest of a member demonstrated a certain level of prestige in Shanghai society. Leo accepted with pleasure.

The chef at the club prided himself on providing traditional English dishes for its members, whose palates were unabashedly unadventurous; that night they enjoyed a hearty meal of roast mutton. Leo was in the process of warming his brandy over a candle, placed on the table for precisely that purpose, when he decided to bring up the subject that he'd been dying to address all evening.

"Lawrence, ever done any trading on the commodities markets?"

"Good Lord, no." A touch of self-righteousness crept into Cosgrove's voice. Leo knew he was about to receive a lecture.

"Commodities? I don't even venture into the stock market. No better than a trip to the Derby, all that nonsense. Hoping the price of this will go up, so that will come down. Ridiculous, I say. A bank is the only decent place to keep your money. Solid interest. That's the only sensible way to hang onto what you've got."

"What if you want to do more than just hang on?" Leo asked with a grin. By now he knew Cosgrove well enough to tease him a bit. When aggravated, Cosgrove rumbled and sputtered like a tea kettle boiling over. Leo found it an entertaining spectacle.

"Then invest in something you can control, not a piece of paper worth no more than what someone else is willing to pay for it at the closing bell. Who knows what your money will be worth the next day?

Why, look at what's happened with the rubber market. First, the financial pages eat up the news that the Bolsheviks are stirring up trouble on the Malay Peninsula, causing unrest on the plantations, destabilizing production. Next the word's out that Japanese troop ships have been seen in the area, and in the Philippines. Then it's not the Japanese or the Reds, it's some disease threatening the whole region. It's not as if any of this can be verified or disproved in time to prevent wild market fluctuations, for the world's full of greedy bastards who lunge at the rumors like starving hyenas. I say leave the whole bloody mess alone."

"Wise advice, but too late."

"Oh, no," Cosgrove replied, not without sympathy. "What did you get into?"

"Rubber futures."

"Good God. How long ago?"

"About five months ago. In late January. Right after I arrived."

"Whatever for?"

"A hunch."

"Hunch? Bloody shame. I wish you'd talked to me first. How badly have you been hit?"

The smile Leo had been trying to suppress finally emerged. "So far, so good."

"Really?" Cosgrove looked skeptical. The rubber situation had been one of the major topics of conversation at the club for three months. Like a bucking bronco, the gyrations of the rubber market had tested the nerves of many a seasoned trader. Most of the men bold enough to jump in when rumors of an imminent supply disruption sent prices leaping up sold out the moment the market headed south. The last dive devastated several prominent Shanghai Club members, who dumped their devalued positions only to see the price soar back to an all-time high within ten days.

"So you're not out yet?"

"Not yet."

"Brave cuss, or stupid. How much longer do you plan to give it?"

"I'm not sure." But this response was disingenuous. Leo knew exactly when he was going to sell his holdings. Tomorrow morning, June 10th, and for no better reason than the fact that it was Liu Tue-Sheng's birthday. *Rubber makes a nice birthday present.*

It had been easy for Leo to find a simple biography of Liu among the many newspaper articles lauding the man's noncriminal achievements; he'd found one after spending a couple of hours in the archive room of the *North China Daily News*. And even if the details revealed to the public about the gangster's life were mostly hogwash, Leo assumed that the June 10th date that he'd uncovered was accurate. At least he hoped it was.

It awed him to think that Liu was behind the rumor mill that had played havoc with the rubber market for the past five months. Maybe he was giving the gangster too much credit; could one man actually manipulate the market for a commodity vital to world trade? Still, Leo had played his part, making a significant purchase just as the market started to rise. He'd held on through the agonizing months of spring, watching as his investment doubled, then quadrupled, then crashed, then soared.

From time to time during those tumultuous months Leo felt a vague sense of guilt, but his own desperation soon silenced his raw conscience. After all, he did nothing more than invest and hang on. He took the same risks as any other investor. He had no guarantee that Liu's plan, if it was Liu's plan, would succeed. He had nothing to cling to other than hope and patience.

His patience, and his gambler's instincts, had paid off. Men whose nerves were not as strong had been broken. But Leo was rich. Very, very rich. Tomorrow he would cash in his chips, and send for Martha.

"Yes, my friend, I managed to survive the rubber debacle. And I have another piece of news for you. I think I'll be staying in Shanghai for some time."

"Really? Taken a liking to the place, have you?"

"It gets into your blood, doesn't it? All this luxury—" Leo made an expansive gesture, taking in the club, its marble floors, the mahogany bar, the attentive waiters—"available for so little. And the anonymity to enjoy it."

"So the anonymity appeals to you, does it?"

Leo contemplated his answer, aware that he had let down his guard. But surely there was no harm in admitting he'd come to Shanghai for the same reason as so many others. He lifted his glass.

"Yes. Here's to Shanghai, Lawrence. The miraculous place where broken lives begin anew."

As Leo offered his toast, Cosgrove gave him an odd look, as if he knew something that Leo did not, but elected to keep it to himself. Yet he raised his glass to Leo's, and, as the crystal goblets rang out their accord, the older man gave Leo his good wishes.

"Very well then. To your new life. May it be a long and happy one."

"For me and my wife."

"Your wife?"

"I mean, the woman I hope will soon be my wife. If she'll still have me."

"My word, all sorts of secrets are pouring out of you tonight, Leo. Is this lucky lady here in Shanghai?"

"Not yet. I'll let you know when she arrives. I don't even know if she *will* come."

Six weeks later her telegram arrived. Martha was on her way.

At night Leo trembled with anticipation at the thought of having Martha in his arms, alongside him in his bed, rising to greet him in the morning. *She had not given up. She was coming to Shanghai.* And now he had the money he needed to take care of her, to protect her. And oh how he would spoil her; nothing was too good for Martha. Nothing.

Every day he toured the Bund, aching to see her. He knew she could not possibly arrive for weeks, yet still he prowled the docks, unable to keep himself away. He could sense her. She was coming to him.

FIVE

Martha stepped onto the dock and felt it lurch beneath her feet. Dazed, she reached out and clutched a pylon to steady herself. The wood felt moist but solid. She realized that the pier she was standing on had not, in fact, moved. The motion of the sea still tormented her brain, that was all: the unrelenting motion of the loathsome ocean.

During her voyage the attentive captain had assured Martha daily that as long as she was able to keep down some of what she ate and drank, seasickness would not kill her. More than once during the past five weeks she would have preferred a quick, painless death to the torment she'd experienced during her journey. The nausea subsided once they reached the China Sea, and she thought the worst was behind her. Until the earth started moving, too.

Another wave of dizziness hit her. She took a deep breath and placed her hand over her mouth as the newness of Shanghai assaulted her senses: the stench from the river; the voices of the coolies unloading cargo with their unfamiliar, rhythmic chants; the horns and bells of the ships, bicycles, and automobiles; the pleas of the beggars and the hawkers; the sticky heat; the sunburned foreignness of the faces staring at her with inquisitive admiration.

It was too much. She was too weak. She stood still, unable to move any farther than the five thousand miles she'd traveled to be there.

Then she saw him, and burst into tears.

In two long strides Leo reached her. Sweeping one arm under her shoulders and the other beneath her knees, he lifted her off her feet and carried her as one would a small child, holding her close to his chest and murmuring comforting words as the anguish of the past nine months poured out of her in a rush of sobs and stuttered sentences. He carried her down the dock toward the shade of one of the trees on the thin stretch of park lawn that separated the river from the hot pavement of the Bund, and sat down on a small public bench, still holding her in his arms, heedless of the curious and critical glances of their public audience. He stroked her silken auburn hair and rocked her, until she pulled her head away from his shoulder and looked at him, her eyes begging for reassurance.

"I love you, Martha Levy," he said.

It was enough.

She said nothing for a moment, then started to talk again, wiping away her tears with the palm of her hand. "I can't believe I fell apart like this. It's just that I've been so sick. The voyage was horrendous. I don't care if I never set foot on another boat as long as I live. Were you seasick?"

He smiled down at her, his heart so full of love he could not speak. Then he enveloped her in another huge hug.

"I promise. No more boats."

"Good," came the muffled reply. She squirmed to get free and, with one last sniffle, looked around.

"Goodness. What a spectacle I'm making. I'm sor—"

Leo touched a finger to her lips to cut her off. "You have nothing to be sorry for, my darling." His face then drew closer to hers, until their lips met. The warmth of her mouth instantly ignited his passion and he pulled away, acutely aware of their surroundings and his overpowering need for her.

"Come on, my love," he said, standing up and easing her to her feet. "Let's go home."

They collected her one small suitcase from the dock, then returned to the busy traffic of the Bund, where Leo hailed a rickshaw. With Leo's assistance Martha stepped up and sat down in the peculiar little cart, her eyes wide with amazement as she took in the small, grinning man who seemed delighted to have been chosen to take them to their destination.

"He can't possibly carry us both."

"Of course he can. Especially you, you tiny little thing. The wheels carry most of the weight."

"But it's barbaric, being toted about by a human being."

"Not as barbaric as letting him starve to death, which, I assure you, is a common alternative. I'm sure that this man considers himself quite lucky to be able to lease a rickshaw. We do him an honor by getting in it and helping him feed his family. Or buy his opium." Leo chanted an address in Chinese. The coolie picked up the handles of his vehicle and trotted off at a brisk pace. Martha was relieved to find the regular, swaying motion of the rickshaw oddly soothing after the unpredictable movement of a ship at sea.

"Did you say opium? Is it true they all smoke opium? Leo, were you speaking Chinese? What is that man selling? My goodness, but it's hot." Despite her queasiness, the exotic panoply passing by filled her mind with dozens of questions. She gave Leo's arm an excited squeeze.

Leo felt a surge of joy at Martha's touch. He shifted to face her and covered the small hand gripping his arm with his own, never taking his eyes off her face.

"Martha, my darling, I hear you speak and I think I must be dreaming. I've dreamed of you so often. Day and night. I can't believe you're really here."

He looked at her like she might vanish. With that look he offered himself to her, all he was and all he would ever be. Martha read his gaze, and understood. All of her doubts settled like dust in an attic corner, far away from her heart.

"I love you, Leo. I will always love you."

He seized her fingers and kissed them, each tip, one by one. After he'd planted a fervent kiss upon her thumb, she brought his hand to her lap and gripped it there.

"Don't ever let go," he said quietly.

"I won't. Never again. Never, never again."

They sat silent for a while, basking in the sweet pleasure of their reunion. Leo could feel the heat of Martha's body as she pressed his hand against her thigh. He would have to wait. Until they were home. Or longer. She might need some time, he chided himself. She'd been through so much on his account. Patience. He should tell her something about her new home.

"Well," he said, "as you can see we're heading into the nicer residential neighborhoods. Shanghai isn't all cargo and beggars and noise.

I know this must seem strange, to find me living on the other side of the world, but I hope you'll grow to like it here."

"It all seems so foreign, yet familiar at the same time. Most of the buildings don't look the least bit oriental."

"Not in this part of town, but wait until you see the old section of the city, or some of the Chinese palaces in the French Concession. By that I mean—"

Martha interrupted proudly. "I know all about the Concessions. And extraterritoriality, and the nationalists and the communists, and Sun Yat Sen, and war lords, and the White Russians, and hundred-year-old eggs—"

"And where did you pick up all this expertise?"

"From the ship's captain."

"I see. So you turned the captain into your own private tutor? That must have been very informative."

"Leo, please." Martha was more amused than insulted by this subtle accusation. "I was so seasick I had to spend a lot of time on deck, and the captain would come up and chat with me. I made clear that I was going to Shanghai to meet my . . . my . . . husband." Her face flushed with a touch of embarrassment. "But there was nothing 'private' about it. He was just passing time, and I wanted to find out something about the place where I was going to live. And he was old enough to be my grandfather." She did not mention that being under the captain's unofficial protection conveniently kept the other men on the ship from making unwanted advances.

Leo's pout evaporated. "Your husband?"

Martha blushed outright this time. "Well, you did ask me to marry you. Or don't you remember?"

Earnestness replaced Leo's lighthearted expression. "Martha, the thought of making you my wife, legally my wife, has never left my mind. That's the whole reason I came to Shanghai."

At that moment the rickshaw pulled up in front of a glorious Georgian mansion. Black shutters accented the cream stucco walls, and the front portico extended from the massive front door in a wide semi-circle, punctuated by four Doric columns. The rickshaw driver laid down his load in front of the main gate and waited patiently for Leo to hand him his fare. Martha did not move.

"Why are we stopping?" she asked. "Who lives here?"

"I do. And so will you, at least as of today," replied Leo, playful again. He leapt down from the cart and extended his hand to help her down. Martha remained motionless.

"What? Here? In this house? This mansion? You're not serious."

"Well, if you don't like it, say so, and I'll buy another. Although I did negotiate a rather good deal on this one. The man who built it was in the shipping business. He lost his fortune a little over a month ago, when a typhoon demolished most of his fleet. Seems there was some scandal involving the maritime insurance. Sold me all the furnishings as well. The interior of the place is quite nice. If you would just come in and take a peek around, then you can pass judgment." He said all this cheerfully, but he was quite serious. He would sell the place as quickly as he'd bought it, lock, stock, and barrel, to please Martha.

Martha stared at the house a moment longer, then her eyes returned to Leo. She gave him a look that could convey only one meaning, and then stepped down from the rickshaw.

In his haste to get her inside Leo forgot to pay the driver, whose loud howls of betrayal forced him to return and hand over the fare. By this time the head household servant, Duo Win, had opened the gate to greet them. The rest of the staff, inherited directly from the previous owner, waited in a dignified line just inside the front door. Dressed in their best white cotton uniforms, they respectfully bowed in turn, to their new mistress.

Seven Chinese faces moved before her in a blur. Martha was conscious only of Leo's arm around her waist, the warmth of his body, the firmness of his thigh as it brushed up against her hip.

"Tea ready. Please to come," offered Duo Win politely, after everyone had been introduced.

"No, thank you," Leo responded. "Madame would like to rest now." *This was taking forever.*

"Very good. Will turn down bed for Madame."

"Never mind that. We'll manage." Leo escorted Martha up the wide marble steps of the double staircase that led to the second floor. Seven pairs of eyes watched with barely concealed amusement. He reached the landing and paused.

"Duo Win, everyone take the rest of the day off."

"Sir?"

"I said everyone is off duty for the rest of the day. Leave the house. Go shopping. Take a holiday."

"All?"

"Yes, damn it. Everyone."

"Cook too?"

"EVERYONE. RIGHT NOW."

Leo's roar scattered the group in the foyer. Taking Martha's hand, he led her down the hall to the master bedroom suite. He did not point out that the rosewood four-poster bed had been carved in Siam, or that the antique mirror over her marble-topped vanity came from Venice, or that the silk carpet on the floor had once belonged to an Indian Maharajah. He brought her to the center of the room, released her, then walked back to the door and shut it, determined to shut out the rest of the world.

Words were no longer necessary. She reached out to him and he came to her, locking her in his arms as their hungry mouths met and opened. Martha moaned, and the sound of her yearning inflamed him even more. Dropping his embrace he seized her face in his hands. He kissed her chin, her cheeks, her temples, her eyes; then returned to her lips, seeking and demanding. With trembling fingers Martha stroked the corners of his mouth as his tongue claimed her again. She stroked his ears, his neck, and his back, urging him onward, lost in an abyss of desire.

He could have taken her immediately, tearing off only the pieces of clothing that barred their essential coupling, but he wanted to relish all of her. He tried to reach behind her and unclasp the top of her dress; after one unsuccessful effort his ardor refused to let him waste any more time on buttons. Turning her roughly he ripped them off in a single effort. Martha's crumpled linen chemise fell to the floor, instantly forgotten.

Martha brought his hands to her breasts. Still behind her, he cupped one in each hand and massaged them upward, fondling her nipples beneath the silk of her short slip. Then he pulled that garment over her head and flung it away. Martha quickly kicked free of her shoes, and turned to face her lover. She stood before him with no thought of modesty or embarrassment, rendered completely comfortable in her nakedness by the force of her need for him.

Leo dropped to his knees and slowly removed her panties, then her stockings. When she was completely undressed, he began to nibble and kiss her inner thighs, first one, then the other, while stroking the backs of her legs with long, fluttering caresses.

Martha rewarded him with a series of short moans, and buried her hands in his hair. He kissed his way up to the small, pointed bones of her slender hips. She rocked them gently, as if he had already entered her. He could not wait much longer. He picked her up and laid her across the bed, threw himself on top of her, still fully clothed, then pinned her hands close to her head and pushed himself against her.

"Can you feel how much I want you?"

She wanted to answer him but a groan of passion was the only sound she could make. Leo kept talking to her, whispering close to her ear.

"You are mine, Martha. Mine forever. Do you know how much I love you?" He stood up and kicked off his pants. Martha tried to sit up, but he guided her back down onto the bed.

"Don't move. Not yet." Still standing, he leaned over the bed, pulled her body toward him, and entered her with one smooth thrust. Martha cried out again, an exclamation of pure joy. She wrapped her legs around his lower back and tilted her pelvis up, encouraging him to enter her more deeply. Holding her hips he pushed further, until their bodies bonded completely.

Leo stood motionless, possessing her, pulsing inside her. He did not move. He wanted this moment to last forever.

Martha's hand traveled toward the point where their bodies became one. She stroked her lower abdomen, welcoming his presence there. She then rocked her hips one time.

Leo exploded. His back arched and he pressed even deeper into her as spasm after spasm rocked his body. A low growling moan escaped him, answered by Martha's cries of delight as she shared his pleasure.

It was several moments before he withdrew from her body. Then he took off the rest of his clothes and pressed his naked body to hers. Their kisses overflowed with tenderness now, their passionate demands momentarily sated.

"You are my wife, Martha Levy."

"And you are my husband, Leopold Hoffman."

"I missed you so much"

"My love."

And so their endearments continued, until at last they nestled down in the big four-poster bed, her back curled up against his stomach, his arm beneath her head, and drifted into a sleep of cozy contentment.

He awoke after dark and saw her standing at the window, his shirt wrapped around her like a nightdress, an apparition of extraordinary loveliness bathed in moonlight.

"Consummation," he whispered, not realizing that he'd spoken aloud.

She turned toward him, smiling.

"What did you say, darling?"

"I said, 'consummation.'"

Her smile deepened, and she moved closer. "Is that an observation or an invitation?"

"Both." He sat up and patted the bed next to him. "I was looking at you, and thinking about how lovely you are, and thought again that our lovemaking is the essence of that word—consummation. That's what I thought the first time we made love, and it's still true." He did not add that he had a generous basis for comparison. There was no reason to hurt Martha with his history.

She sat next to him and tucked her feet under his thighs. "Would it be possible to consume something of a different nature first? For the first time in weeks, I'm hungry."

"If you insist. Supper will be ready in a moment." Leo reached over to pull the bell cord that summoned Duo Win, then stopped, his hand in midair, when he realized that no one would be in the kitchen to hear it. Deciphering his movements, Martha laughed.

"I don't suppose we can give the whole staff the day off every time we make love, can we?"

"Guess not. I would have to make every day a holiday."

"What a pleasant thought," she said, abandoning her seated position and curling up next to him.

"House would be a wreck, though," he added absent-mindedly as she began to stroke his chest. Could he persuade her to wait a few minutes before heading to the kitchen? Then again, why not make love there, too?

Leo did not get the opportunity to make this suggestion. Martha bolted upright, eyes full of anxiety. "Leo, what is going on? How could you afford all this? What have you been doing for the past six months? How do you go from being a concierge to lord and master of a place like this?"

Because I killed, and stole, and gambled. Because I had to find a way of staying alive and out of prison, to be with you again. Because I had to have money to protect you and make you happy. But would you, could you, still love me, knowing what I have done? No, he could not tell her his story, at least, not all of it, for he could not bear to lose her if she could neither understand nor forgive him.

Leo pulled Martha back down next to him. He turned to face her, so that they were laying side by side, hands clasped between them, their faces only inches apart. Her eyes were serious now, and so full of love that Leo felt a lump form in his throat. What had he ever done to deserve love like this? That this beautiful woman would wait for him, and cross the world for him, bringing a heart so full and pure? He closed his eyes and inhaled again. Then he began to speak.

"Martha, I was not in Paris on a holiday. I was there to function as an interpreter for a group of businessmen."

"As an interpreter?"

"Yes. You noticed when we were in Paris that I speak several languages. We're speaking German now, because that's your first language. But I seem to have a special talent for languages. I pick them up easily.

"Someone I knew in Budapest decided that I was the person he needed to facilitate an international business transaction. It wasn't really legal, for it involved buying weapons for the Hungarian army in violation of the peace treaty. But this man, and the group he was with, appealed to my sense of national pride, and, I suppose I have to admit, to my vanity. So I agreed to help them. I thought I would be helping myself, and Hungary."

He shifted onto his back and stared at the ceiling, choosing his words carefully, anxious to get close enough to the truth to be credible without incriminating himself too deeply.

"You know I'd just arrived in Paris when we met. The morning I left you in front of Notre Dame, I learned that the men I was helping were not working for the Hungarian government at all. They were members of the Hungarian Fascist Party, attempting to acquire weapons for their own organization. Rather than cooperate, I decided to foil their plans."

"What did you do?"

"There was a story in the paper that morning about a Hungarian army officer who'd been arrested at the Hague passing counterfeit French francs. That gave me an idea. I contacted one of the man responsible for selling the weapons, drew his attention to the article, and warned him, in confidence, that he'd better make sure the Hungarian group he was dealing with did not intend to pay him with fake francs. I assumed, of course, that the deal would be called off immediately, or at least delayed. I planned to lay low for the day, meet you at five o'clock, go with you to Munich, and be done with the whole business. But when I returned to my hotel to collect my passport, I discovered that I'd underestimated the people with whom I was dealing. There was another man in my room. Dead."

"Dead? How?"

"If you mean how was he killed, I don't know, exactly. There was too much blood to tell easily, and I didn't want to examine things too closely."

"Oh my God, Leo, how awful." Martha threw herself across Leo's chest, her eyes filling with tears. She knew that he had abandoned her for a reason, but she never imagined anything so appalling. How could she have ever felt a moment of self-pity?

Leo continued, stroking her hair as he spoke.

"I knew then that I was meant to take the blame for the murder. I suppose the leader of the group I was with thought the dead man was the one who'd betrayed them, and that I was expendable. At any rate, I had to leave the country immediately."

"But couldn't you prove you were innocent? I would've told the police that you were with me all night, and couldn't possibly have killed anyone."

"Martha, I'm Hungarian. You're German. The French hate us. What's more, we're Jewish. I learned after the war that Jews make the most convenient scapegoats. The murder was orchestrated by powerful people with international connections. There was no way the French police were going to let me off the hook, not even with an alibi as beautiful as you."

"But why didn't you go to Germany? Or England? Somewhere closer?"

"I'm a Hungarian citizen. I can't travel freely in Europe without both entry and transit visas. I didn't know how far they would look for me. I knew I had to get beyond their net as quickly as possible."

"So you came to Shanghai."

"So I came to Shanghai."

"But will you be safe here?"

"I think so. As safe as I could be anywhere in the world. I was a little fish, and people don't tend to ask questions here. No one cares much about the past. It's amazing that way."

"And the house?"

"The murdered man evidently had some scheme of his own going on the side, something the rest of them must not have known about. You see, he had a lot of money with him. That money brought me here."

Martha gasped. "You stole money from a dead man?"

"I didn't go through his pockets while he . . . I mean, he must have taken off his coat before he was killed. I saw it and went through it, looking for some identification. That's how I confirmed who he was: Imre Károly, the police chief of Budapest. He was an outspoken member of the Fascist party, and had a personal reputation for being corrupt, so I was pretty sure he hadn't made that money lawfully. Maybe he'd played a part in the counterfeiting scheme, I don't know. At any rate, given what his fellow Fascists had done to him and were trying to do to me, taking his money was the only way I could think of to escape from them."

"But Leo, didn't it occur to you that taking the money would make you look guilty? And that you could be charged with another crime for stealing it?"

"So they could put me in jail for theft and then hang me for murder? No, Martha. I saw my chance to evade their plans for me and I took it. Unfortunately, I couldn't take you with me. I didn't know how to find you, and every moment I stayed in France placed me, and our future together, in greater peril."

"But why did you take so long to send for me?"

"I didn't want to put you in any danger. I needed some time to make certain that I was safe here. And, I needed to know that I could create a future worthy of sharing with you. Until then, it was pointless. It was better for you to just forget about me."

"As if I could."

Hearing the tenderness in her voice, Leo felt relief flood through every limb of his body. Martha was satisfied with his story. She could still love a man falsely accused of murder, who had taken what was not his out of self-defense.

"When I arrived here, I discovered that I have a talent for investing, and, after a rocky start, managed to turn my initial investment into a tidy sum."

"A tidy sum? This must cost a fortune. The house, the servants—"

Leo grinned. "That, my dear, is one of the luxuries of Shanghai. I can keep seven servants for the price of one decent gardener in Europe. The house was not inexpensive, but didn't cost nearly what it would have anywhere else. To make money is the main reason people come to Shanghai. The life you can lead after you've made some here is one reason they stay. Will you stay and be the queen of my castle? Could you be happy here?"

"Anywhere, with you, my love. Anywhere."

And they decided to put supper off for a while longer, after all.

They were married four days later, at eleven o'clock in the morning, in the office of a Justice of the Peace in the French Concession. Martha wore a simple ankle-length wedding dress, created especially for her by the leading American designer at one of Nanking Road's finest dress shops. He designed the dress in pale green silk embroidered with violets, saved, he claimed, "for the purpose of adorning a truly beautiful redhead." Lawrence Cosgrove and the Justice's elderly secretary served as their witnesses. At the proper moment, Leo held Martha's hands, and uttered the vow he'd longed to make since meeting her in Paris.

"I, Leopold Gustave Hoffman, take you, Martha Katrina Levy, to be my lawful wedded wife; to have and to hold from this day forward, for better, for worse; for richer, or poorer; in sickness, and in health; to honor and cherish, forsaking all others in steadfast love, 'til death us do part."

" 'Til death us do part," repeated Martha, in turn. And then, flooded with emotion, she looked at the diamond band encircling her finger and thought, *no. Ours is a bond not even death could break.*

They celebrated with a festive brunch at the dining room of the Palace. "So this is what it feels like to be blissfully happy," sighed Martha, leaning against Leo's shoulder, feeling giddy and more than a little tipsy. She wasn't used to champagne and felt its effects very quickly.

"I want you to be this happy every day," said a slightly less tipsy Leo, meaning it.

"Leo, may I see the license?"

"Why? Don't you believe that we're married?"

"You silly darling. I just want to read it. I want to see it, in print. With my own two little eyes, where it says, 'Mr. and Mrs. Leopold Hoffman.' "

"All right then." A guarded note had entered Leo's voice, but Martha did not notice. He pulled an official-looking piece of paper out of his breast pocket and handed it to his wife.

"Ah, there it is." She sighed another happy sigh and carefully spread the document out on the table in front of her. A quizzical expression soon wrinkled her forehead.

"Leo, what's this?"

"I thought you spoke French," he answered, his tone deliberately light.

"You know I do. What I mean is, why does it say here that we're Catholic?"

"Does it? What an embarrassing mistake."

"Well, shouldn't we have it corrected?"

"Why?"

"It's an official document. This is our marriage license. I don't want to start our marriage with a lie."

"A lie? That is a bit harsh, isn't it? Most Hungarians are Catholic. The old girl at the notary's office probably just assumed I was, and that, therefore, you were, too. Doesn't change anything. We're not any less married. French law respects the civil ceremony, not the religious one. It's not worth the trouble to correct it."

"But it's not right. It's not who we are."

"And just who are we?" Leo asked, serious now. He lowered his voice. "Did you decide to be Jewish?"

"Don't be ridiculous."

"Do you go to synagogue?"

"No."

"Do you follow the laws of Jehovah?"

"No, but—"

"Did your parents?"

"No, but Leo—"

"Do you even know a single Hebrew prayer?"

"No, but it doesn't—"

"But what? When I was a boy, growing up in Budapest, I was taught that one's religion was irrelevant. It was the age of science. The age of reason. Talent and hard work were all that mattered, and God was a matter of conscience. Well, it seems that's only true when there's enough to go around. When someone goes hungry, the hungry blame the Jews. When there's a war, the losers blame the Jews. When the country collapses, the bankrupt blame the Jews. I won't have my children blamed: not for famine, not for financial chaos, not for war. I didn't choose to be born Jewish, and I choose for my children not to be born Jews."

Martha stared hard at the piece of paper in front of her, trying to make sense out of Leo's words. Through the diminishing fog of her champagne euphoria, she comprehended that the misinformation on their marriage license was not the secretary's mistake. Leo had given the wrong religion on purpose. This fact troubled Martha, in a vague, inexplicable way. She'd never felt as if she'd had any meaningful religious connection to her Jewish heritage, but it didn't feel right to have it snatched away from her with the stroke of a pen. It seemed blasphemous, somehow. She thought of her father and her sister. Living under some false pretense would make her feel even farther away from them. How could she make Leo understand?

He interrupted the growing silence, correctly reading her thoughts. Taking her hand, he asked gently, "Do you think God cares? Don't you think that our relationship with God can transcend the label others have given us?"

"I don't know, Leo. It doesn't seem right, somehow. It seems like a charade."

"Listen, my darling." His face was close to hers now. "We've come to a place where we can begin our lives all over again. Without stigma, without fear, without poverty. Why handicap ourselves? Why handicap our children? We have nothing to lose."

Martha pondered all that he had said. The idea still disturbed her, but she couldn't find a way to contradict Leo's logic. As a young girl she'd seen, firsthand, a man called Adolph Hitler try to take control of the government of Bavaria, mesmerizing his followers with a speech given in a Munich beer hall, preaching hatred of the Jews. Hitler had gone to jail for his attempted coup. But what about the ones who listened so raptly to his hateful words? Were there others like Hitler out there?

Martha looked at her husband, who was toying with the remains of his dessert, similarly lost in thought. He was so handsome, so intelligent, so tender. Why should it matter if he chose to evade a heritage to which he felt no connection? A heritage that had probably caused him only pain. Many people in Germany were aware of what had happened in Hungary after the fall of the short-lived communist government: the slaughter of the communist ministers, the massacres that followed in the countryside, and the killing of people whose only crime was their Jewish ancestry. Had Leo's family been caught up in the bloody aftermath of the war?

She started to ask, then relented. She would ask someday, but not today. Not on their wedding day. She did not want him to relive any nightmares today. There was so much about him that she did not know. She would have years to solve Leo's many riddles. For the time being, she must be satisfied with his explanation; he wanted to protect her and their children.

Her glass of champagne had gone flat. The violets on her wrist had wilted. Her giddy mood had evaporated, replaced by a sleepy melancholia. She wanted his arms around her; to fall asleep surrounded by his strength. She touched his sleeve.

"My husband, let's go home."

"Whatever you desire, my love."

"Could we just spend the rest of our wedding day in bed?"

"Why of course, Mrs. Hoffman. Of course."

Later that evening Leo gave Martha a wedding present.

"But Leo, that's not fair. I have nothing for you," she insisted, making an effort to hand him back the small silver box.

He pressed it back into her hand. "Martha, your presence is the only present I will ever need. And no more struggling, or I will open it for you. It's fragile."

Enticed by her love of surprises, Martha yielded and opened the box. She lifted out a miniature porcelain swan, no more than six inches long, but so lifelike it seemed ready to float from her hands into the air. Two tiny emeralds glittered in its eyes.

"How lovely," she exclaimed, genuinely pleased. She placed the swan on her dresser. "He'll be there to greet me every morning."

"Perhaps if we ever run out of money, it will lay us a few golden eggs, too."

"Sorry, sir. I think it was a goose that did the golden-egg laying. Swans are only useful for decoration."

"Then he will be in good company in this room." Leo took her in his arms and planted a barrage of kisses on her hair.

Martha pretended to be insulted. She dodged her head this way and that to avoid his continuing kisses. "Are you implying that I am only good for decoration?"

"Far from it," he replied, his forehead touching hers. "I meant only that you are the most beautiful thing I have ever seen."

"Why thank you, Mr. Hoffman."

"You are most welcome, Mrs. Hoffman. Come to think of it, I know a very good way for you to thank me."

Martha rolled her eyes and giggled, her good humor completely restored.

"Again?" she asked, with false exasperation.

He grinned a truly lascivious grin. "And again and again and again and—"

Martha interrupted him, putting a finger to his lips. Her other hand reached out to his waist and untied the loosely knotted sash of his dressing gown. Her eyes glowed.

"With so much to do, we'd better get started."

And so, they did.

SIX
SHANGHAI, 1927

During the 1920s the collective consciousness of the civilized world turned its back on the horror of the Great War and concentrated, instead, on the pursuit of pleasure. Fed up with sacrifice and responsibility, the citizens of the victorious countries threw themselves into a celebration that lasted for close to a decade. Life became an unending party. And nowhere was the party longer, louder, or more festive than in Shanghai.

Flush with new wealth and inebriated by love, Leo and Martha cheerfully joined the revelry. They danced away the afternoons at the tea dances hosted by the Astor House Hotel; dressed in white tie and sequins to attend the latest Hollywood movie at the new cinema in the French Quarter; led the charge to investigate the newest, most promising restaurants; and were regularly seen at the clubhouse of the municipal racetrack, where Leo's love of horses grew to include the stubby, native Mongolian ponies that only the smallest jockeys could ride.

Often, they finished their evenings in the company of gossipy friends at the glamorous Club Casanova, or took in a show at the notorious Lido. They entertained frequently at their home, and at their country club, the newly built Cercle Sportif Français, which boasted a roof garden for summer dancing, a ballroom for winter parties, and a magnificent indoor swimming pool decorated in vivid Art Deco style, as well as badminton and tennis courts.

During the searing heat of summer they fled north to Tsingtao, the heart of "the Asian Riviera" on the western coast of the Yellow Sea, where they stayed in the historic Grand Hotel, an imposing white structure decorated like a fanciful gingerbread castle. Beauty and laughter floated through their lives with the welcome regularity of a sultry summer breeze.

Martha was rarely homesick. She soon abandoned her native German, speaking only the more popular tongues of French and English. She took great joy in little frivolities, activities that would have caused her father to shake his head in disapproval. She joined a garden club, a music appreciation club, a literary society devoted to the popular novel, and an amateur drama society. Her lifestyle was not atypical, for while the men of Shanghai made money, their wives had to keep busy, and with a house full of servants there was little to do in the way of household chores, other than plan menus and periodically redecorate.

At times Martha felt as if she'd been given a second chance at childhood, untainted by tragedy and war. She knew she was ridiculously lucky, but seldom questioned why she deserved her new life. Leo loved her. That was reason enough.

Occasionally she would rebel against the self-centered nature of her daily routine, and throw her boundless energy behind one of the charities attempting to do something about the plight of the poor in

Shanghai: the beggars, the abandoned children, the homeless families. But the infinite scope of the poverty and suffering she witnessed would soon overwhelm her, and she would retreat to the security of the celebration that was her life with Leo. Leo, who spoiled and pampered her, who brought her laughter and made endless, enchanting love to her, who never talked down to her or made her feel foolish or unintelligent. Leo, who made her life begin.

Leo loved being responsible for Martha. He took delight in all of her accomplishments, from a beautifully executed dinner party to her mastery of a new English phrase. His heart told him that he'd been given custody of a special treasure; he was the devoted trustee of an incomparable work of art. It was his duty to ensure her happiness.

It struck him hardest when he caught sight of her suddenly, hurrying through the front door, back from one of her social gatherings, or emerging from the bath, her glorious auburn hair wrapped up in a towel. At those impromptu moments the depth and intensity of his love for her seized him with a physical force that could have been agony. But it wasn't, any more than the violent muscular contractions of an orgasm could be called pain. She was part of him.

They were gregarious and generous with their time, but their special closeness to each other excluded all others from any bond deeper than casual friendship. Both enjoyed the companionship of their own gender, but they never lingered long within it. Lawrence Cosgrove was the closest friend Leo ever made in Shanghai. His return to England six months after Martha and Leo's wedding caused a moment of sorrow and gave them a good justification for a lavish party, but it caused no deep sense of loss. The company of others was a pleasant entertainment, but only Martha was essential. And only Leo was essential to her.

"It's so unseemly," complained one wealthy British widow, whose long list of companions included many married young men new to the wicked ways of Shanghai, "for such a handsome young man to be so blatantly in love with his wife." And the men of Shanghai felt the same way. It was heartlessly unfashionable for anyone as enchanting as Martha to be so taken with her husband. Such a shame. Her brilliant smile and charming conversation yielded occasional comfort, but no hope, as she and Leo moved like brilliant particles through the kaleidoscope of concentric circles that shaped Shanghai society.

And so the party continued, until the winter of 1927. Then, for a few brief and bloody days, the music stopped.

Leo woke with a start. He lay rigid in his bed, his heart beating ferociously in his chest. The nightmares came so rarely now. He had forgotten how real the terror of war felt when recaptured in the silence of his dreams.

In this dream he lay in a ditch, trapped beneath barbed wire, struggling to free himself. The wire cut into his flesh, and the stench of blood and sulfur was suffocating. Then a hand stretched toward him. "Get out man; get out," a male voice bellowed. Leo closed his eyes, trying to recall the image. Whose face had it been, reaching down to him?

The soldier trying to help him had been Lawrence Cosgrove.

Martha stirred beside him. Leo rested a hand along her thigh, seeking comfort in the peacefulness of her sleep.

Lawrence Cosgrove. How odd.

Then he heard it, in the distance, a sound like thunder that was not thunder. The low, booming rumble set his heart hammering again, with renewed vigor.

Mortar fire.

The bedroom window rattled slightly as the echoes of sound reached the panes. Leo slid cautiously out of bed, making sure not to wake his sleeping wife. He crept toward the window, and drew the curtain back.

Nothing.

The glow from a three-quarter moon revealed only the familiar shadows of homes and gardens, tranquil in the chill of a frosty February night. No strange lights on the horizon. No fires. Nothing to suggest war or catastrophe.

But there it was again, coming from the direction of the river. Another booming rumble.

Leo quickly donned his cashmere dressing gown and headed downstairs. He could not see the river from their house, but someone would be on duty at the desk of the Palace Hotel. Someone there would know what was happening.

He went to the telephone in his office and rang the hotel. The clock on his wall showed four thirty. Two rings. A dignified British voice answered.

"This is the Palace Hotel. How may we be of service?"

"Leo Hoffman here. Who is this speaking?"

"Mr. Hoffman, good to hear from you. This is Richard Fletcher. I was the bell captain when you were residing here."

"That's right. Good to speak to you, Richard. So you're working the night desk now?"

"Yes, sir."

"Well, congratulations on the promotion. You'll soon be running the place." Leo had little patience for small talk at the moment, but small talk, especially flattery, was a necessary precursor to the extraction of significant information. Patience.

"Thank you, sir. So kind of you to say so. What can I do for you this evening? Or rather, this morning?"

"I've been hearing some thumps and bumps that sound like mortar fire. Is that possible?"

"I am afraid so, sir. It seems that General Chiang Kai-shek is making his presence known."

"What? Is the bastard actually going to attack Shanghai?"

"Well, we all hope not, sir. But he did a nice job of it in Nanking, didn't he?"

"Almighty God. What's being done?"

"Well, I've heard the Americans are moving their warships down the Yangtze to protect the harbor here. I imagine the others will jump in soon. No one would want the Yanks to get all the credit for saving us, eh?" The young Englishman chuckled at his own slim wit, and Leo joined him, feigning amusement. He had to know more.

"So what's the artillery fire about? Who's Chiang fighting?"

"Well, it's not really clear at the moment, sir. Civil war does get confusing, doesn't it? Last report is that he's just shelling a bit as he goes, to ward off potential resistance from Sun Chuan-fang, the reigning warlord at the moment. We can't see anything burning from here."

"Good."

"You should think about coming down, Mr. Hoffman. There's quite a party going on. Loads of reporters. Most of the Municipal Council. They're running between here and the Astor House like it was a relay race. Highly entertaining."

"Thank you, but I think I'll wait for the sun to come up. There's no serious danger at the moment? No call for evacuation?"

"No, sir. No real trouble yet. Just Chinaman against Chinaman. They all know better than to bother the International Settlement or the French Concession. A few European warships would make pretty short work of the whole Chinese Nationalist Army."

"Right you are. Thank you for the information. It's been a pleasure talking to you."

"And you, sir."

They rang off. Leo lowered the receiver back in its cradle. No danger. Was such unruffled bravado justified? He knew this wasn't the first time that political unrest had threatened Shanghai. China had gone through varying degrees of internal revolt since the collapse of the Manchu dynasty. But for the most part, other than the inconvenience of an occasional influx of Chinese refugees, the Concessions of Shanghai were unaffected by the war raging between Peking and Canton. They stood untouched: a rich, glittering sanctuary from civil war, a tribute to capitalism and the power of gunboat diplomacy. And, the Shanghai-landers believed, an invincible one.

Until now. For this new general, Chiang Kai-shek, in his quest to re-create a nation out of the private kingdoms of China's many warlords, seemed willing to take on the foreign powers as well: those countries that had, for close to a hundred years, kept strategic pieces of his homeland as private playgrounds. Worse, he had the backing of Soviet Russia. The general and his troops had already forced Britain to return its concessions further north, at Hankow and Kiukiang. Would Shanghai be next?

The Western powers were not willing to take any chances. Too much money was at stake; they moved quickly to protect their investment. Britain, America, Japan, France, Italy, and Spain rushed troops to Shanghai. They were to serve as a warning to the general, and to the Soviets: leave Shanghai alone.

Their faith bolstered by this evidence of the world's commitment to their safety, the Shanghailanders turned the threat of invasion into yet another excellent excuse for a party. They arranged entertainments for the arriving troops, ranging from brothel trips to hockey games to billiard tournaments, and waited for the general to arrive.

Now, one month later, he was pounding on Shanghai's door. For the first time in over a year, Leo felt fear. But he had nowhere to go. No safe place to take Martha. They had to wait and hope the foreign powers were prepared to back up their bluster with action.

When the sun came up the following morning, residents of the Concessions found themselves inhabiting an armed camp. Barbed wire barriers had been erected around the Settlements. Military guards patrolled the streets.

Within a few days the real show began, and the Shanghailanders discovered they once again had front row seats to the Chinese civil war theater. Smoke clouded the horizon. Gunfire and mortar shells could be heard above the usual panoply of commercial noise. But as the Shanghailanders had hoped, the violence remained strictly confined to the sections of city under Chinese control, and the fighting lasted only a few days. With the help of communist forces loyal to Soviet Russia, Chiang Kai-shek conquered the Chinese sections of Shanghai.

Then, nothing. For weeks there was no significant military activity. Spring came, and the foreign residents began to relax. It seemed the general would respect the Concessions after all.

To celebrate the end of the hostilities, Leo and Martha decided to go in search of a Russian teahouse Leo had visited once, before Martha's arrival. Leo loved the ritual of late afternoon tea. It reminded him of happy times at home with his foster mother, Erzsebet: a time when life was civilized, and his expectations knew no limits.

"Isn't it lovely to walk outside again, without worrying?" sighed Martha with languid contentment, hugging Leo's arm as they strolled along the Avenue Joffre. The April air was cool and crisp, and the heavy fragrance of cherry blossoms blotted out the smell of the river. Leo could not remember the precise address of the tiny establishment they were seeking, so they explored at their leisure, poking their noses around every corner. Soon they left Avenue Joffre behind, and found themselves on the outskirts of the French Concession, where restaurants and cafés competed with innumerable small shops for space and the attention of the passing public.

Leo found a small street that looked encouragingly familiar and started down it, Martha in tow. He was by this time so intent that he scarcely noticed the small group of Chinese men huddled across the street. Chinese men always gathered on the streets in the early evening to gamble, gossip, or to argue about politics; they were part of the scenery.

But Martha noticed something unusual, and slowed her pace. Three men stood in a semicircle with their backs to the street, clad in the ubiquitous blue cotton suits worn by the working class Chinese. Two more men stood in the center of the circle, and another, a young man, knelt in the center of the small ring. Why was the young man on his knees? Were his hands tied? Martha tugged on Leo's arm.

"Leo, look, there's something strange going on there—"

He did not hear her, having just located the teahouse. "There it is, just across from the lantern shop—"

"Leo, look."

This time Martha's voice caused Leo to spin quickly on his heel. As he turned he heard a shout, full of youthful defiance. He knew enough of the language to understand the words.

"Long live the revolution!"

A burst of gunfire followed. The small group scattered in five differ-ent directions. The young man lay on the ground, blood pouring from the wound where a portion of his skull had been blown away. Bits of his brain stuck to the pavement. His legs still quivered.

Martha screamed. Leo grabbed her shoulders and spun her around, pressing her head to his shoulder.

"Don't look, Martha. Let's get out of here." Her screams turned into whimpers.

Leo heard a whistle blow. Within minutes the sidewalk could be swarming with French police. He had no desire to serve as a witness. He had no useful facts to share, and did not want his own background investigated.

"Come on." He grabbed Martha's hand and pulled her along behind him. They walked quickly away from the scene without encountering anyone. No one at all. When they reached the Avenue Joffre Leo hailed a cab. They did not leave the house for five days.

All around the city, the massacre continued. Day after day, night after night, the Shanghailanders closed their doors and averted their eyes while mercenary thugs controlled by the nationalists slaughtered the communists within their ranks. After all, the foreign residents told themselves, there was no reason for the Europeans to get involved; this was a Chinese political problem, and the Chinese had a different no-tion regarding the sanctity of life. Perhaps because there were so many of them.

And so with guns, knives, and treachery, Chiang Kai-shek consoli-dated his power. He was supported this time not by the Russians, but by the wealthy Chinese without whom he could not rule the country.

Wealthy men who wanted a unified China, but did not want their property nationalized by the communists. Men who owned banks, ships, and factories, and the souls of other men. Men like Liu Tue-Sheng.

The remaining communist members of the liberation army soon fled the city. The general then left Shanghai to establish a nationalist government at Nanking. On his arm was his new bride, Maylong Soong, sister of Mr. T. V. Soong, the new government's Minister of Finance and one of the wealthiest men in China.

The Concessions remained inviolate. The wire fences came down. The soldiers came into town to drink and purchase the favors of women, and merchant ships returned to the harbor. Life resumed its normal frenetic pace. A short memory was a handy attribute if one wanted to live at ease in Shanghai.

Leo was not so sanguine. The sight of the factories burning across the river lingered in his mind. Just as the Derkovits family had linked their fortune to the fate of Hungary, he had linked his fortune to Shanghai's future. He'd invested in several businesses operating in the war-damaged industrial zone. He owned rental property in the Chinese districts and undeveloped real estate outside the French Concession. Luckily, this time his losses had been minor, but the next time, if there was a next time, he could face a major financial setback.

War was a risky business, and there was no guarantee that the political situation in China would not adversely affect Shanghai's economy in the future. Without another country that would take him in, he was not free to leave Shanghai, but his money could travel. Money could not be so easily seized or burned or destroyed by revolution. At least, not money that was invested in the safest, strongest country in the world: the United States of America.

By the end of the summer Leo had sold everything. With the help of a broker he invested his entire fortune in the stocks of American companies. He could not go to America, but his money could. It could grow there. And keep Martha safe.

In the interest of continued economic cooperation between the International Settlements and the new government of China, Sir Elly Kadoorie, one of Shanghai's wealthiest men, decided to host a gala honoring Chiang Kai-shek and his new bride. He invited the elite of Shanghai society, Western and Asian, to a dance at his home, Marble Hall, named for the tons of Italian marble he'd imported to build the mansion's massive stone fireplaces.

On the night of the party, Leo surprised Martha with an early Christmas present.

"My darling, it's so beautiful," Martha exclaimed as she lifted an emerald and diamond necklace from the velvet box he'd just handed her.

"Not as beautiful as your eyes."

She batted her lashes at him. "Thank you, kind sir. Could you help me put it on?"

They moved to stand in front of the mirror in the foyer so Martha could admire her new gift as Leo placed it around her neck. "Well, now there's a good-looking couple," Leo quipped as he closed the clasp.

The light faded from Martha's eyes. "They should have beautiful children, don't you think? But that doesn't seem to be in the cards, does it?"

Leo planted a few kisses on the back of her neck, just below the edge of her bobbed hair. "Darling, the doctor keeps telling us there's no reason why we can't have children. We just have to keep trying. If you like, I'll take you back upstairs and we can try again right now."

A smile replaced Martha's wistful expression. "And miss a chance to dance in Marble Hall? Not likely."

"Well, I won't allow you to dance with anyone else tonight, that's certain. I couldn't stand it. You're irresistible in that dress." Despite the trend toward heavily beaded, calf-length chemises for evening wear, Martha wore a long gown of emerald-green satin. In back, the fabric draped in a long cowl to her waist, exposing the creamy skin of her back and shoulders to maximum advantage.

She turned to face him. "I promise not to test you. Just one dance with old Silas Hardoon."

"The old man's ticker couldn't possibly take it."

"Don't underestimate him. I heard he bought his wife in a Chinese brothel."

"And to think I was lucky enough to find you in a pastry shop. Saved all that money."

Martha playfully clubbed her husband on the head with her small velvet bag, and they made their way to Marble Hall.

It was the party of the decade in a city whose population lived for fine parties. Bejeweled revelers danced under the radiant light of thirty-six hundred electric bulbs, clustered on massive Bohemian crystal chandeliers that swayed from the sixty-foot ceiling. Towering champagne fountains poured gallons of bubbly wine into crystal glasses, and banquet tables offered up delicacies from every nationality represented in Shanghai: Chinese dumplings shaped like swans and stuffed with shrimp, French cheeses, Italian pasta and bread, blintzes stuffed with caviar, beef tenderloin medallions, and desserts of every kind.

By midnight, the heat of the many electric bulbs caused the crowded ballroom to become uncomfortably warm. When Martha excused herself to go powder her nose, Leo decided to step out onto the balcony on the lower terrace to cool off.

To his dismay he was not alone. Also on the balcony, enjoying the fresh but frigid night air, were none other than Chiang Kai-shek himself, along with his wife. And Liu Tue-Sheng.

There was no way for Leo to back away and return to the ballroom without being rude, for all three people had turned to look directly at him. Nonetheless, he tried.

"Excuse me. I didn't mean to interrupt what must be a private conversation. Good evening."

No luck. "Mr. Hoffman, please, let me introduce you." The awkward cadence of Liu's speech rang in Leo's ears like a warning, but how could he turn down the honor of meeting the general, the man who might one day rule all of China, without insulting everyone present? He stepped forward.

"Good evening, Mr. Liu. It's been some time since we last met."

"Yes. I trust life in Shanghai has treated you well?"

"I have no complaints, thank you."

"Nor have I. General, please allow me to present Mr. Leopold Hoffman, a successful Shanghai businessman."

"It is an honor, General Chiang." Leo knew better than to shake hands. He acknowledged the general's bow by responding in a similar fashion, making sure that his own head descended a noticeable distance lower, to show his respect.

"And, Madame Chiang, Mr. Hoffman."

Here Leo was free to display his Hungarian courtesy. He bent low over the dimpled hand that the general's wife offered him from beneath her sable wrap, bringing his heels together smartly as he did so, and pressed his lips to the back of her palm for a fraction of an instant.

Then he committed an unforgivable breach of etiquette. He did not let go of her hand. He held it, staring at the ring she wore: a five-carat, emerald-cut diamond, winking up at him like an old menace.

An uncomfortable cough from the woman whose hand he clutched brought Leo back to his senses. He released Madame Chiang's hand. His head jerked up with a snap and he met Liu's eyes.

The man was smiling.

Leo managed to regain his composure. "It's an honor to meet you both, and may I offer my sincere congratulations on your marriage. Now, if you will please excuse me, I must meet my wife before she is lost in this crowd."

"Of course," Liu replied. "One must not leave such a beautiful woman alone too long."

Leo did not like the thought that Liu even knew of Martha's existence. Without another word, he turned and left the terrace.

Within a few minutes Martha rejoined him, but Leo's encounter with Liu had taken the pleasure out of the evening. He saw only the diamond on Madame Chiang's hand. Liu had given the Cartier diamonds to the general to help finance his war, of that Leo was certain. Had those stones helped pay for the guns that Chiang used to massacre his communist brethren, once the general decided he'd toss his lot in with the likes of Liu rather than rely on the Russians?

Leo felt like a pawn on a chessboard, the size and scope of which he could not ascertain. He did not like the feeling. He wanted to leave, to get away from Liu and the general and the crowd of people celebrating the survival of a city that had no right to exist, yet continued to do so.

Martha looked up at him. "Leo, do you feel unwell?"

"Fine, just tired. I don't know that I'll last much longer."

She acquiesced immediately when he suggested they leave; she could tell he was no longer enjoying the evening. They'd reached the entrance to the ballroom when Martha hesitated, listening.

"A waltz. They're playing a waltz. No one plays waltzes anymore. Could we please dance one more time?"

He could never refuse her. "Of course, my darling."

The waltz, which had been the scandal of their grandparents' generation because it called for such close physical contact between the sexes, was now viewed as hopelessly old-fashioned by the emancipated libertines of the roaring twenties. However, Leo was a child of the land of the waltz, and to the offspring of the Austrian-Hungarian Empire, the waltz was a romantic ritual, not a mere dance that could fall out of favor as quickly as yesterday's hemline. Leo could waltz more gracefully than most men could breathe.

He took Martha's hand in his and led her back to the all but empty dance floor. They paused for an instant to catch the rhythm of the music. Then with one quick step backward, Leo and Martha floated into the dance. They moved in effortless unison, gliding in swift circles around the room, stepping and turning as though the music emanated from them, as if their dance granted the spectators permission to share, for a moment, the magic of their special union.

Leo could sense every eye upon them, and his heart filled with emotion as he looked at Martha. He was dancing a waltz with his beautiful wife, his most beloved treasure, making love to her through the music, and he knew he was the envy of every man in the room.

"By God, you're worth a revolution," he whispered in the air above her ear. She did not catch his words, but heard the love with which he uttered them, and turning slightly to face him, she smiled.

SEVEN
SHANGHAI, 1929

"Missus sick again today, Mistah Leo. She no come down."

Leo took a last sip of his coffee and put down the newspaper he'd been reading. "I think it's time to take her to see the doctor, Wei. Yesterday she was too tired to move, and it's not like her to skip breakfast." As modern as Shanghai was, they were nonetheless exposed to a myriad of tropical diseases, from malaria carried by the voracious mosquitoes to dysentery spread by vegetables washed with tainted water. Martha was not running a fever, but there was no easy explanation for her illness. He did not want to take any chances.

When they left the house to take Martha to her doctor's appointment, it was just before nine o'clock on a cold and dreary Tuesday morning. Fog horns boomed loudly across the water as boats tried to navigate their way through the thick haze blanketing the river. The whole city seemed subdued.

The doctor's office was located a few blocks off the Bund. The nurse admitted Martha quickly, leaving Leo to wait uneasily in the sitting room. He told himself that there was probably nothing seriously wrong with his wife, but where Martha was concerned, he was not a patient man. He tried to occupy his mind by rereading yesterday's edition of the *North China Daily News*, but the stale stories did nothing to curb his agitation. It occurred to him that he could run up the street to his broker's office, and ask him about the status of his latest investment: shares in a coal mining company in the American state called Pennsylvania. Leo tapped on the glass that separated the waiting area from the nurse's station.

"Excuse me. Do you have any idea how long my wife will be?"

"I'm sure it will be at least an hour, if not more. With all that nausea the doctor will want to run some tests. Would you like a cup of coffee?"

"No, thanks, but I may run out for a moment. Please tell her I'll leave the car and driver for her, but that I'll be right back."

"Of course, sir." The nurse shut her glass barrier with an indulgent smile. Feeling a touch of guilt and a hint of relief, Leo left.

He quickly covered the few short blocks to the Bund and stopped at the Ewo building, where the offices of Jardine, Matheson and Company, the largest trading company in the Orient, were located. Leo's securities broker leased an office on the third floor.

Leo's investment advisor was a man by the name of Burton Damion. He was American, New York born, Harvard educated, and well-respected for his ability to make money for his clients, and himself. A rumor traveled around Shanghai that an investment scandal in New York was responsible for Burton's relocation to the city, but one never knew the truth behind the story of anyone's decision to come to Shanghai. His references were good, and with his hands-on experience as a trader in New York, his presence allowed some of the wealthy Shanghailanders to tap into the New York stock exchange with relative ease. Leo liked him. In the two years since he decided to put his money into the American stock market, he'd made an excellent return following Burton's advice. Lately, encouraged by his success, he'd started engaging in margin trades: he could diversify his portfolio by using part of it as collateral for loans to buy more shares. So far the strategy had worked quite well.

Leo tapped on the door to Burton's office. He didn't want to leave Martha for long; he did not want her to be alone if she received some distressing news about her health. If Burton was free, he'd be back at the doctor's office in ten minutes, and it would be ten minutes he did not have to spend sitting, worried and restive.

Hearing no answer, he stepped inside. He saw no sign of Burton's secretary, but the door to his private office was closed. Leo thought he heard the sound of someone sobbing. Without thinking he opened the inner door.

The secretary was there. So was a policeman, and so was Burton, or rather, the remains of Burton. The back of his head was plastered all over the window, a red and brown patch of gore, blotting out the gray view of the Bund.

"What in God's name has happened?"

At the sound of Leo's voice the woman looked up. Her eyes were swollen from crying.

"And who might you be?" the policeman asked, blustering with British efficiency.

"Leo Hoffman. I'm a client."

"Well, Mr. Damion won't be keepin' any more appointments, sir.

He's checked himself out. The gun's still right there on the floor, right where it ought to be, so there ain't no doubt about what's happened. This poor lady heard the shot."

Leo stared, dumbfounded. "Burton? Killed himself?"

"I'd say so. Didn't take any chances, on missin', did he? Awful business." He made a notation in his notebook, and continued to talk.

"He must've had quite a hot wire to the States. The word is just now gettin' across the water. 'Black Monday,' they're callin' it. Didn't have much money in the stock market stateside, yourself, did ya sir?"

The bottom fell out of Leo's stomach. He swallowed, then bit his lower lip. "A bit," was all he managed to say.

"Well, that bit's probably gone up in smoke, sir. The New York stock market crashed. I heard there's stock brokers poppin' out of windows like champagne corks in Manhattan. Pitiful blokes. It's only money, after all. Well, you better go now, sir. I'll see to this poor lady. What a mess. Poor bastard." Clucking and muttering, the man turned his attention back to the corpse.

Out on the street, Leo noticed a small cluster of men gathering on the steps of the Hong Kong and Shanghai Banking Corporation. The impressive entrance to the city's most prestigious bank was flanked by two enormous bronze lions, whose paws were kept shiny by innumerable Chinese who did not pass by without rubbing them for good luck. Leo felt tempted to go and rub one now. He went to join the group on the stairs, under the massive white dome that symbolized the wealth and power of the men who owned Shanghai.

As he approached, he caught bits of conversation: some highly agitated, some curious, some smug. Leo stepped up to listen.

"No, there's no doubt about it. The whole market's been wiped out, and the world financial markets are already following Wall Street's lead. This is a disaster of unprecedented proportion."

"Wonder how many chaps will be busted flat. We surely don't need another bunch of well-to-do beggars. That White Russian business was enough."

"I can't believe it could happen so quickly. How could it all collapse so quickly?"

"Surely it will pick up again."

"You will need a miracle the likes of which has not been seen since Jesus walked the earth to salvage anything out of this mess."

"I wonder who'll feel the worst of it. Thank God I wasn't in."

Leo could stand no more. It was true. He was ruined. He'd put all of his faith in the American stock market, to share part of the wealth of a great nation he knew he'd never see. And now he was left with nothing.

He staggered backward and came close to tripping down the stairs. A friendly arm reached out to steady him.

"I say there, are you quite all right?" Leo shrugged off the helpful stranger's assistance.

How am I going to be able to tell Martha?

He stumbled back to the doctor's office in a daze. Martha was standing in the waiting room.

"Leo, how troubled you look. You're so pale. But everything is fine, darling. It's better than fine; everything is wonderful." Tears filled her eyes; her voice caught in her throat, but she was still smiling.

"We're going to have a baby. The doctor says I have to be careful, but if I follow this special diet and don't tax myself too much, there shouldn't be any problems. Oh Leo, darling, we're going to have a baby." She threw her arms around his neck.

Leo held her tightly. He'd held Erzsebet, and Martha, and other women whose tears mattered much less, as they cried in sorrow, and in joy. But the tears confronting him now were his own. Tears of jubilation, and tears of anguish.

Once again, within the space of a few short hours, his life had been radically altered. Somehow, he must find a way to start over again. He crushed his beloved Martha to him, and thought about the new life inside her, a life for whom he was responsible. A life so much more important than his own.

He couldn't tell Martha about his financial losses; he couldn't stand to bring her any grief or anxiety now. Nor did he want to have to admit to her how badly he'd failed. He would have to keep up appearances, somehow, pretending that nothing had changed, at least until the baby came.

Later that night Leo sat alone in his library, sorting out his options. According to the financial information he'd been able to scrape together, they were not completely destitute, but close to it. He could mortgage the house to buy time. But he had to produce some income. He'd have to get a job.

He needed a position that would allow them to continue their current lifestyle. He could not bear to ask Martha to abandon the life of luxury he'd created for her. And he wanted no less for his child.

He was fluent in five European languages, and could now also speak and understand a good deal of Mandarin, and some Cantonese. He was able to get along well with people from diverse backgrounds. He possessed a modicum of financial knowledge. Given the economy of Shanghai, it all pointed in one direction: a bank.

But how to go about getting a position? He couldn't just wander up to the door and drop off a resume. He wouldn't be hired at any of the city's truly prestigious institutions if the word got out that he really needed a job. No one wanted to pay top dollar for a "well-to-do beggar." Not in Shanghai.

He would have to conduct his search by word of mouth, in the most informal settings. *I'm interested in carving out a place for myself in the business community. Want to put down some roots, now that a baby is on the way. Might be amusing to learn something about the banking business.* He'd put the word out casually, at the country club, on the golf course, and over a glass of brandy at the Astor House. At least, he could start his search that way.

To his delight, his plan worked. Within a few weeks he received a telephone call from Maximillian Berbier, a vice president of the Commerce Bank of China.

"Mr. Hoffman, I'm pleased to find you at home," the Frenchman began. His English was heavily accented, but more than acceptable. "I don't believe that we've actually met before, but I know that we have many mutual acquaintances, especially among the members of *Le Cercle Sportif*. I know that I've seen you and your lovely wife there on many occasions."

"How kind of you to remember us."

"Well, it's not kindness at all that motivates my call to you today, but good business sense. I understand from some conversations with colleagues at the club that you might be interested in a position with a financial institution."

Leo kept his tone nonchalant. "Why, yes, actually. Funny you should hear about that. What a little fishbowl we live in."

"Yes, no doubt. Well, we've been looking for some time for someone to help us in the area of business development. Would something of that nature interest you?"

"I'd be happy to discuss it."

"Could you come in tomorrow? That is, if you have no other pressing engagements?"

"I think I could find time to slip in during the morning."

"Excellent. Shall we say, ten o'clock?"

"Yes, that should work out nicely."

"Good. And I'm sure you know the address—"

"Certainly. On the Bund, next to the *North China Daily News* office."

"*Exactement*. I'm looking forward to meeting with you."

"The pleasure is all mine."

Berbier turned out to be a small, fidgety man, whose thinning hair and full mustache made him look older than his forty-five years. He'd been in China since 1910, he told Leo. It was a difficult place to leave, once you got used to the small inconveniences of malaria-laden mosquitoes and civil war, *n'est-ce pas?* One could live so well in Shanghai.

Leo listened attentively to Berbier's routine description of the bank's history, its growth, and current assets with growing impatience. He finally interrupted.

"And how do you think I may be of service to this prestigious institution?"

"Ah, yes. Well, in fact, I believe that one of the members of our board of directors would like to discuss that with you. He is waiting in the president's office. I will show you in."

Curious, Leo followed the small man up the grand mahogany staircase leading away from the main banking floor to the office suites located on the second story. Why would a board member be interviewing him? Why not the president of the bank? Well, he didn't really know that much about the banking business. He had a lot to learn.

Berbier crossed the second floor lobby. Leo could not help but notice the presence of several armed guards. Here was a bank that took security seriously.

The Frenchman led Leo through a set of double doors, intricately carved with scenes from Chinese history. These doors opened into a small outer office: an executive secretary's work station. No one sat at the desk.

Berbier knocked on the door to the president's office. Leo heard a muffled response. Berbier did not open the door. Instead, he walked away, saying as he did so, "I will leave you now. You may go in."

Startled that he was expected to make his own introduction, Leo conjured up all of his self-confidence, opened the door of the inner office, and walked in.

There was a tall man, an Asian man, seated at the elaborate *bureau plat* that served as a desk. He was gazing out of a large picture window that presented a panoramic view of the Bund, with his back facing the door. Leo did not have to see his face to know who he was.

Liu Tue-Sheng swung his chair around slowly, almost regally. Leo stood in front of his desk, saying nothing, feeling as if his life in Shanghai had somehow come full circle.

"Mr. Hoffman. Good morning. I do apologize for this subterfuge, but I was not . . . altogether sure that you would accept my invitation for another . . . business meeting. Please, sit down."

Leo debated making a quick departure. He was sure that he did not want to be a part of anything this man would have to offer, but he sensed that he had been lured into a trap, and had to learn the nature of it before he could plan his escape.

Leo dropped into a chair and crossed an ankle over the opposite knee, wanting to give the impression that he was comfortable and not at all surprised. "Of course, Mr. Liu, I knew of your affiliation with this bank," he lied smoothly, "But I didn't think that my presence here would concern you."

"Ah, but it concerns me exclusively, Mr. Hoffman. You see, it has come to my attention that you are seeking employment."

"I thought it might be amusing to learn something about the banking business."

Liu did not acknowledge his remark. "It has also come to my attention that you recently lost a great deal of money, that you have mortgaged your house, and that your lovely wife is expecting a child."

Leo flushed with humiliation. He leapt up, determined to avoid any more embarrassment.

"Please," Liu went on in a cordial tone, "these are simply facts that have come to my attention. I do not mean to insult you."

Defensive anger tugged at the edge of Leo's self-control. "Not much gets by you, I suppose. But why are you so interested in me?"

Liu considered this query, apparently unperturbed by Leo's hostility. "If you will retake your seat, I can explain." They stared at each other for a moment. Leo, torn between his pride and his need to know the answer to the question he'd just posed, deliberated silently. Liu waited, still as a spider in its web. Leo sat down. Liu spoke.

"You see, Mr. Hoffman, at the time of our first transaction, I surmised that you were a man of unique talents. I am engaged in a variety of business enterprises, some of which, such as this bank, are quite straightforward. Others are more complicated."

Like running revolutions and smuggling opium, Leo thought to himself. He kept his face blank as Liu continued.

"For these, more complicated enterprises, a man with your particular talents could be very useful. However, when we first met, I suspected that, for you, mere financial reward would not produce the . . . flexibility . . . required to assist me in those enterprises. So I waited. And I collected information.

"It is true, I have made it my business to know yours. I know many, many things about many people. As I told you at our first meeting, nothing is as valuable as information. Information overlooked by others often proves helpful. When I learned that you were seeking employment, I thought that now would be an opportune moment to discuss your talents, and that we could once again prove useful to each other."

Leo could sense the bait dangled before him. It had been so easy the first time; one compromise and he'd made a fortune. He was embarrassed and angry, but he was also curious.

"What did you have in mind?"

"You have an unusual ability to make a singular impression . . . while at the same time blending into your environment. An old Russian believes you are a Russian aristocrat. A concierge insists you are a British lord. An American tycoon thinks you are a self-made millionaire, months before you have succeeded in making a fortune. And while Shanghai is not a closed society, after a short period of time, you and your wife . . . what is the expression? You are 'rubbing elbows' with our town's most elite citizenry, in a manner that is particularly impressive given that your fortune is . . . was . . . comfortable, but not grand enough to buy that much influence.

"All this goes beyond your skill with languages; men trust you, and women find you desirable. Your charm is a key to many doors. Doors I need to go through, and cannot, because I have a certain reputation, and because I am Chinese. Frankly, I need ears behind those doors. You can be those ears."

Leo was flabbergasted. "Are you telling me that you want me to spy for you?"

"An indelicate description of your duties, but not entirely incorrect. Of course, you would be given a regular position, with the title of vice president, at this bank. You would assist in garnering new business; meet potential clients, explain our services. All quite legitimate. A business conducted over dinner and on the golf course, with the assistance of a generous expense account. In exchange for all this, I will occasionally ask that you execute a special errand. But, for the most part, you will just . . . keep your ears open."

Leo could not believe what he was hearing. It was all so simple. So easy. And so vile. Any information he gave Liu would surely be used for nefarious purposes. He would never work for this man. He stood up again.

"Thank you for the compliment," Leo said, his sarcasm contradicting the meaning of his words. "I am deeply honored that you think I'm worthy of your consideration. But I'm afraid that I cannot accept your offer." With this, Leo stood up and took three steps toward the door.

He reached for the doorknob, but his hand never touched it. His fingers halted, inches away from the crystal orb, as he heard Liu serenely inquire:

"Are you aware, Mr. Hoffman, that under the Napoleonic code there exists no statute of limitations for the crime of murder?"

Leo dropped his arm and turned around. Liu was still looking directly at him. His impassive expression had not changed. Leo knew what he was about to hear.

"You may not know that I have a very good relationship with the French Prefect of Police here in Shanghai. Letters and warrants regarding crimes committed in every French-speaking corner of the world pile up on the poor man's desk, just in case a perpetrator or two sneaks into the French Concession of Shanghai. My friend would drown under these papers, if I did not help him sort through them.

"After our original transaction, I became curious as to the origin of your diamonds. I wondered if perhaps any of my friend's papers pertained to the theft of a quantity of perfect stones. I discovered this document. Of course, I have made photographic copies. Important documents have a way of disappearing. One must protect them."

Leo took the proffered piece of paper. It was a warrant, issued in Paris, for the arrest of an unnamed Hungarian national, on charges of theft, counterfeiting, fraud, and murder. The document contained a precise physical description of Leo. It was dated December 23rd, 1925.

Liu kept talking, never taking his eyes off Leo's face. "My friend has never seen this. He is a busy man. He does not have to see it. He will not. If you will agree to be . . . flexible."

Leo's brain was churning. He tried to think of a way out. He must take Martha and leave Shanghai.

And go where? Brazil? In her condition she would never survive an ocean crossing; the trip from Europe had nearly killed her. He wouldn't take any risks with Martha's health. Back to Germany? There was no guarantee he could even get into the country. Hong Kong? Even if he could get in without proper documents, the gangster had connections there as well. He would not be beyond Liu's grasp.

Within a few brief seconds he considered and rejected a dozen alternatives. There was nowhere for him to go. He was trapped. He knew it. And Liu knew it, as he waited for Leo's response.

"My wife must never find out about this. I must have your word on that."

Liu leaned forward and took the warrant from Leo's hand. "A most excellent decision, Mr. Hoffman. Most men find me a very reasonable employer . . . as long as I receive their full cooperation."

EIGHT
SHANGHAI, 1934

"Mr. Hoffman, your wife and daughter are here."

"What a nice surprise. Please send them up."

In a moment his four-year-old daughter stampeded into the room, followed closely by a breathless Martha. "Madeleine, no running inside," she exclaimed as they burst in.

Maddy stopped short. Then, with a mischievous grin worthy of a leprechaun, she began to tip-toe with exaggerated stealth to where her father squatted, arms outstretched. She didn't fly into his embrace as she usually did; instead, she paused a few feet in front of him, and pointed down at her feet.

"New shoes. New shoes. New shoes!" she cried with delight, picking up one foot and nearly planting it in Leo's face.

"Oh, my. Those are beautiful, Maddy."

Maddy put her foot back on the ground and beamed. Then she stamped her feet and spun in a circle, arms outstretched like a whirly-bird.

"She just had to have the red ones," Martha explained.

Maddy stopped spinning. "My shoes have a name, papa. They are MARY JANES. And they're made of PATTED leather. That's why they're so shiny."

"Madeleine's marvelous Mary Janes," Leo said warmly, finally getting his hug, which his daughter returned with enthusiasm. He lifted her up and sat her down on his desk.

"Did I ever tell you the story about the princess with the magic shoes?"

Maddy's little face glowed. "No, papa. You haven't told me that story."

"Well I'll have to remedy that. Those shoes were red, too. Red and gold. They were given to the princess by a powerful wizard."

Maddy clapped her hands with eager anticipation. "Can you tell me the story right now?"

Martha interrupted. "No, darling. Papa is working now."

Maddy pouted. "Tonight?"

"I'm sorry, little love. I have a business dinner tonight."

"You do?"

Leo turned to his wife. "Yes. I'm sorry. It came up very suddenly. A couple of prospective clients in from the States want to be shown around."

"Then, tomorrow? Can I hear the story tomorrow?" Maddy asked sweetly, and Leo was once again struck by her resemblance to her mother. She had Martha's green eyes, heart-shaped face, and enchanting smile. All he'd added to her beauty was a mane of curly black hair, just like his own.

"Yes, *ma princesse*, I promise, I'll tell you the story tomorrow," Leo replied as he helped her jump down off the desk.

Maddy dashed back to her mother. "Is it time for ice cream now? I ate all my lunch."

Martha smiled and looked back to Leo. "Our visit has two purposes. One, to show you Maddy's new shoes—"

"My Mary Janes," Maddy added.

"—and to ask you if you could join us for an ice cream."

"I'd love to." He leaned over his desk and pushed the button on his intercom. "Miss Yu, I'll be going out for an hour or so. I've been invited to accompany two beautiful ladies for ice cream."

"Yes, sir."

He glanced at the papers on his desk. Liu's note still lay there, unopened. Well, it could wait.

He walked over to Martha and gently caressed her cheek. "Have I told you today how much I love you?"

"You don't have to tell me every day, darling," she answered, looking both pleased and slightly embarrassed.

He picked Maddy up. "But I should. I love you both. And I want you to know that every minute of every day."

"And we love you," Maddy declared, depositing a kiss on her father's face with a loud smack.

"Oh, I think this little girl might get two scoops of ice cream today," he said, and his heart soared again at the sight of his daughter's joyful smile.

One of Liu's shadowy minions had left the note on Leo's desk at the bank earlier that morning. He ignored it for hours, struggling with his conscience, trying to convince himself that there was still a way out. He could send Martha and his daughter somewhere safe, then wait for

Liu to summon him and refuse to submit to this request. He would go to jail; Liu would manufacture whatever evidence the French police needed to make sure of that. He might even hang. But at least he would be free.

And never see his wife and child again. Never feel Martha moving underneath him, never feel the warmth of her breath on his neck, never hear his precious daughter's laughter, or watch her beautiful green eyes grow wide with excitement as he told her a thrilling story about princesses and dragons and knights who rode magical horses and came to the rescue.

No, he could lose his liberty and survive. But he could not lose them.

For the first four years it had been bearable. With a working knowledge of all the major languages spoken in the Concessions, Leo became a fly on the wall of the Tower of Babel that was Shanghai. In fact, his meetings with Liu were rare. At times he received a note containing a name, and he would undertake to find out all he could about that person. Or about a pending business transaction, or a government raid. It was not difficult work. Just distasteful.

And Liu kept his word. He paid Leo handsomely to lead his double life. Established at the bank, Leo continued to live the life of a well-to-do businessman during a time of worldwide economic depression. No one in Leo's social circle knew that he was on Liu's generous payroll. No one knew that a confidence whispered at the bar might make it to Liu's ears. No one knew that a boast about a business coup might be used to help a competitor. No one knew that Leo Hoffman could not be trusted, because everyone did.

He tried not to connect the information he'd passed on to Liu with the arrest of one man; he closed his eyes to the financial ruin of another. Those men were not innocent. They'd made their choices. Leo was paying the price for his own mistakes; and they paid for theirs.

But now Liu had raised the price. Leo had access to women who were unable to keep their desires, or their husbands' secrets, to themselves, he'd explained. Another valuable source of information. Liu expected Leo to exploit it.

Amelia Simmons, he'd said. She was a former cabaret singer, now married to one Reginald Simmons, who worked for a tobacco export company but lived a lifestyle not in keeping with his salary. Liu then handed Leo a picture of the woman, one that had been cut out of a local newspaper. It was a photograph of a throng of people outside the Cathay Theater, waiting to attend the Shanghai premier of *It Happened One Night*, starring Clark Gable. Although Amelia was just one person in a very large group, her face, circled in the photograph, was clear enough for Leo to be able to recognize her later. "Become friendly with Amelia," Liu instructed, "and find out how Simmons really makes his money."

Leo told himself that he wasn't really being unfaithful. He told himself he was just like an actor paid to play a love scene. He was no different than Douglas Fairbanks or Errol Flynn, except he had no choice but to follow Liu's direction. He was not allowed to walk off the set.

Just before the bank was about to close for the day, he picked up the note and tore open the envelope.

The Black Cat was all it said.

The Black Cat fell several levels below the fashionable clubs that he and Martha frequented. It was the type of establishment where a reasonably wealthy person would only go when seeking an opportunity for extracurricular entertainment while minimizing the chances of running into one's reasonably respectable spouse.

He'd been there about an hour before she came in. Amelia looked like many of the dance hall girls in Shanghai, or, as in her case, a dance hall girl who'd married into a better situation: blond hair cut in a fashionable bob, long legs well-displayed under an expensive dress that was cut just a little too low. She was with a man who looked to be several years younger than she was, probably still in his early twenties. He was already staggering when they sat down. Amelia looked around. It didn't take long for Leo to catch her eye.

Leo smiled and gave a nod indicating the presence of Amelia's inebriated escort. She rolled her eyes. He went over to their table.

"Mind if I join you?"

"Not 'f you pick up the next round," the young man slurred.

"My pleasure. What are you drinking?"

Amelia answered. "Champagne."

"Done." The waiter, smelling new blood, was already hovering behind Leo. "Champagne, please. House best." Leo did not expect the Black Cat's bar to carry any champagne that was remotely drinkable, but it would be overpriced nonetheless.

Amelia reached for her cigarette case. "Allow me," said Leo, taking it from her. He removed a cigarette, placed it gently between her lips, and lit it for her, gazing into her eyes the whole time.

The unexpected intimacy of this maneuver seemed to please her. She blew out the first puff of smoke and smiled back at him.

"And you are?"

"Leo."

"Amelia."

Her escort put his head down on the table and began to snore. Leo gave him an amused look. "Wore him out pretty early, didn't you?"

"Oh, not me. He's just a baby. My cousin."

"I take it your cousin is just visiting?"

"You could say that."

"From where?"

"Wherever inconvenient cousins come from."

Leo smiled. "And if you want to send him back to where he came from?"

"You have to come up with cab fare, I suppose."

"Allow me."

"That's very gracious. But give the poor thing a minute to collect himself. I'd hate for him to be carried out horizontal."

"Whatever you desire, Madame."

This evening is definitely looking up, Amelia thought. The kid had gotten drunk so quickly, she figured she wasn't going to get what she wanted out of the evening, which was a disappointment. Amelia liked getting what she wanted.

In fact from birth Amelia had focused on just one goal: her own satisfaction. She ran away from home at the age of fifteen to escape the drudgery of her family's working-class existence in a small town in Michigan, and going to San Francisco would have been a good start, except that the man with whom she left neglected to mention that he was already married. He handed her over to a friend in the entertainment business, who took one look at Amelia's legs and decided that she ought to be a dancer.

Her troupe came through Shanghai in 1922. By then she'd learned that the quickest way to a man's bank vault was through his bedroom door. Tempted by the knowledge that many wealthy Shanghailanders desired female company and asked few questions, she located a nightclub owner who agreed that her long legs, firm white breasts, and throaty voice would fill up more than a few seats in his cabaret, and then rented a tiny apartment in the International Settlement.

Amelia soon enjoyed a steady stream of generous sponsors. Two years later she startled a middle-aged patron with an affirmative response to his spontaneous marriage proposal, and Amelia Grogan became Amelia Simmons.

In Shanghai a tarnished past was no more than an inconvenience; an impressive marriage could whitewash a background more sordid than Amelia's. But to her disappointment, she soon realized that her husband's position as a vice president of a tobacco export company did not produce what she considered sufficient income. After warming Reginald Simmons's bed, Amelia proceeded to chisel away at his conscience. She eventually convinced him that honesty was an admirable trait only in children, priests, and idiots. He started to embezzle, and she began to live the life she felt she deserved. And she deserved more, she thought, than sex with Reggie.

She tried to be discreet, but there were only so many places a decent woman could go alone in Shanghai, and only so long Amelia could go without the attention she wanted from a more attractive man than her husband. And the man she sat across from now was very, very attractive.

He was wearing a wedding ring, but in Shanghai that didn't mean much, and his willingness to come over to her table suggested that he was interested in an entertaining evening. But how entertaining? It was easy for a man to get a prostitute in Shanghai, if all he wanted was a bit of what he wasn't getting at home, or if he was looking for a more creative version of what he normally got from his wife. So what did this guy want, exactly? She'd have to feel him out a little.

"So, Leo, do you live in Shanghai?"

"For the time being."

"Well that's true of us all, isn't it? Where are you from?"

"Germany," he answered, as the waiter brought their champagne.

"Funny, you don't speak with a German accent."

"I do when I speak German."

Amelia laughed. Her young companion muttered something unintelligible, and Leo glanced over at him. "Would you like to dance while he's taking his nap? The orchestra's not bad."

"Are you a good dancer?"

"You'll have to judge that for yourself."

Amelia stubbed out her cigarette. "I guess I will."

The orchestra, made up entirely of musicians from the Philippines, was playing "Somebody Loves You," a popular hit that had jumped quickly across the Pacific from America. Leo wove them smoothly onto the crowded dance floor, holding Amelia a respectable distance away from his body.

"Okay, you're definitely a good dancer," she said after a moment. "Is that why you're here tonight? Did you come here to dance?" She punctuated her question with an inviting smile.

"I'm not sure why I came here. I was restless, I suppose. I just wanted some time away from everything and everyone."

Amelia moved a little closer to him. "Life gets that way sometimes, doesn't it? One minute you feel like you have everything you've ever wanted, and then you wonder why you ever wanted any of it."

"And what do you want, Amelia?"

Right now I want you, she thought, but came up with a different answer. "I just want to enjoy my life more."

"And what is there about your life now that you don't enjoy?"

"This is sort of a serious conversation to be having while doing a foxtrot, don't you think?"

"Sorry. I just don't usually find myself in this position."

"Dancing?"

"Dancing with a beautiful woman who is so intriguing."

"And what about Mrs. Leo?"

"I'd rather not talk about her."

"Suits me."

They danced without talking for a while, and Leo could feel that silent communication beginning, the conversation that occurs between bodies, not hearts.

I can't do this, he thought.

Amelia felt him slipping away from her. "It's okay," she said. "I don't really do this kind of thing, anyway. Maybe we should leave. I'll just pour my poor little cousin into a taxi and go home. I don't want to interfere with your life."

It's too late for that. I'm about to interfere with yours. "I don't want you to go, Amelia. Maybe we should just seize the moment."

"Is that something you do often? Seize the moment?"

"I don't have many moments like this."

"Neither do I," Amelia answered, knowing at that instant she'd said exactly the right thing.

———————————————

It was easy to find a room. Most of the hotels in the area were designed to facilitate this sort of assignation. Amelia walked in ahead of Leo and lay down on the bed, stretching seductively, like a lazy lioness reigning over a kingdom of cheap satin and worn velvet.

Leo looked at her and felt nothing except intense apprehension. *Leave. Don't do this. You can't do this.* Then, suddenly, he thought about the war, and what it had been like to slip into the role of a soldier: to kill other men to keep from being killed himself, while trying to keep a piece of who he was separate from the bloody anarchy surrounding him. He'd been able to play that role and survive.

Amelia lifted one of her elegant legs and pointed her toe at him. "I've heard that the way a man undresses a woman says a lot about his . . . talent. Why don't you start with my shoes?"

He didn't move. "Don't you have a husband who'll be worrying about you?"

She let her leg fall back to the bed and sat up. "The only thing Reggie worries about is how to make enough money to keep me from leaving him."

"And he does that well, I suppose."

"Well enough." She gave him another inviting smile. "Are we going to talk all night?"

Martha was asleep when he got home. He immediately went into a guest bedroom and took a shower, to rid himself of the sickening odor of another woman.

His wife reached for him as he got into bed. "Why is your hair wet?" Martha mumbled sleepily as he kissed her. "Did it rain tonight? I didn't hear anything, but I've been asleep for a while. Madeleine and I went for a long walk today. She's so proud of her new shoes."

"It only rained a little, but one of the clients we were entertaining got so drunk he slipped in the mud and then pulled me down with him when I tried to help him up. I had to shower."

"Oh, dear. Leave your suit on the chair. I'll have it cleaned tomorrow."

"I'll get the boy at the bank to take it in. They should pay for it anyway. Damaged in the line of duty, you might say."

"Hmm." Martha was soon asleep again.

Damaged in the line of duty, thought Leo. He did not fall asleep until sunrise.

NINE
SHANGHAI, 1937

"Your mother and I have a surprise for you, little love, but you'll have to come downstairs to see it," Leo sang out as he entered the playroom. Without hesitation Maddy dropped the book she was reading and stretched out her arms. She loved to be picked up by her father. She especially loved it when, with a sudden cry of "*Allez*," he lifted her high above his head and then lowered her onto his shoulders, as he did now.

"And, mademoiselle, how is the view from the top of the world?" he asked, knowing what the reply would be.

"*Comme c'est beau*," the little voice answered. "Papa, it's beautiful here on top of the world."

"Ah," he always replied, "then that is where you shall stay."

Martha abandoned her own perch on the window seat and followed them as they headed into the hall. "Leo, please. A seven-year-old is too big for such behavior," she said, but her smile belied her words.

Maddy clasped her hands under her father's chin to keep from falling off his shoulders as they bounded down the stairs. "Is it a big surprise, or a little one?" she asked.

"It's bigger than you are, *ma princesse*." Leo trotted across the foyer, then pulled up in front of the closed parlor doors, waiting for Martha to catch up. When she reached them he slipped Maddy back down to the floor and gave his daughter a slow, exaggerated wink.

"Go in and see what it is."

Giggling with anticipation, Maddy opened one of the double doors and peeked inside. Her eyes swept the familiar room, searching for something new. In the corner, gleaming in the midmorning sun, stood a baby grand piano.

"Mama, Papa, I can't believe it!" Maddy rushed in to admire her new possession, her parents close behind.

"Gaston, one of the musicians at the club, said you were very interested in his piano, and that you even tried to play it; your father and I thought your interest in music should be encouraged, my darling. You'll have lessons now, and play as often as you like."

"It's so beautiful." Maddy climbed up onto the ebony bench, and then brushed her fingertips across the keys without making a sound. "I'll have to learn a song to play for Grandpa. Does he have a piano?"

She looked up to see the light fade from her father's face. Her mother turned away and said something sharply in German.

German. That other language, the one she did not understand. Maddy used to think of it as the language of happy surprises; German preceded Christmas presents, picnics, and birthday parties. Now it meant something different. German meant bad secrets. German meant something was wrong.

She hung her head. She must have asked the wrong question. Again.

Maddy heard her mother leave the room. Her father let out a deep sigh. Then he was sitting beside her. They both stared down at the keyboard.

"Maddy, listen to Papa," Leo said at last. "I know that Mama told you that you were going to visit Grandpa in Germany, but I'm afraid that's not going to happen just yet."

"We're not going?"

"Not yet. I don't think it's safe to travel right now."

"Oh." More silence. She was still afraid to speak. What if she asked another wrong question? But she had to know.

"We will go to Germany *someday*, won't we?"

"Someday, I'm sure you will go, my darling. Now, can you play a song for Papa?"

"I don't know any songs yet. But I'll learn some soon. I listen very well. May I go see Mama now?"

Leo nodded, his thoughts already elsewhere. Maddy slipped off the bench and tiptoed to the door. She hated the thundercloud of tension that could burst into a room without warning. She was not capable of predicting it, but she did know how to react to it. Do not ask what is wrong. Just be quiet.

Pausing in the doorway, Maddy peered back over her shoulder. Her father was standing now, staring out the window, hands thrust deeply into his front pockets. He looked worried. Still unnerved by the thought that she was to blame, Maddy dashed out of the room.

Where could Mama have gone? Maybe to their bedroom?

Normally, Maddy relished any opportunity to go into her parents' bedroom. It was a fantastic place, an oasis of interesting and beautiful things. She loved to sit at her mother's dressing table and pretend the beautiful crystal perfume bottles were elegantly dressed courtiers, dancing at an imperial ball. Her favorite was the porcelain swan, who presided over the entire menagerie, an enchanted prince greeting his guests. The swan occupied a position of honor in front of a photograph of Leo and Martha taken on their wedding day. Martha was looking straight at the camera, her face full of joy. Leo was looking down at Martha, his complete devotion visible even to the camera's detail-blurring eye.

There were other pictures in the room, mostly of her parents at fancy grown-up parties. Maddy loved helping her mother get ready for a party. First, her mother would flood her room with music; she kept both a radio and a Victrola in the bedroom. Then Maddy helped her mother decide what to wear. Together they would carefully evaluate the selection of appropriate garments laid out earlier by the maid. Her mother always made Maddy feel that her opinion was a critically important factor in making the final choice.

After choosing a dress, there came the cosmetic ceremony. Maddy, fascinated by the whole elaborate procedure, handed pencils and pots to her mother on command, like a sous-chef assisting the master.

Once her mother had finished dressing and applying her makeup, she would put on her jewelry. What would it be tonight? The pearls? Or the emeralds that were the same color as Maddy's eyes? Maddy's last duty was to hold a hand mirror behind her mother's reflection at the dressing table, so that Martha could assess the final result. Then Martha would reward her daughter with a big, loving hug. "How could I get dressed without you? You have the eye of an artist."

"But this is not a party day," sighed Maddy to herself as she trudged down the hall. Wait—wasn't that the radio playing in her parents' room? Heartened, she closed her eyes and wished that her mother would sing along: but when Maddy reached the doorway she saw her sitting motionless on the bed. She, too, wore a fretful expression.

"Mama," began Maddy as she crept into the room, "I don't mind about not going to Germany—" She stopped in midsentence. Her mother was holding a gray velvet box. It was the home of her mother's golden songbird.

From the time Maddy was old enough to sit still, the appearance of the slim gray box signaled the beginning of her very favorite game. "Should we see if Mr. Songbird is home? Would you like for him to sing?" her mother would ask, then rap sharply on the top of the box.

"*Bonjour, Monsieur. Êtes-vous là?* Are you home? Little Maddy would like to hear you sing." Next Martha would whisper, "*Oui*, I think he is home today," and carefully remove a necklace from the box. Out would come a nightingale, carved onto a gold medallion, hanging on a thick golden chain. Maddy would watch and listen, entranced, as Martha swung the medallion from her fingertips, and sang, and sang, and sang, with a voice every bit as captivating as a real nightingale's.

She'd not seen Mr. Songbird for nearly a year. More than a year. It had been just before her sixth birthday. She and her mother were upstairs, sitting on the floor in the master bedroom, and Mr. Songbird was in the middle of a wonderful concert.

Over her mother's shoulder Maddy saw her father appear in the doorway. She was about to greet him when she saw the look in his eyes. At first warm and tender, they shifted with mercurial speed into icy blue pools of wrath. Speaking in rapid German, he stormed into the room, snatched the necklace from Martha's fingers, and flung it savagely against the wall.

Stunned, Maddy burst into tears. Without a word, her mother scooped her up and carried her out of the room, down the stairs, into the living room. She settled into a large chair by the fireplace.

"Hush, hush, *ma chérie*, *mon enfant*, it's all right, he didn't mean to scare you, he didn't mean to scare you," she crooned, rocking Maddy until she fell asleep, exhausted by her tears.

No mention was made of the incident the next day, and no apologies were given. Maddy dared not broach the subject, so frightened was she of her father's inexplicable rage. But after that day, the game stopped. Martha still sang to Maddy, but the necklace never reappeared.

Once or twice, when Maddy was feeling particularly brave, she asked if Mr. Songbird could come out to play. Her mother would only shake her head sadly. "No, *chérie*, Mr. Songbird is not home today."

Excited at the sight of the box, and hopeful that her mother might remember their game and sing for her, Maddy was about to ask if Mr. Songbird was home when her mother used her free hand to cover her eyes.

"Mama, do you have a headache?"

"No, Maddy. Please, *ma petite*, run to the kitchen and ask Wei Lin to give you some lunch. I think she has a cake for you to taste."

"But I'm not hungry, Mama. Could you—"

"Go now, *chérie*, Wei Lin will want you to taste it while it is still warm."

Her voice sounded so strange, like she was about to cry. Maddy sometimes heard voices raised in anger in the middle of the night. But she had never, ever seen her mother in tears. Petrified of doing something to make the situation worse, she turned and fled the room.

Unaware of his daughter's distress, Leo stared out the front window of his home and tried to empty his mind. He gazed at but did not see the curiously European houses lining the street, each one built in homage to a country on the other side of the world. He saw but did not notice the elegant gardens, all carefully tended by Chinese servants. He saw but did not see the family's new Cadillac, basking on the driveway in the blistering August heat like a huge black beetle. He saw nothing.

He paged through the dictionary in his head. "*Nem*," in Hungarian. Then French: "*non*." German: "*nein*." English: "*no*." Russian: "*nyet*." In Mandarin: "*bu*." He often found that the simplest words worked best to clear his mind, as he leafed through the catalogue of nouns, verbs, conjugations, and cognates he'd committed to memory. *Hideg*, he continued in silence. *Cold. Froid. Kalt. Lerng*.

But today the technique did not work. He repeatedly lost his place in his drill. Words eluded him. He thought only of the journey his wife wanted to undertake: back to Germany, to see her father.

The violence of the changes he'd experienced in his own life left no room for nostalgia. He had no intention of going back to Europe. Ever.

Silently he cursed Bernice, the sister-in-law he'd never met. He didn't know her, but Martha's descriptions made him feel as if he did. The telegram she sent last week was just what he would have expected. No sentimentality. Just the facts:

Situation intolerable. Have opted for France over Shanghai.
Will leave when father improves or dies. Good luck to you.
B.

Leo winced as he recalled the argument that had followed Martha's receipt of the telegram.

"Leo, I want to go and see them before they leave. Before he dies. To let him meet Maddy. He's my father. I owe him that much."

"It's too dangerous. Don't you listen to what people are saying? People of Jewish decent aren't wanted in Germany. It's insane for you to go back now. We've invited them to visit time after time. I've offered to pay for their passage. Now they have refused, again, to come join us. Why should you have to go all that way to apologize for falling in love?"

"He's my father. He's dying. My sister and her husband are leaving their home soon, to start over, just as we did. Who knows what will happen? This may be my last chance."

"Last year your father was removed from the university faculty because Hitler made it illegal for Jews to teach. Do you think the Nazis will have a 'welcome home' banner waiting for you? How could you even consider going back to Germany with those lunatics in charge?"

"The danger is exaggerated. You make it seem like our lives would be in jeopardy. The Nazis are throwing Jews out, not locking them up."

"They may lock me up."

Martha let out an exasperated gust of air. "It's been over eleven years. They couldn't still be looking for you."

Leo could not tell her that Liu Tue-Sheng would make sure he never even made it out of the city. He came back with a credible rejoinder.

"And what if my name is on some list somewhere when I apply for a visa? Is this trip worth that much to you?"

Her aggravation deepened. "It may be just as unsafe to stay here. The Japanese are going to invade any day now. How do we know that this time the Settlements won't be involved?"

"Because the Japanese have picked a fight with Chiang Kai-shek, not the rest of the world. There's no reason to think the Japanese won't respect the treaty rights of the European countries, even if they do grab the Chinese sectors of the city away from Chiang. Troops are already in place to protect the Concessions, just like last time. We'll be safe. Nothing has changed."

"I'm going, Leo, with you or without you. I am going to Germany."

"I forbid it. I won't pay for your passage."

"I'll find a way to go without your help."

"You stubborn little fool, how can you even consider doing this? Traveling alone, just you and Maddy? To a country run by Nazis? I won't permit it."

"I must. I have to go. I just have to."

In a burst of clarity, Leo understood the source of his fear. Maybe she wasn't just going to her father. Maybe she was leaving him.

There had not been many women. The affairs were brief, and the women discreet, at least about their sexual adventures; they'd all been very willing to complain about their husbands, and Leo learned everything he needed to know, quickly. He had no choice, he told himself. Those women meant nothing. But his guilt ate away at him, like a sour leprosy of shame.

He knew his guilt had affected his relationship with Martha. He flew into jealous rages, as if she were the one being unfaithful, as if she were the one leading a double life. Sometimes he made love to her with a fervor bordering on desperation; at other times he could not bring himself to touch her, thinking that his caresses would corrupt her. He knew his behavior was ridiculous; he knew he was hurting her. But he could not help himself. His self-loathing lit a monstrous fire within him, and the flames scorched them both.

It had taken her threat to leave to make him realize how close he was to disaster. And he did not know what to do, except to tell her everything. And that, he was sure, would drive her away completely.

The day after their argument he'd locked their passports in a safe at the bank. He knew that if she discovered what he'd done it would lead to another, even more bitter confrontation. But he had to take the chance. He could not let her go.

He walked away from the window and collapsed, head in his hands. Perhaps there was still time to convince her to change her mind.

Martha had trouble explaining, even to herself, why she felt compelled to go to Germany without Leo, or why she discounted the risk involved. Bernice's telegram had given her a reason to leave Shanghai. She did not yet connect her desire to leave with the gradual changes in her husband: the jealousy, the over-protectiveness bordering on lunacy, the outrageous accusations.

Initially, when his behavior started to change, Martha thought Leo must be hiding some financial problem. She did not have a clear idea of where their money was, or how much they had, but this had never worried her in the past. Of course, they'd stopped spending money as lavishly as they had before the Depression. Even though Shanghai's economy had been hurt less than most other port cities, the mood had changed. It was impolite to flaunt one's wealth when so many people had lost so much.

But her cautious inquiries among their acquaintances confirmed what Leo claimed; he was doing quite well at the bank. Money did not seem to be the cause of the turbulence in their lives.

And it was difficult to stay angry, for Leo always took the blame for their arguments. Apologies followed every outburst; self-re-crimination countered every groundless accusation. Sometimes, he seemed better, less volatile, and she thought she had her husband back. Then the arguments started again. Yet, as bad as the situation was at times, she could not imagine life without him. At least, not in Shanghai.

Shanghai, too, was changing. Every day it became a more danger-ous place. At the moment it seemed certain that the Shanghailanders would be treated to another violent spectacle. The Japanese were intent on expanding their holdings in China. Chiang Kai-shek had to stop them.

For weeks the Chinese residents of Chapei, Nantao, and Hong-kew—all the Chinese sections of the city—had been flooding into the International Settlement and the French Concession. Those who could afford it rented rooms at inflated prices from landlords always ready to profit from the misery of their human brethren. Others squatted in the blistering hot streets of the city, surrounded by their meager pos-sessions and their screaming children. When the complaints from the Shanghailanders grew vociferous, the Municipal Council started herd-ing the peasants into temporary refugee centers.

Everyone knew why they were coming. They were clearing the bat-tleground.

All summer Japan had been moving against Chinese positions to the north. Chiang did not respond. He knew his army could not with-stand a long campaign, stretched across the country from Nanking to Peking. So he challenged the invaders in the place the western powers cared about most, in the arena he knew best: Shanghai.

Martha was afraid. Despite Leo's confidence, the idea of living through another war scared her. In the past Leo's love and reassurance had been sufficient to calm her fears. But this time his explanation did not seem to help.

Her sister's telegram had given her a legitimate reason to leave. She wanted to return to Germany to make amends. Her father had never been cruel, just emotionally incapable. She wanted to make her peace with him before he died. She could see her sister, and meet her brother-in-law. She could reconnect with her family, and have some time to think. To think about why her marriage was crumbling, about why loving Leo had become so painful.

Martha sat on her bed, holding tightly to the golden necklace. The first time she wore it in front of Leo, she'd told him about Harry, and he never seemed to mind that she kept the necklace as a keepsake, a gift given to her by an old friend. Until the last time he saw it, when he'd terrified poor Maddy with one of his sudden rages.

Dear Harry. She heard from her sister, in one of her early letters, that he'd been devastated by the news of Martha's hasty marriage. Martha truly regretted having hurt Harry and her family. How had things worked out for Harry in America? Had he married an American girl? Her own life would have turned out so differently had she joined him there. At first, she and Leo had been so happy. Now, she felt trapped by her choice.

Unless.

They kept her good jewelry locked in a vault, and she couldn't get to it without Leo's knowledge. But Harry's necklace was made of gold. She could sell the medallion to pay for her passage to Germany.

Tomorrow, she would take the necklace to a jewelry store and find out how much it was worth. Perhaps she could rely on her dear friend Harry to help her again, after all.

An overnight rain did little to dissipate the sticky heat. Leo was already gone when Martha awoke. She donned a light cotton dress and went downstairs. Maddy was having breakfast in the morning room, under the strict scrutiny of the cook, Wei Lin.

"No egg, no grow. Too skinny to get husband," admonished the diminutive Chinese lady, herself a grandmother several times over.

"But the yolk is runny. It makes me sick to look at all that oozy stuff. Please tell Wei Lin I don't have to eat it."

Martha inspected the offending egg. "Wei, it is a little underdone. You know how picky she is. But you must eat your toast, Maddy."

Vindicated, Maddy spread a dollop of strawberry jam on her toast. Martha reached for a croissant. She never had more than bread and coffee for breakfast.

"Wei, where is Mr. Hoffman?"

Wei snorted before answering. "He say, good breakfast, Wei. He like egg. He say, tell Miss Martha be home soon." With another injured sniff she scooped up Maddy's plate and stalked off to the kitchen.

At that moment Leo walked through the front door. The sound of his footsteps made Maddy leap up from the table.

"Good morning Papa," she greeted him, arms outstretched.

Leo kneeled down and gave his daughter a hug and an absentminded kiss. He looked at Martha, an unspoken question in his eyes.

"Good morning, Leo," she said quietly. "Where have you been this morning?"

"To check on the hostilities. Shots were fired yesterday to the north, at Yokohama Bridge. Chinese soldiers have taken up positions along the northern edge of the city. Warships are moving up the Whangpoo. The Settlements seem well protected."

"So we get to watch another war," Martha commented dryly, helping herself to milk and sugar.

"It seems that way."

Martha thought furiously while she stirred her coffee. Leo did not seem too apprehensive, but she didn't want to go on her secret errand if it was truly dangerous to do so. Nor did she want to cause Leo any unnecessary distress. Normally he played tennis on Saturday afternoons, just before tea. She quickly thought of a legitimate reason to leave the house around that time.

"Leo, I was to stop by the dressmaker today, and thought I might bring Maddy along. We could have tea at the Cathay after my fitting. Do you think it would be safe?"

Leo considered her question. "I suppose so," he answered, after some deliberation. "You should be safe on the Bund. Take the car. I'll have one of the regulars fetch me for my tennis game at the club."

Martha gave him an appreciative smile. She had not lied. She'd told him two-thirds of the truth. Later she and Maddy would visit Madame Olinov, Shanghai's most exclusive dressmaker, whose shop was in the ground floor of the Cathay Hotel, the newest architectural showpiece on the Bund. They would have tea in the hotel lobby lounge. Then they would slip up Nanking Road and pop into a jewelry store or two. She wanted to go to Germany, and she was not going to give up easily.

Their car turned left off Foochow Road onto the Bund at just after four o'clock. The normally busy street was packed with people: refugees, school children and their mothers, rickshaw drivers, beggars, coolies, shoppers and tourists, call girls, bankers, merchants and businessmen. The mass of people covered the street, the lawn, the docks, and the sidewalks. Even the rooftops of the Bund's stately towers were being used as observation platforms. Everyone was watching some activity across the river.

"What on earth is going on?" asked Martha with apprehension as Maddy pressed her face to the car window.

"Look, Mama, the planes." Across the water, less than a mile away, ten Chinese warplanes buzzed and spun like wrathful insects over a Japanese battleship anchored near the Hongkew wharf. Over the din of the carnival atmosphere Martha could hear the rattle of anti-aircraft artillery.

Their driver rolled down his window for a brief conversation with a Russian compatriot who was watching the action through a pair of binoculars. He then turned to Martha. "Well, Mrs. Hoffman, this man says the Chinese bombers have been at it for some time. First they attacked the Japanese factories over in Hongkew, now they're trying to blow up their flagship, the *Idzumo*. Says they haven't hit a thing yet."

Martha surveyed the scene with foreboding. By now they were packed in on all sides; the car could neither move forward, nor turn back. This was insanity. It wasn't safe. If they couldn't leave, she thought, at least they could get out of the road.

"Maddy dear, we may as well get out and walk. The Cathay is only a few blocks away, and the car will never make it through all this."

A loud boom brought a loud cheer from the crowds. Maddy pointed out the window, her eyes wide. "They've blown up the Hongkew dock."

"That's quite enough sightseeing for one day," said Martha emphatically. "Pick us up at the Cathay at six o'clock," she instructed, opening her own door. Ahead she could see the stately pyramid-shaped roof of the Cathay Hotel. Soaring twenty stories high, the luxurious structure sat on the Bund across Nanking Road from the Palace Hotel, completely outclassing its older rival.

As they approached the hotel Martha sensed the crowd dispersing. Glancing back up to the sky she saw the Chinese planes breaking formation, and felt a rush of relief. It was ridiculous, standing around to gawk at a bombing raid as if it were a target shoot. Even though they were landing several hundred yards away, those bombs were real. But the spectators acted like the air raid was nothing more than an interesting show: a comedy, given the inexperienced pilots' lack of skill in hitting their targets.

Martha and Maddy walked into the air-conditioned lobby of the Cathay, stopping to give the doorman a friendly greeting. She would skip Madame Olinov's. They would have tea, and stay at the Cathay until things settled down outside. The rest of her plans would have to wait.

Martha requested her favorite table, near the rear of the lobby, with a nice view of the Bund. It was the best place for people-watching in all of Shanghai.

She had just taken her seat across from Maddy when a thunderous noise caused everyone to look out at the Bund. Martha jerked her head up just in time to see a huge wall of water rise up from the Whangpoo, like a hideous brown monster emerging from a swamp. It towered over the Bund for a fraction of an instant and then crashed down on the street, drenching everything and everyone for a block and a half.

There was no time to react before the second bomb fell. A crater opened in the pavement in front of the Cathay doors. Somehow, her reflexes took over, and Martha threw herself over her daughter's body, tipping over the child's chair and sending them both to the floor as hot air and glass blasted into the room.

Every window along the front of the building shattered from the force of the explosion. The doorman who had greeted them a minute earlier was blown backward through the door and into the lobby, where his body skimmed across the smooth marble until it hit the reception desk, lifeless.

For a moment there was silence, punctuated by the sound of people thrashing through broken glass. Then the screaming began.

Martha pulled Maddy under the table. They crouched there, petrified.

"Maddy, oh my God, Maddy, are you hurt? Are you all right?" Martha tried to hug her daughter and inspect her for wounds at the same time. Tiny shards of broken glass clung to their clothes.

"I think so," replied Maddy, her voice low and quivering.

"Are you bleeding? Does it hurt anywhere?"

"No. Except my ears feel funny."

Martha realized that her own ears were also numb from the sound of the explosion. Not knowing what else to do she frantically tried to brush the fragments of glass off Maddy's clothes. As she did so tiny splinters of glass pierced her gloves. Small red stains appeared on her white linen fingertips.

Maddy stared at the blood on her mother's gloves. She emitted a whimper that grew into a howl. "What is it, Mama? What happened?" the terrified girl shrieked, thrashing in her mother's arms.

Martha held fast to Maddy's shoulders, afraid to move for fear another bomb was already on its way. "It was a bomb, Maddy. One of the planes dropped a bomb. But we're all right, darling. We're safe now." To her own muffled hearing, her voice sounded far away and unnaturally calm. Maddy continued to cry but ceased struggling. They would wait, for the moment, huddled under the table. Until someone came to tell them what to do.

Two miles away a group of four men dressed in pristine tennis whites were engaged in a competitive game of doubles at the *Cercle Sportif Français*. Leo tossed the ball to serve. He watched as it reached the perfect spot in the air, two feet above and slightly forward of his head, but he did not swing his racquet, and the ball fell back down to the ground. Something had distracted him. A noise. A noise like thunder. Thunder on a sticky, hot, sunny day. Thunder from the direction of the Whangpoo.

"Did you hear that?" he asked, not really needing confirmation, but soliciting it nonetheless.

The other men looked at each other. One of them shrugged. "The Chinese have been trying to bomb Japanese positions in Hongkew all afternoon. Maybe they finally hit something."

"If that was a bomb, it was closer than Hongkew," Leo's partner commented.

Leo dropped his racquet and headed off the court at a trot. As he mounted the steps of the club he heard another distant boom. Chills ran up his spine and he started to run, not stopping to give a word of explanation to the puzzled friends he left behind or the surprised club members he passed, as he sped through the clubhouse and out the front door, yelling to get the attention of the taxi driver who habitually parked in front of the club at this hour for the convenience of members who drank too much whiskey with their tea.

He wrenched open the cab door and jumped into the car. "The Bund," he barked in Russian to the startled driver. "To the Cathay Hotel. Go. As fast as the devil or I'll drive this goddamn thing myself."

They got as far as the intersection of Avenue Edward VII and Szechuan Road, one block behind the Bund, before the mayhem in the street completely blocked traffic. Leo bolted from the car. The driver did not even try to ask for his fare.

A crazed mass of people fled in every direction. Leo grabbed the arm of the first white person he saw. The man's face was ashen. Bloodstains covered his trousers.

"What's happened?" Leo bellowed.

"They've bombed the Settlement," the bewildered man answered. "They've blown away the Palace and the Cathay Hotel. There are so many people dead. So much blood. So many people . . ."

Leo jerked back as if he'd been struck in the face. The man turned and wandered away, still mumbling to himself.

"It's not true," Leo shouted at the retreating figure, unwilling to believe what his senses were telling him. Then Leo began to run again, as fast as he had ever run in his life. He shoved or sidestepped the motionless and the hysterical, thrust aside anyone who got in his way. He was at Nanking Road. He turned the corner. He stopped short.

Nothing during the time he'd spent as a soldier during the Great War had prepared him for the human carnage that assaulted his eyes. The Chinese planes had dropped three bombs on the Bund. One bomb landed in the Whangpoo, another in front of the Cathay, and a third dropped straight through the roof of the Palace, exploding inside the building and blasting away one whole side of the hotel. Mutilated bodies dangled from the wreckage of the Palace like pieces of twisted laundry. Clouds of acrid dust hung low in the air, hovering over loose piles of glass and steel and mortar, now mingled with severed bone, flesh, and blood. A chorus of terror and pain rose from the throats of five hundred wounded. Seven hundred lay dead. European and Asian, young and old, rich and poor, innocent and evil; all were united in a sudden, grisly execution.

A wave of nausea swept over him. *Martha. Maddy.* He ran once more, tripping over bits of rubble and slipping in the blood that ran in the street like rainwater. He repeated their names aloud, over and over, until the mantra became a frenzied cry of horror and hope.

He saw the Cathay, and the crater in front of it. Something caught at his foot, causing him to stumble and fall. It was a small Chinese boy. The bone of his left shin had broken completely through his skin. He howled piteously for help. Leo pushed himself up off the ground and dashed forward. His hands and knees were now drenched in blood.

He climbed through what had been the grand entrance to the Ca-thay Hotel, calling out the names of his wife and child. There were so many people hurt. Others were there helping, clearing away glass and debris so that the injured could be freed from the wreckage.

And then he heard it, the shrill voice of a frightened little girl, call-ing to him through the chaos.

"Papa!" Maddy screeched. She raced to him and wrapped her quak-ing arms around him. Martha was right behind her, tears streaming down her cheeks.

Leo hugged Martha to him, wrapping Maddy between their two grateful bodies. He closed his eyes.

"Oh thank you, dear God," he sobbed, the first real prayer he had uttered since childhood. "Thank God, thank God. Thank God." Wiping his eyes, he took one step back to inspect them.

"You aren't hurt?" It was a plea, not a question.

"No, we're all right," replied Martha, as if she didn't quite believe her own words.

"Then let's get out of here." He wiped his hands off on his tennis shorts, then whipped off his shirt and tore off a long strip of fabric, trying to use a piece that was not sullied with blood.

He squatted down next to Maddy, gave her a kiss, and another big hug. Then he looked her straight in the eyes. "My brave little princess, I'm going to cover your eyes with this and carry you away from here. You put your face in my shoulder and don't even think about looking up until I tell you to. Do you understand?"

Maddy nodded, her little chin still trembling. Leo turned the strip of fabric into a blindfold and tied it around Maddy's closed eyes. Before picking her up he said to Martha, "Keep your eyes on the ground, Martha. Don't look around you. Hold onto my arm. You've already seen enough."

"I'll try." She managed a weak smile.

"That's my girl." Picking a careful path through the rubble and the gore, Leo led his family home.

He waited until they had each taken a warm bath, changed into comfortable silk pajamas, and had a bowl of hot broth, provided by a pinch-faced Wei Lin. He waited until Maddy fell asleep on the big bed in her parent's room, nestled between her parents, one small hand holding that of her father, the other tucked into her mother's. He waited until he and Martha were settled together on the overstuffed leather couch in the parlor, a decanter of brandy on the table in front of them. Then he began.

"Martha, we have to leave Shanghai."

"I know."

He picked up a lock of her hair and let it ripple through his fingers. What would he have done if he had lost them today? What reason would he have to go on living? He must find somewhere safe for them. He did not care what price he had to pay, as long as they were safe.

"It may not be so easy for me to get out. There are . . . well, there are some things about me that you don't know."

He stood up, and took a step away from her, running his hand over his head and down the back of his neck as he did so. When he turned around to face her he saw the question in her eyes.

"You see, Martha, I was not entirely truthful with you about why I came to Shanghai. There was more to my story. But I was afraid that you'd leave me if you knew the truth. I was afraid I would lose you. And I knew I couldn't bear it."

She did not interrupt. She looked at him and waited. He had no idea how long she'd been waiting.

Leo paused again, not sure where to start. Then the truth poured out.

"I killed a man. When I was in Paris. Imre Károly, the chief of police in Budapest, was found dead in my hotel room because I killed him. I killed him in self-defense, but there were no witnesses. And I probably could have gotten away without killing him, but I wanted him dead.

He'd murdered my foster mother and uncle. And then I stole a diamond necklace from him, a necklace I knew had been paid for with counterfeit francs. I stole it because I knew it was the only way I could ever hope to be with you."

Martha listened, immobile on the couch.

"When I came to Shanghai I sold the diamonds to one of the most powerful men in China. You know of him. Liu Tue-Sheng. He's powerful because he's rich, and ruthless, and behind almost everything illegal that happens in this part of China. But I sold him the diamonds anyway, because I was desperate. And then I made even more money in a commodities market manipulation that Liu somehow pulled off. So I was rich. Then you came to Shanghai. I had everything.

"But the stock market crash wiped me out. I didn't have the heart to tell you then. You were so excited about the baby, and I so badly wanted to give you both a beautiful life. Liu found out about my predicament and he, well, he made me go to work for him.

"I really am wanted for murder, Martha, and Liu is holding a valid warrant for my arrest. It may be, with all the time that has passed, that I'd be safe, that no one is still looking for me. But they'd start looking the minute that Liu turned me in. He'd make sure of it. Not only because I'm a valuable commodity for him, but because to do otherwise would show he was merciful, a weakness that a person in his business can't afford. So I'm stuck here. But you aren't. So you and Maddy must leave."

He sat down in a chair across from her, afraid to go any closer. A long, fluid silence filled the space between them, ebbing and flowing into different emotions: remorse and anger, contrition and indignation, sympathy and sorrow.

Fighting back her tears, Martha finally spoke. "What do you mean, you work for Liu Tue-Sheng? You work at the bank. How can Liu keep you here?"

"I spy on people, Martha," Leo said flatly, his self-deprecation obvious. "I eavesdrop, and uncover secrets, and collect dirty laundry. I'm an informant. And in exchange for the information I provide, Liu Tue-Sheng, member of the board of the Commerce Bank of China, puts money into my account every month. I chalk it all up to commissions on new business."

Martha looked down at her hands, then up at the ceiling, then to the door. When she faced Leo again, her face was twisted with pain.

"I could forgive you for almost anything, Leo," she began. "I know that if you killed that man in Paris, you had a reason. And I know that if you took something or did something to survive that you did what you truly believed you had to do. I'm not as naïve as you think I am. I know that after the war people did things they wouldn't otherwise do, just to survive, and these times we live in are in some ways no less challenging. But it's so hard for me to accept that you didn't trust me. That from the very beginning, you didn't trust me. That you couldn't trust me to forgive you for what you did, out of love for me, thinking that an easy life was more important to me than the truth. And I don't know if I can forgive you for what your guilt has done to you. And done to us." She buried her face in her hands.

The sight of Martha in tears sent a fresh torrent of guilt raging through him. He pressed his fists together, fighting the urge to reach for her, searching for words to explain why he'd taken so long to confess.

"At first I thought I was protecting you; first you, and then Maddy. I wanted you to be happy. To be with me, and to be happy. I didn't know what love was, until I met you. I thought that true love was fragile and precious, and I was afraid to test its limits. I'd already put you through so much, abandoning you in Paris and then asking you to come to Shanghai. I thought that by not telling you the truth I was keeping you safe. But now I see that I was only protecting myself. Not just my life, but what I wanted our life together to be."

Leo's voice caught in his throat, and he did not know how much longer he could go on talking. "All I can say is, I am so sorry, my darling. I never wanted things to be this way. I just wanted you to be with me, and be happy. But now you and Maddy are better off without me. You must go to a place where you can be safe, and I can't keep you safe here. I want you to join your sister and her family when they get to France."

Martha did not answer. She continued to cry as Leo took a seat beside her. He stroked her shoulder tentatively, still afraid to touch her, afraid he would upset her even more.

"Whatever I've done, Martha," he said, his voice breaking, "whatever I've done, I've done loving you."

He closed his eyes and kissed her hair; tenderly, reverently, trying to convey in that single act how precious she was to him.

Still crying, Martha jerked her head away. As she moved she felt him cringe. Then, like a disciplined rider pulling hard on the reins of a runaway horse, she pulled herself away from her anger. *There's no time for this. There's no time for anger. Not now.* If it was within her to forgive him then she must forgive him now. Their circumstances could not tolerate indecision. She took a deep breath and turned her head toward his.

Engulfed by grateful passion, Leo kissed her face, her throat, and her neck. He swept her silk pajamas off her body, and he worshiped her.

Lost in his ardent caresses, she smiled. She had her husband back. The man she loved; the man with whom she shared her life, a life that could not be beautiful or complete without him. Yet something that had been perfect was no longer so, and would never be again.

"I won't leave without you," she whispered later, as they drifted into a healing sleep.

"We'll see." Leo's heart glowed with renewed strength. Martha loved him. She would always love him. He felt invincible.

TEN

The next day the Chinese government issued its official apology. An accident. The bombing of the Bund by the Chinese pilots had been an accident. And fifteen minutes after the first three bombs had devastated the Bund, two more fell at the intersection of Avenue Edward VII and Tibet Road. One struck the Great World Amusement Center. On Thursday it had been a six-story fun house, entertaining visitors with tight rope walkers, acrobats, gambling tables, slot machines, professional letter-writers, fortune tellers, shooting galleries, ice cream shops, dumpling stands, prayer temples, and women of ill repute. On Friday it had been converted into a refugee center. On Saturday it became a pyramid of death for a thousand people, most of them Chinese, who'd come to the Settlement to escape the war. Flesh and shrapnel from the explosion rained down on the Englishmen playing cricket at a nearby park. Also an accident.

The significance of what had happened was not lost on the Shang-hailanders. Intentionally or not, Chiang had broken the rules. If the

Taipans and their families, their homes and their silver, their port and their ponies, if all that could not be safe, then Shanghai would cease to exist. Already, the evacuations had started. The British wives and their children boarded the *Rajputana*, bound for Hong Kong. American families sailed away on the *President Taft*, Germans on the *Oldenburg*. Shanghai was now a war zone, the myth of its sanctity exposed. It was time to leave.

But for the outcasts, for all those no longer welcome in their native land, leaving the city was not so easy. To leave, you needed permission to enter another country, permission that was not easy to obtain.

The grim reality of the situation soon became clear to Leo and Martha. The Nazi government would not allow Martha to return to Germany, for she was of Jewish heritage. The French government would not allow her to enter France until she could prove she had relatives established there. The United States was similarly out of the question. Even visas for Hong Kong were restricted to British nationals until the immediate refugee crisis had abated. For the time being, there was no decent place for Martha and Maddy to go, even if they were willing to leave without Leo. They would have to wait.

After a few uneventful days, the remaining foreign residents of the city emerged from hiding. Perhaps the boundaries of the French Concession and the International Settlement would be respected after all; there did not seem to be any compelling reason to stay inside. If not, well, an errant bomb could land on one's house as easily as it could land on the country club. *May as well go have a drink*, mused the Shanghailanders as they studied the night sky, painted a macabre red by the incendiary blaze of Japanese bombs pulverizing Hongkew and Nantao. Life was too short to stay thirsty.

Martha and Leo felt safer at home. Their house was in the heart of the residential district of the French Concession; they hoped that its distance from any likely targets would keep them safe. Still, Leo ventured out from time to time for news, and Martha went in search of groceries and other staples, for their Chinese servants refused point-blank to leave the property for fear of being shot or captured by the Japanese.

Nine days after the bombing of the Bund, Maddy bounded into the breakfast room where her parents were finishing their coffee and reading the morning edition of the newspaper. She jiggled her mother's knee.

"Mama, I have to show you something."

"Oh yes?" Martha put down her section of the paper. "Should I come see it now?"

"Yes. And you too, Papa."

"I'll be along in just a minute, little love. Just let me finish my coffee."

Maddy made a face. "Finish your *paper*, you mean. Well, then, Mama will be the lucky one, and you'll have to be second." With this admonishment, she dragged her mother from the table and into the parlor. Martha saw her daughter's entire collection of dolls and stuffed animals arranged on the sofa, creating an attentive audience.

Maddy pointed her mother to a vacant chair. "Madame," she announced solemnly, "the concert is about to begin."

"Why, thank you." With gracious decorum, Martha took a seat.

Maddy skipped over to the piano bench and executed an elaborate curtsy. Martha applauded. Her daughter then climbed onto the piano bench, her small feet dangling four inches from the floor. For an instant she posed her ten little fingers over the keys. Then she began to play.

Within seconds Martha's mouth fell wide open. She listened, astonished, as Maddy played, from beginning to end, an energetic rendition of Scott Joplin's "Maple Leaf Rag."

Martha flew to where her child sat beaming with delight and wrapped her in an ardent hug. "That was fantastic. How long did it take you to learn that? Who's been teaching you? Is this a secret between you and Papa?"

Radiant, Maddy shook her head. "No, Mama. There's no secret. Gaston, who plays the piano at the club, showed me how to play it. Then I came home and figured out how to do it by myself. I told you, I listen very well."

"But how did he . . . could you explain to me a little bit more about *exactly* how you learned to play it?"

"Well," said Maddy, swinging her feet as she thought about her answer, "Gaston played it for me at the club when we were there for dinner with Janine and her parents, so however long ago that was, you know, since you bought the piano for me, I guess. A few days. But I can do it faster now, because now I know where all the sounds are in the keys. But I can't reach the pedals. It would sound better if I could reach the pedals."

"Leo," called Martha, moving toward the door. "Leo, come here. You have to hear this."

They bumped into each other at the doorway. Leo caught sight of the pile of stuffed animals and dolls on the couch.

"How marvelous. A concert. May I listen to the encore?"

"By all means. Go ahead, darling, play your song for Papa."

Maddy gave Leo a sly sideways smile then turned her attention back to the keyboard. She played the piece once again, flawlessly.

Leo clapped enthusiastically. "Brava, Brava," he called as Maddy stood up to take a bow. Then he turned to Martha. "Well, I guess the joke's on me. How long has she been taking lessons?"

"She hasn't had any lessons. She taught herself. In just two weeks. Isn't that right, Maddy?"

"Hmm hmm." Maddy turned a fidgety pirouette. She was starting to get nervous. Her father had a funny look on his face. Maybe it was time to stop talking.

Leo motioned for Maddy to sit back down on the piano bench, and then sat beside her. Martha started to speak, but Leo held up his hand to silence her.

"Maddy, did you really teach yourself how to play that song?"

Maddy nodded.

"How did you do it?"

Maddy hesitated. She so wanted her father to be happy with her. She hoped her explanation would please him.

"Well, Papa, you see, each of these keys makes a sound. Gaston told me it is a special musical sound, called a 'note.' Here is 'C,' then 'D.' It goes up to 'G,' but that's all, and then it just repeats itself, so it's really easier than the alphabet. The black keys are 'sharp' for up, and 'flat,' for down. If you fall, you fall down flat, so that's easy to remember.

"Gaston played this song for me, a few times, and I listened very well, and then I came home and learned where each note lives on my piano, so that I could play it. So that's all. It wasn't too hard." She flashed him an uncertain little smile.

Martha could not restrain herself. "Leo, is that possible? Could she really be so talented? Just naturally gifted?"

"I suppose so." He thought about his own gift. Words were, after all, sounds. They made sense to him in a way he knew made him different from other people. Musical notes could live in Maddy's little head just as easily as six languages now inhabited his.

Then he noticed the look on his daughter's face.

"Maddy, my magnificent Madeleine, don't be afraid. We think it's wonderful. *You're* wonderful." He picked her up and spun her through the air before setting her down in front of the crowded couch. Her concern alleviated, Maddy giggled, basking in her father's praise.

"Now," Leo said in a mock-serious tone, wagging his finger at the population on the sofa, "if we are to have concerts here fit for royalty, don't you think a new doll is in order? A new queen for your collection? Someone worthy of your performances?"

"Really, Papa? But my birthday is past already, and Christmas is so far away."

"Nonsense. A pianist with your talent deserves a regal audience. You will have lessons starting tomorrow. And I will ride my stallion to court and invite her highness, the queen of fairyland, to come and pay you tribute."

Maddy glanced at her mother, expecting her to intervene. But Martha's face showed no disapproval; her eyes glowed with pride. She looked back at her father. He, too, was gazing at her with unabashed adoration.

Normally, Maddy was not a greedy child. But there was one thing she wanted with all of her girlish heart; she saw her opportunity, and took it.

"Papa, there is a doll. She's so beautiful. We saw her at the department store. Do you remember, Mama? The ballerina? She's a queen, I guess. She's wearing a tiara. Mama, would it be all right?"

"Of course, darling. I think if we are to have such fabulous concerts in the house, a new doll would be perfectly appropriate."

Leo tapped his blissful little prodigy on the forehead. "Then you shall have it; and you shall have it in time for a concert at tea."

"Can we all go?" Maddy asked, her face full of joyful expectation.

Again, Martha looked at Leo. He considered Maddy's question carefully before answering. "It should be safe. The department stores are as far from the harbor as our house, and even farther away from the French Concession border. It will do us good to get out. We can even see if there is anywhere open for lunch."

The cheerful group set out on its expedition just before noon. Refugees were still flooding into the Settlement from the Chinese Municipality of Greater Shanghai, as well as the surrounding countryside. Their street-clogging presence made driving difficult. It took a good thirty minutes to make what should have been a ten-minute trip.

When the car reached the point where the two huge stores, Wing On and Sincere's, flanked Nanking Road, they discovered that parking was impossible. Leo tapped their driver on the shoulder.

"Just leave it running right here. I'll dash in. You can't cause any bigger traffic jam than what's already here. Shouldn't take five minutes."

"But you don't know which doll it is, Papa," Maddy pointed out logically. "I have to come, too."

A uniformed traffic policeman tapped on the windshield. "Please keep it moving, sir. With all these extra bodies in the road, we can't be blocking traffic. Move along."

"Leo," Martha broke in quickly, "I know just which doll it is. You stay here with Maddy in the car, and drive around the block. I'll be back here in five minutes, and we'll just go home for lunch." She leaned over and gave her husband a quick kiss, then hopped out before he could protest.

"Five minutes," he called after her, savoring the taste of her kiss.

The policeman tapped on the window again. Maddy opened it and looked up at him. "My mama went to get me a doll."

"Very nice," he replied cheerfully. "Now tell your daddy to move along, or I'll have to give him a ticket."

Leo playfully saluted the officer. "As you wish, sir. Go around the block, Peter. In this traffic that alone will take us more than ten minutes." The driver complied, edging the car into the morass of automobiles and other wheeled contraptions.

Martha quickly maneuvered her way into the busy department store. She went directly to where a display of porcelain dolls from Austria were arranged in a large glass case and spotted Maddy's choice immediately. Sixteen inches tall, with fair pink skin and blushing cheeks, the doll's chestnut hair was braided around her head and adorned with a tiara of Bavarian crystal. Martha flagged down a saleswoman, who unlocked the case and retrieved the coveted dancer.

"A pretty doll for a pretty girl?"

"The best, the most beautiful little girl. I'd like it gift-wrapped, please."

"Certainly, Madame." Martha followed the saleswoman to her register. She opened her purse and dug around for her wallet. As she did so she heard a noise. An odd noise, above the din of the crowd.

She looked around. What was that strange sound? It was high and thin, like a shrill voice stretched taut, melting into a scream. No, a whine. A metallic, whistling whine.

Within seconds the laws of physics ruthlessly eviscerated the expectations of humanity. The first floor of Sincere's was obliterated. One side of Wing On collapsed. A thousand people died instantly, or bled quickly to death. The hysterical survivors, insane with fear, screamed and stampeded through the forest of broken glass and dismembered bodies. Outside the corpse of the traffic policeman dangled from the electric wires overhead, like a gruesome marionette, directing the dance of death beneath him. A broken water main sent a bloody waterfall cascading into the street.

Martha had no time to react, no time for fear, and no time for regrets. She had no time to remember the sweet touch of Leo's caress, or the feeling of Maddy's slender arms around her neck. She had no time to remember the smell of Bavarian wildflowers in early spring, the sound of her mother's voice, or to picture her husband and daughter together at the breakfast table. She heard a wall of noise, and felt a rippling sheet of pain. And then, darkness.

ELEVEN

Amelia Simmons stood on the Hoffman's doorstep and waited for someone to answer the doorbell. She did not fidget, nor exhibit any visible sign of irritation as the seconds became minutes, and still no one responded to her summons. She waited. Then she rang again, and she waited again. She did not tap her slim crocodile-clad foot, check her lipstick in the reflection provided by the decorative brass doorknocker, or readjust the hat that covered the smooth chignon into which she'd twisted her hair. Her demeanor was neither patient, nor benign. Hers was the menacing forbearance of the scavenger.

The sticky Shanghai heat sent a bead of sweat rolling down the back of her long white neck. *God, I detest this place.* She hated the heat and the noise and the stench of it. But like many of the human scavengers and parasites found in Shanghai, she stayed because the city's decadent prosperity provided a better home for their kind than anywhere else in the world.

Now Shanghai was dying, giving her the perfect reason to leave: self-preservation.

Amelia could have left Shanghai when her husband Reggie died. She had her own hefty little nest egg, expertly skimmed from Reggie's ill-gotten gains. But something—or rather, someone—made her decide to stay.

The possibility of seeing Leo again brought back a flood of erotic memories. Their affair had lasted only two weeks, but no one with an ounce of pride could have objected to how Leo had handled himself, and Amelia had plenty of pride. But she still remembered the feel of his hands, and the taste of his kiss. The smell that was most distinctly *him*. Most of all she remembered the distant look in his eyes, a distance she'd thought, for one small moment, she could breach.

At first she did not connect Leo with the scandal that resulted in her husband's suicide. Reggie was not confronted by the people at his firm until a year after Leo broke off their liaison. She did not really miss her dearly departed. His money and her independence were more than sufficient consolation for the loss of his stodgy company. But it was inconvenient for his life to have ended the way it did.

Then, one sultry evening six months after Reggie's death, Amelia saw Martha and Leo dancing together at the popular nightclub on top of the Cathay Hotel. Her heart leapt at the sight of him, but she wisely kept her distance and studied the two of them.

The expression on Leo's face as he looked at his wife gave her the first clue. Amelia was a woman of considerable experience. She knew that his gaze was not the look of a man who searched elsewhere for entertainment.

Ever since that moment, she couldn't shake the notion that Leo had played some role in Reggie's demise. In her clever brain she replayed every conversation she'd had with Leo during their two-week affair. It seemed to her that she never really told him that Reggie was stealing; however, looking back, she'd probably said enough for a suspicious, insightful mind to put two and two together.

It wasn't until afterward that she'd learned her dear Reggie had jumped from embezzling to smuggling opium, using his tobacco shipments as a convenient cover. While a lucrative move financially, cutting into the opium market made Reggie an inconvenience for Liu Tue-Sheng. And Leo worked at the bank that many whispered was a cover for Liu's other, more profitable businesses.

A wry smile played upon her lips as she thought again about how coolly Leo had used her. Of course, she'd exploited many people in her life, but she never expected for anyone to give her a taste of her own with such finesse.

For a while she was tempted to plan some revenge, but Amelia never acted rashly. After critically examining her situation, she realized that vengeance was not her true goal. What she wanted was Leo.

She'd felt something different when she was with him, something more than pleasant physical passion. In his arms she'd remembered the few things she actually liked about herself, and was even able, for a few tantalizing moments, to abandon all of her disciplined self-control. She'd felt free.

Yes, Amelia wanted Leo. She wanted him back in her bed. And she wanted him to look at her the way he'd looked at Martha.

With her usual pragmatism, Amelia discerned that destroying Leo's marriage would be counterproductive. That would only make him hate her. And she had to hope that Leo didn't know much about her past. Unlike Reggie, Leo did not seem like the type of man to take home used merchandise, no matter how alluring the packaging.

No, given her colorful track record, she couldn't hope to break up his marriage. She would have to wait and capitalize on someone else's mistake. Someone else would expose Leo for mixing sex and business (for she had no doubt he had done so before and would do it again), and then she, Amelia, would swoop down and snatch Leo away from Martha's wounded little paws.

For three years she waited. Then an errant bomb suddenly eliminated Martha from the equation. No matter. Once again, Amelia's perseverance had paid off. This was her moment. She intended to seize it.

He can't love a dead woman forever, she thought, as the manservant, Duo Win, finally answered the door in response to her persistent ringing. The fact that Martha had been dead less than forty-eight hours did not give Amelia a moment's hesitation. She did not see herself as callous; she was merely practical. She wanted to leave Shanghai. In light of the dangers posed by the Japanese invasion, it made good sense to leave immediately. She wanted Leo to go with her. To accomplish this, she had something to offer him, something she thought Leo would be unable to refuse: an American passport.

Duo Win looked at her in annoyance. He did not recognize the woman on the step, and he did not wait for an introduction before dismissing her.

"No come in, Missy. Mista Leo no see. No talk. Missy Martha die. No come in."

Amelia came prepared for such a rebuff. As Duo Win closed the door, she swiftly pushed an American twenty-dollar bill into the crack between the door and its frame, just above the door knob. When the door slammed shut, it trapped the bill so that a few inches stuck out on either side.

It was a staggering amount of money, probably more than the poor servant had ever seen so close to his own nose. Amelia clutched her end tightly. After a moment she felt a tug. She tightened her grip.

"No, my dear. Wantchee money, open door."

There was silence, then another tug. Amelia waited. The door creaked open. Duo Win's guilty face peeked out.

Amelia pressed into the room, skillfully tucking the twenty into Duo Win's hand as she slipped by him.

"Let's say I pushed my way in, why don't we? Go ahead and make a fuss." She moved quickly to the center of the foyer.

Duo Win, grateful to have an alibi, started to yell. "I say no come in. Bad lady. Mista Leo too sad. No see no one."

After a moment of this ranting Leo appeared on the first floor landing. Maddy was right behind him. Amelia looked up at them. She scarcely noticed Maddy, whose pinched and tear-stained face peered over the railing with a pathetic stare that would have melted anyone's heart—anyone but Amelia's.

Leo looked wretched. His face was gray, his skin unshaven, and two deep lines were now visible on his broad, square forehead. Amelia was not deterred. She was relying on the fact that, in time, his grief would pass. He would recover, and be deeply grateful that she had saved them.

"Leo, I came as soon as I heard. I can't tell you how badly I feel for you. For both of you. I know how you loved her."

Leo looked at her with consternation, not conveying any indication that he understood what she'd said. He made no move to come downstairs. After a moment he cleared his throat. Ragged words emerged. "Amelia, I appreciate your coming, but we are not up to receiving visitors. I'll have to ask you to leave."

Amelia knew that additional pleasantries would serve no purpose. She came directly to the point. "Leo, I need to speak to you. Immediately. About your future. And Madeleine's," she added, baiting her hook. Leo did not say a word. She walked to the bottom of the stairs, looking up at him with all the sweetness she could muster.

"Amelia, this is really not the time—"

"Leo," she implored, "how much time do any of us have left here? I know you'll want to hear what I have to say."

Leo sighed, conveying the impression that he would agree to listen because he did not have the energy to argue. He said to Duo Win, who was still hovering furtively near the front door, "Please take Miss Maddy down to the kitchen, and see if Wei Lin can tempt her into eating something."

Duo Win scampered up to collect his small charge. Maddy allowed herself to be led away. She cast one panicked look at her father before exiting the foyer.

Leo showed Amelia into the front parlor. He waited for her to take a seat on the sofa, then positioned himself on a chair near the fireplace, politely communicating that he intended to remain as far away from her as possible. Amelia decided not to be insulted.

She was nervous. It was an unfamiliar sensation. She thought about lighting a cigarette, then decided not to. Better to plunge ahead.

"Leo," she began, "please believe that I'm here only as a concerned friend. Have you thought about what you and Maddy are going to do?"

Do? What was there left to do? What did it matter, now that Martha was gone? He'd thought about nothing but the explosion for the last forty-eight hours. He saw the buildings collapse, and heard Maddy's screams. His life had stopped at that moment.

"Look," he said, after a significant pause, "this is pointless. What-ever you have to tell me—"

"Marry me and come to America."

He stared at her, shocked beyond words. She rushed into the void, explaining and cajoling.

"Leo, I know it's ridiculous, my coming to you this way. You and Maddy are safe here for the moment, but for how long? No one knows if the Japanese will respect the International Concessions, and the Chinese army is going to abandon Shanghai any day now. The rest of the world has given up on us. No one is willing to rescue Shanghai this time, because this time the war between Japan and China will destroy the city's ability to keep making money. And where can you go? Back to Vienna? If you'd been comfortable there, you wouldn't have come to Shanghai."

She paused, allowing the truth of her words to sink in. "Maybe you don't care about what happens to you, but I do. And Madeleine deserves a chance at happiness, in a place where the death of her mother won't haunt her. I know it may seem cruel, even obscene for me to come here, today, with an offer like this, but we've no time for proper etiquette. I've booked a first-class cabin on the *President Jefferson*. It leaves in five days. Once its berths are full, no more American ships will be leaving Shanghai until God knows when. Everyone who could get out already has."

Leo still stared at her. She looked down at her own slim ankles, neatly crossed in front of her, and finished her speech.

"I know you don't love me, and I know our marriage will exist only on paper. We can get a divorce as soon as you like, or as soon as the law will allow without jeopardizing your American residency. But at least you can get out. I don't want to leave you and your daughter here, not knowing if the next bomb will fall on you and Madeleine. Or to find out one day that you were killed, and that she was left alone in one of those ghastly orphanages—" She stopped short as real tears filled her eyes. The idea of Leo's dying really did upset her.

Leo sat back heavily in his chair as the pain of his loss once again overwhelmed him. A question hissed out of his lungs, like stale air from a balloon.

"Why are you doing this?"

But he knew why, even as he asked. Women like Amelia always found a way into his life. They were like cockroaches, crawling in and out of the cracks of human weakness, surviving no matter what the cost; women like Amelia and his first lover, Countess Podmaniczky.

In his life there had been only two women he'd loved and wanted to protect: Erzsebet and Martha. He'd failed them both. He covered his face with his hands.

Then he was aware of Amelia's presence next to him. She put her hand lightly on his shoulder. "I won't lie and say that I grieved over Reggie the way you're grieving over Martha. But I do know what it's like to be alone. And I know this isn't the right time, but I've never had the chance to tell you that during the time we were . . . that is . . . the time we spent together, it really meant something to me. More than you ever knew."

She leaned in closer. "I know that I'll never replace Martha. I'm not trying to. But I do care about you, and at the very least I can help you escape from this hell hole. And maybe, at some point in the future, you and I can help each other overcome our loneliness."

Leo's self-hatred responded instantly to her words, raging inside him like a caged animal in search of violent release. His entire body flexed with tension as he fought his urge to hurt this woman. Instinctively he clutched the arms of his chair to keep himself from striking her.

Amelia could see the outline of his erection through the linen of his trousers. Encouraged, she did not guess he was inspired by fury and not desire. She took off her hat and knelt on the floor next to his chair, ready to service him then and there.

As she started to bring her head to his lap Leo grabbed Amelia by the hair. She looked up at him, her light brown eyes glazed with lust and anticipation, excited by what she mistook for passion.

Leo returned her stare with cold malice. For the second time in his life he felt overcome by a thirst for revenge; but this time, there was no one to blame for his pain but himself. *He* had killed Martha, by keeping her in Shanghai. Why bother to go on living?

For Maddy.

If he threw away this chance to elude Liu's grasp, he might not get another. And to go to America? Under different circumstances, it would be a dream come true. Leo forced himself to relax his grip. He had no reason to be angry at this woman. On the contrary, he had used her. As far as he knew, Amelia's sins were no worse than his own.

Now Amelia was trying to help him, just as the Countess had tried to help him so long ago, when she'd warned him not to go back to the villa on the night Károly murdered Erzsebet and József. His anger ebbed away. When he spoke his voice was dull with resignation.

"I'll take you up on your generous offer. But we can't celebrate prematurely. Are you sure I can get into the country?"

Amelia stood up and straightened her skirt, subduing the exhilaration she felt.

"We can be married in two days. Spouses of American citizens are being given immediate permission to enter the States in light of the crisis here. All we need to do is show up with your passport and our marriage license." She stood before him, meekly waiting for him to tell her what to do.

Leo rubbed his hands across his unshaven face. He must salvage a life for his daughter.

"No one can know I'm leaving. I have my reasons. Can we get married just before we board the ship?"

"Of course."

Leo stood up. He looked drained. "Amelia, I don't want Maddy to know about our marriage until the absolute last minute. As you can readily understand, she may not take it well. Please be patient. And, thank you."

Amelia managed to keep her smile small and humble.

TWELVE

Later that day, Leo placed a call to Tokyo and contacted a wealthy Japanese client of the Commerce Bank who'd once mentioned how much he wanted to relocate to Shanghai. Life in Japan under the new military regime was becoming too Spartan, too restricted, he'd complained. Even jazz music had been outlawed. Shanghai glittered across the China Sea like a pulsating, decadent oasis. Now Leo offered to sell the man his own glorious Georgian manor, with all its furnishings, at a very reasonable price. Rejoicing over his good luck, the client agreed to wire the funds directly to a specific bank in New York, and made plans to move to Shanghai the moment the Chinese retreated from the city.

Leo knew that by selling his house he was taking a chance, for it gave Liu the opportunity to discover that he planned to leave. But Leo did not want to rely on Amelia for money, and his home was his most significant asset. He was counting on the fact that Liu would be preoccupied by the war, and that hostilities between Japan and China would necessarily limit Liu's contacts with the Japanese. Things were not going well for Liu's friend, General Chiang. Under the circumstances, Leo hoped the gangster wouldn't discover that one of his minions was planning to escape.

He waited until the morning of their scheduled departure to go to the bank and wire the remainder of his savings to his new bank account in New York. He executed the transaction himself, then went upstairs to his private office, to empty the small vault containing Martha's jewelry and their passports.

Once in his office, Leo locked the door, then squatted on the floor behind his desk and tossed back the rug covering the safe. He opened the steel door and started to transfer the boxes containing Martha's jewelry to a briefcase. Here was the string of pearls he had bought her for her thirtieth birthday, and the emerald set he had given her one Christmas. Then came the Art Deco bracelet, studded with onyx and tiny diamonds. Each jewel glinted with painful memories. He tried not to think about the childlike joy with which Martha had received each present, or how each piece had looked against the soft marvel of her skin. His hands began to shake.

The safe was now empty. Still overcome by his grief, it took him a moment to realize what was wrong. The passports. The passports were not there.

Leo groaned. He slammed the door of the small safe shut. There, along the outside edges of the lock, he could see the small holes testifying to where the lock had been drilled.

"Damn." He slammed the side of his fist against the metal door. His hand vibrated with pain from the harsh contact, but his brain paid no attention.

"You filthy son of a bitch," Leo growled, standing up and shaking his bruised fist at an imaginary Liu. "You have no power over me now, you bastard. Do you hear me? You can't thwart a man with nothing left to lose. You'll give me back those passports or you'll have to kill me. And then you'll be doing me a favor, you understand? A favor. If you'd killed me years ago Martha would be alive now. *She'd be alive.*"

A knock on the door brought him to his senses. "What is it?"

"Is everything all right, sir?" a voice inquired. His secretary. She must have heard him.

"Yes. I'm fine. My wife died. Now go away." He heard the sound of her heels clicking down the hall as she retreated.

He could not give up. There might not be any hope for him, but the one thing he could do for Martha was to try and save their daughter: to get her away from the dangers of the war, and the threat that Liu might ultimately try to use Maddy as leverage over him.

By now it was almost noon. Their ship was due to sail at six. He was to meet Amelia at the Justice of the Peace at two o'clock. Two hours. Two hours to find Liu Tue-Sheng and win his life back. No. Maddy's life. His life was over. He picked up his briefcase and walked out, back down to the Bund where his car and driver were waiting.

He stopped at his own home for a moment, then proceeded to Liu's compound. The guard waved his car in, as if he'd been expected. Leo was not surprised. Liu knew him well enough to know that he would come.

This time he was not escorted to Liu's study. After the anticipated body search the houseboy took him outside to an enormous greenhouse. At the far end of the structure Liu sat in one of two high-backed wicker chairs, surrounded by rare orchids. *Like the snake in the garden of Eden*, thought Leo. In front of Liu a small bamboo table was set for lunch. A bodyguard kept watch at either end of the glass-enclosed building.

Leo knew he must stay composed. Rude demands would be futile. For all of his Western attributes, Liu still had the soul of a Chinese. Leo could not succeed unless he allowed Liu to lose gracefully. To save face. He had to stick to his plan.

"Good . . . afternoon," Liu greeted Leo with his stilted speech. "Please sit . . . down."

Leo forced himself to sit.

"Mr. Liu," he began, "I believe that you have some property of mine. Some property that I need to retrieve."

"And what would that be, Mr. Hoffman?"

"My passport. And my wife's."

"Ah, your wife. I am so sorry to hear about your wife. A beautiful woman, with a good heart."

A muscle twitched in Leo's lower jaw as he fought to control himself. "Thank you. She, of course, will no longer need a passport, but my child is listed on hers."

Liu raised a thin black eyebrow. "You are planning to leave Shanghai?"

"I think you knew that."

"Yes. However, from my point of view your departure would be most inconvenient. If General Chiang retreats, as I am afraid he soon will, I shall have to move my operations to Hong Kong. I have already reserved a suite at the Peninsula Hotel there. I could use a man of your talent here, in Shanghai, to help me stay informed. In fact, it would be . . . essential to many of my business arrangements."

Leo shook his head. "You don't need me, Mr. Liu. Shanghai is dying.

There's no more money to be made here. You and the general must concentrate on winning this war. I'm afraid I'm no longer able to offer you my services. I am resigning my position at the bank."

"And if I refuse to accept your resignation?"

"Then I will kill you."

The faintest hint of surprise flickered across Liu's features. "But of course, you will also die."

Leo leaned forward. "You can't kill a man who is already dead. I died when my wife died."

"But you are unarmed," Liu pointed out. He remained unruffled. He could have been discussing strategy during a friendly game of chess.

Leo held out his hands, never taking his eyes off Liu's face. "There are many ways to kill a man. Neither of your bodyguards speak English, and I speak Chinese. If you call to them you'll be dead before they can reach you."

"And your daughter?"

Leo twisted his lips into a barren smile. His hands dropped to his knees. "Ah, for my daughter I am willing to gamble." He paused. He must choose his words carefully.

"You said once that you were a gambling man. This time, I'll make you a proposition. We'll play a game of cards."

"And what do I stand to gain?"

Leo reached into his breast pocket. As he made this motion the two bodyguards approached, poised for action. With a subtle wave of his hand Liu sent them back to their stations.

From his pocket Leo removed the swan he had given Martha as a wedding gift. He placed it on the table.

Liu looked at it impassively. "The swan is pretty, but not much of an incentive, Mr. Hoffman."

Leo raised his hand over the fragile porcelain trinket. "Appearances can be deceiving." With one swift motion, he brought his palm down on the swan's back, crushing it. From the shards and dust of porcelain he removed the last four of the Cartier diamonds. One by one he laid them on the table in front of the gangster.

"I propose that we cut a deck of cards and each draw one. The higher card wins. If I win, you will give me the passports, I will leave Shanghai, and you will keep these diamonds. If you win, I will stay in Shanghai and continue to work for you. But you will, with your usual methods, use the diamonds to arrange for my new American wife to get immediate custody of my daughter, so that she can leave Shanghai on the *President Jefferson* this evening."

"And if I refuse to play?"

"Then I will kill you. By the time the order to kill me has sprung from your throat, you will be dead."

"And your daughter will be dead soon afterward."

Leo flinched. The only way he could protect Maddy was to get her out of Shanghai: away from the bombs, away from the Japanese, away from the clutches of this monster. And the only asset he could use to buy her freedom was himself.

"Another reason for both of us to take this wager, Liu. If you play, you keep something of value: your life. And no matter who pulls the higher card, you win, for you will retain either the diamonds, or my services. And either way I win, for my daughter will get out of Shanghai. But if we do not play, we both die."

There was a brief moment of silence. In the distance a bird sang out three shrill notes, and was quiet.

"And I suppose, Mr. Hoffman, you brought a deck of cards with you?"

From his pocket Leo silently removed a deck of cards. The seal was unbroken.

A tiny smile touched Liu's face. "Mr. Hoffman, you never disappoint me. But tell me, what makes you think that I will let you leave this room alive after threatening me, no matter what the outcome of our little game of chance?"

Leo looked Liu in the eyes. "Because you are a man of your word. As am I."

Liu acknowledged the statement with a slight incline of his chin. "You may shuffle the cards, Mr. Hoffman."

Forty-five minutes later Leo was in the attic of his house, retrieving two large suitcases. He brought one with him into Maddy's room, where he found her staring out the window, while Wei Lin read her a simple story. He could not tell if Maddy was listening.

Leo excused Wei Lin, then sat down on Maddy's bed. He held out his arms and she came to him, sitting on his knees and wrapping her fragile arms around his neck. She looked so much like Martha, lying there against his chest, that for a moment Leo thought he would break down again. He waited until he could speak.

"Maddy, we're leaving Shanghai."

Maddy looked up at him, struggling to make sense of his words. She had difficulty understanding anything said to her since the explosion. Words floated into her ears and rested there, waiting for her to go back and listen to them later. Later she would hear their echoes, and force herself to understand.

Having grown up in Shanghai, where men picked up dead beggars off the street every morning and women left unwanted infants out to die every night, Maddy understood death. She understood that death meant gone forever, that dead things did not wake up, and did not come back. But death was something she associated with stray animals, and poverty, and Chinese people. Maddy did not understand why it had happened to her mother. All she knew was that her mother's presence in the store had been her fault.

She tried again to listen to what her father was saying.

"I want you to help me pack, *ma princesse*. You can fill up one big suitcase with your favorites. Clothes and toys. Whatever you like."

Maddy made no comment. Leo hugged her, then slid her off his lap. When Maddy saw the suitcase she understood.

"Are we coming back?"

He shook his head. "No, *ma princesse*. We're going to America to live."

She looked around her room. "Can I bring whatever I want?"

"Yes, Maddy. Anything you want, as long as it fits in this suitcase."

Maddy walked out of the room. Leo followed her down the hall to the master bedroom. He watched as she strode purposefully to Martha's dressing table and carefully picked up the wedding picture. A puzzled look crossed her face as she regarded the dresser, searching for something she did not see. She turned to face Leo.

"The swan, Papa. Where has the swan gone?"

Again Leo's voice caught in his throat. "It flew away, *chérie*. It flew away when Mama died."

Leo could see Maddy trying to comprehend what he'd said. In a moment she went over to Martha's lingerie dresser and rummaged through the top drawer, eventually withdrawing a gray velvet box. With the picture and the box in hand, she walked back over to Leo.

"This is what I want to bring, Papa. It doesn't matter about the rest."

Hot tears burned the back of Leo's eyes as he gazed at his daughter, looking up at him so matter-of-factly. Grief crowded every other emotion out of his heart.

After convincing Maddy to put some clothes and a couple of toys in her suitcase, he called all the servants into the foyer. He told them he was leaving, gave each one a small bundle of cash, and assured them that the new owner had agreed to keep them on. He did not know if they would stay to work for a Japanese boss, but he felt he had done his duty.

The ceremony at the Justice of the Peace was brief and sterile. They did not exchange rings, and did not kiss. Amelia knew better than to push her luck.

At six o'clock Leo and Maddy met Amelia on the Bund, at the edge of the wharf where the *President Jefferson* was anchored. A brass band played cheerful American tunes. People surged around the dock, shrieking last minute instructions and receiving farewell hugs, deliberately ignoring the nearby wreckage of the Cathay and Palace Hotels. A long low whistle from the ship signaled the final call to board.

Maddy held tightly to her father's hand. As the threesome boarded the ship, she did not ask Leo who Amelia was, or why she was there.

The bursar approached them as they stepped on deck. "Passports, please. Tickets. Thank you."

Amelia handed over the ticket for a first-class cabin, and her passport. Leo handed the officer a passport and an official-looking document. The man inspected each document in turn, then handed back everything but the tickets.

"I'm sorry, sir, but you will have to say goodbye to your wife and daughter here; we can't let anyone below deck today."

Amelia corrected him. "No, he's coming with me."

"No, Amelia, I'm afraid that I'm not."

The look on Amelia's face instantly convinced the bursar that he wanted no part of this conversation. "I'm sorry, ma'am," he said, edging toward the next two passengers. "You'll have to step aside and sort this out. I can give you five minutes."

Leo took a few steps away from the crowd, pulling his hand away from Maddy's as he did so. After a moment's hesitation Amelia followed. Her eyes narrowed in anger as she faced her new husband.

"What the hell do you think you are doing? I didn't agree to bring her without you."

"I can't come with you. Not yet. Because we're married, I'm able to give you custody of Maddy. Please take her to New York, and take care of her. I'll join you as soon as I can."

"As soon as you can? Leo, this is ridiculous—"

Her protests were cut off by Leo's lips against her own. His arms surrounded her. His kiss was urgent, passionate. It left her breathless.

"I will join you as soon as I can," he said again.

Amelia's head was spinning. She could capitalize on this turn of events, she thought as she caught her breath. She looked down at her new ward, aware of the little girl's anxious eyes upon her.

Leo knelt down to talk to his daughter. "Maddy, this is Amelia. She's going with you to America."

Maddy smiled with dutiful politeness, her stance edged with wariness. Amelia wondered what the child thought about that kiss.

Leo grasped his daughter gently by the shoulders. "Amelia is going to take you to New York." He waited for her to say something. A light of comprehension dawned on Maddy's face.

"Is she going to be my new nanny?" she asked innocently. Amelia quickly stifled an incredulous snort.

Leo glared up at Amelia, then quickly turned his attention back to his daughter.

"Not exactly. You see, for us to be able to go to America, I need to be married to an American citizen. Amelia is American, and she agreed to marry me, so that we could leave Shanghai, and be safe. There won't be any bombs in America. But I can't leave quite yet. I'll come for you soon. In the meantime, you must be a good girl, and mind Amelia. I promise I'll come for you as soon as I can."

Again, it seemed to take a while for Maddy to absorb this. Then she looked at Leo in horror. "You mean, she is your *wife?*" she shrieked, "Your *new wife?*"

"Maddy, please. It's all right." Leo tried to hold Maddy still, but she would not be comforted. She hit her father, flailing away at him like a crazed demon.

"I hate you. I hate you. How could you?" she screamed over and over again, writhing and pummeling Leo with all her might. Not knowing what else to do, Leo twisted her around and pinned her arms behind her back. She ended up facing Amelia, and the sight of her new stepmother caused her to fall instantly and eerily silent.

"I apologize. I should have expected this." Leo said gravely, looking at Amelia over Maddy's shoulder.

Amelia did her best to arrange her features into what she hoped was an expression of maternal concern.

"That's okay, Leo. Of course it's upsetting. Madeleine and I will soon be friends, you'll see." *And if not, I'm sure we can find a lovely Catholic boarding school near Manhattan. Let the nuns beat some manners into the little bitch.*

THIRTEEN
NEW YORK, 1938

"Again, Madeleine. And please, this time, *try* to concentrate on the rhythm," Sister Edwina admonished her pupil, not bothering to temper her exasperation. The small wooden piano bench upon which both she and Madeleine sat creaked nervously as the heavyset woman shifted her weight.

Maddy took a deep breath and began to play again, striking each note on the shabby old upright piano with stiff, awkward movements of her fingers. Unforgiving echoes bounced off the barren plaster walls. An hour locked in a dark closet in the Mother Superior's office had finally convinced her to take piano lessons, and several sharp raps with a ruler persuaded her to hit the right notes as she learned how to read music. But nothing could make her play well.

Six iron bars secured the room's one window. The scant sunlight that slipped through this barricade cast long, striped shadows across the scarred wooden floor. An amateurish oil portrait of the Virgin Mary provided the only decoration on the dingy gray walls. The Holy

Mother's eyes were upturned, as if she, too, were begging for some heavenly miracle to assist the unwilling student who now sat in the room.

Sister Edwina closed her eyes and grimaced as Madeleine once again assaulted Bach. She'd never seen a pupil put forth so much effort only to attain such mediocre results. The girl had been taking lessons for over a year. She thought the girl's father must be delusional to think that his child had any sort of musical talent. But his letters to Sister Gabriella, the school's headmistress, always contained generous bank drafts, in part "to cover the cost of Maddy's musical instruction." Unfortunately for Sister Edwina, Sister Gabriella knew a gold mine when she saw one. Leo Hoffman's wish that his child learn how to play the piano would be granted, whether Madeleine liked it or not.

Sister Gabriella administered Madeleine's punishments with a clear conscience. It was her duty to teach the child obedience and humility. If that was all she learned from her music lessons then her father's money was, in Sister Gabriella's view, money well spent, despite the child's lack of musical success.

"Enough," Sister Edwina snapped as Maddy finished her soulless rendition. She hefted her considerable bulk off the bench. "You may be excused. But you must ask Sister Constance to allow you to listen to a recording of that piece. Then try to capture some of the *essence* of the music. I've told you a hundred times. There's more to playing the piano than just hitting the right notes."

Maddy sprang up, eager to escape her ordeal.

"Yes, Sister Edwina. Thank you, Sister Edwina," she said politely, without a trace of the resentment she felt. In an instant she collected her books and her sweater and sped out the door.

The majority of the one hundred girls enrolled at St. Mary's Elementary School were day students, dismissed at three o'clock into the waiting arms of nannies and mothers. The school could accept only half a dozen live-in students, for it had not been designed as a boarding school. The six small bunks and six chests-of-drawers that lined the walls of the attic room where the boarders stayed were put there as a temporary concession to a few particularly wealthy parents whose schedules made it hard to deal with the special challenges posed by children deemed "difficult." When it became clear to Sister Gabriella that the school could charge a significant premium for the extra attention given to such students, the arrangements became available on a permanent basis.

For the past year Maddy had been one of the six. It was a convenient arrangement for Amelia; Madeleine was out from underfoot but only a moment away if Leo should make a sudden appearance. As one month drifted into another, Amelia almost forgot that she had a stepdaughter tucked away in a convent school. Oh, Leo knew that Madeleine was at a Catholic school; Amelia had obtained his consent to that much. Why would he object to a boarding school? After all, he'd abandoned his daughter. Madeleine was a well-tended little piece of bait, luring her father to come for her. To come for her, and back to Amelia.

Her one assurance that her plan was still working were the letters that Leo sent every month, containing a simple note and a bank draft. Every letter made the same promise; he would come within six months. As long as Leo covered Madeleine's expenses and the nuns took care of her, Amelia tolerated the wait. Still, she did not take any chances that her plan might go awry. She screened every piece of mail that traveled between Shanghai to New York, including all the letters sent to and from the sour old headmistress at St. Mary's. Madeleine had not once written to her father.

Amelia enjoyed her life in New York. She picked her escorts from a pool of rich, bored young men, whose trust funds enabled them to ignore the unpleasant consequences of what people were referring to as "the Great Depression." She could wait for Leo, she decided, as long as she stayed adequately entertained.

Most of the girls who boarded did so only for a short time: a month, a weekend, or a two-week holiday. Maddy became friendly with one of them: a plain, shy little creature named Jennifer, who screamed at night with nightmares that seemed as terrifying as Maddy's own. But when the spring term started, Jennifer's parents divorced, and she was sent to Vermont to live with her father's family. Maddy did not try to stay in touch with her. By now she accepted the fact that people simply disappeared.

She was pleasant to the rest of the day students, yet did not have one real friend among them. There were so many things that set her apart. She knew nothing about American life; she even spoke English with a British accent. She knew songs and games in French, not English. She accepted what was given to her, but never asked for anything, not so much as a glass of milk, for she could not forgive herself for making the request that had killed her mother.

The defiance she felt played itself out in subtle ways. She said the rosary backward, or tucked unwanted bits of Friday's fish into the pockets of her school uniform, until she could excuse herself to the bathroom and flush them down the toilet. For the most part her rebellions went unnoticed. But the piano lessons were another matter.

She could not find a voice for the terror she felt when Sister Gabriella first told her to sit down and play. There was no way for Maddy to explain to the unsympathetic headmistress that she had killed her mother and lost her father by playing the piano. When the sisters convinced the anguished child that she must play or suffer unrelenting punishments, she capitulated. But she deliberately played badly, using her skill to turn the music into noise. The look of suffering on Sister Edwina's face was her only comfort.

She took her lesson at four o'clock on Thursday afternoons, and it was supposed to last for one hour. Luckily, half an hour was generally all that Sister Edwina could bear, and rather than escort her to the library where the other borders remained confined until time for evening prayers, Sister Edwina just instructed Maddy to "go join the others."

The first time this happened Maddy dawdled in the hallway for the better part of half an hour, knowing that she was not expected until five. To her amazement, no one asked her any questions when she slipped into the dreary room where the other boarders sat reading and working. She realized that as long as she showed up to study hall before vespers at six o'clock, the nun in charge did not know that Maddy was not at her piano lesson, and no one else knew she was not in the library. For over an hour, once a week, she was free.

At first she spent her stolen time in the small powder room underneath the stairs, hiding and reading a Bobbsey Twins novel left behind by a former boarder. When she finished that book, she became bolder. Maddy had the convent to herself, as long as she kept away from the library and the sisters' sleeping quarters. She would creep from room to room, not disturbing anything, just exploring and relishing her solitude.

Today it took her just five minutes to reach her goal: the kitchen. She took a full twenty seconds to open the door, moving the iron handle in minuscule increments, making sure it didn't squeak. Once inside, she walked around with practiced, silent steps, delighted just to be where she shouldn't be.

She saw the cookie jar on a high shelf and decided it was well out of reach, so she decided to investigate the small room next to the kitchen. It was full of white linen bags, each one half as big as herself. She cautiously peeked into the closest one. Laundry.

At the other end of the tiny room she saw a heavy wooden door, gray with age. A sliding bolt across the center kept it securely shut. Maddy stared at it in fascination. What was behind that door?

She checked the time. She had a good twenty minutes before she had to be back. Heart pounding, she reached up and tugged at the bolt. Once released, it slid easily to the side. She turned the handle. The door swung open.

She found herself looking out into the service alley that ran between the convent and the building next door. The door led outside. It was a door to the world. She could feel the cool autumn air brushing her face, tempting her to step out. Dare she? Dare she?

She took a few timid steps toward the street, then remembered to turn back and shut the door to the laundry room, checking first that she would still be able to open it from the outside. This accomplished, she took a deep breath, and ran.

She stopped when she reached the edge of the alley. She knew that six blocks away, straight down Eighty-sixth Street, was Central Park. And she would go there. But not today. She didn't want to risk discovery, and she didn't have much time.

Ten minutes later she was in the library. The thoughts in her head had nothing to do with the history book in front of her. The boldness of her plan made her shiver with anticipation, but she could wait. One of the things she'd learned during the past year was patience.

It was three weeks before she was able to antagonize Sister Edwina into cutting her piano lesson to a mere twenty minutes. By four-thirty she was on the street, skipping happily toward Central Park, with almost ninety minutes to spend any way she wished.

As she approached the park, she saw a crowd gathering on the lawn just inside the park's entrance. Several people were waving signs, and one person seemed to be getting attention by shouting some sort of slogan, which was greeted with roars of approval.

Maddy edged closer, curious but cautious. She read two of the placards. One read, No More War in big red letters. Another read, Don't Sacrifice Our Sons.

On the outskirts of the crowd she saw a girl with thick, fiery red hair, who looked to be about her own age. The girl also wore a parochial school uniform, though hers consisted of a green plaid skirt, white blouse, and green sweater. She sat on a large rock, scribbling furiously on the page of a notebook. Every few seconds she paused, looked back at the crowd, then started writing again. When she stopped to listen she would stick the end of her pencil between her teeth. Having had her wrist slapped with a ruler for absentmindedly engaging in the identical habit, Maddy was immediately envious. Her curiosity got the best of her.

"Hello," Maddy said when she got within talking distance.

The girl lifted her head. "Hi. Isn't this just the keenest thing you ever saw?"

Maddy looked over again at the crowd, which now seemed to number close to fifty people, most of them women. One woman was standing on a wooden crate, talking about the death of her sons in a war in Europe. Around her chest she wore a silk banner, emblazoned with the words MOTHERS AGAINST WAR.

"What's all this about?" she inquired.

"Just a sec," the girl answered, still writing. When she finished the sentence, she looked up again.

"It's a protest, to tell people like President Roosevelt that we should mind our own business if there ends up being another war in Europe. You know, people who don't think that what Hitler and Mussolini do is our problem."

"What's not our problem?"

"Hey," the girl responded, eyes alight with interest. "Where are you from, anyway? You talk just like Vivien Leigh."

"Do I?" Maddy had never seen a movie featuring Vivien Leigh, but she'd seen her picture in a movie magazine left behind by one of the day students.

"Sure. Are you English like her? I should interview you. What's your name?"

"Wait," Maddy said, both embarrassed and pleased at the attention she was receiving from this outgoing American. "I'm not English. I'm from Shanghai. And I don't know anything about any war in Europe, although there was a war going on in Shanghai when I left . . ."

Her words trailed off into silence as she thought about what the war in Shanghai had cost her. Her father sent her to New York with Amelia because he blamed her for Martha's death. And why shouldn't he? It *was* her fault. If she hadn't asked for that doll, her mother would still be alive. Maddy regretted having started this conversation, but her engaging companion gave her no chance to retreat.

"Shanghai? You mean, Shanghai, *China* Shanghai? You must be kidding. You don't look Chinese."

"There are loads of people in Shanghai who aren't Chinese." It didn't seem to matter where you were from in Shanghai; there you were either Chinese, or you weren't. She assumed it must be the same here in America. One was American, or one wasn't. She knew she wasn't, or rather, she knew that she didn't want to be, if for no other reason than Amelia was an American. Then what was she? French was the language most often spoken at her home in Shanghai, and she'd attended a French school, where French nuns taught her French history and began the day with *La Marseillaise*. Maddy quickly decided that French would do as a nationality of choice.

"I'm French."

The girl seemed doubly impressed. "No kidding? French? Do you speak French?"

"Bien sur, je parle le français."

"What did you just say?"

"I said, 'Of course I speak French.' "

"Wow. Now I *have* to interview you. I'm from Ireland. Well, not exactly. My parents were. We were all born here—"

A cheer from the crowd interrupted the delivery of her autobiography. The redhead pointed. "Oh, gosh. The cops are here to break it up. We better scram. I'm probably related to one of them, and if Ma hears I came to the park alone again, I'm gonna be blistered for sure."

The girl grabbed Maddy's hand, and together they ran across the lawn and through the park gate, out onto the crowded sidewalk of

Central Park West. Behind them police whistles blared, as the men in blue demanded to see a permit for such a gathering, and, shown none, quickly dispersed the crowd.

"That was close. I don't wanna get in another jam."

By this point the young American's slang had Maddy completely lost. "Jam? What do you mean? Why were we running because you don't want a blister?" she asked, wary and bewildered, but too curious to flee.

"Hey, you really are a foreigner, aren't you? Look. A jam is a scrape, you know, to get in trouble. Blistered is what my Ma will do to my rear end if she catches me in the park alone again. Haven't you ever caught a good whipping for something?"

"I see. Yes, I have, in fact. Sister Gabriella is very good at 'blistering,' as you say."

"As you say," repeated the girl, mimicking her accent. The look on Maddy's face made clear to her new acquaintance that she did not appreciate being teased about it.

"Aw, don't get upset. I just like the way you talk. It's really classy. My name is Katherine. Mary Katherine Anne O'Connor, actually, but I go by Katherine. Just don't call me Kate. Or Mary. And especially not Mary Kate. I hate that."

Maddy tried to take in this avalanche of information, then smiled and politely held out her hand. "How do you do, Katherine. My name is Madeleine Hoffman. But you—" she stammered, trying to summon enough courage to finish her own introduction "—you may call me Maddy. Please."

Katherine shook her hand. "Madeleine, huh? Wearing a uniform, too. So you're Catholic. Well, we have that much in common. Where do you go to school? Listen, let's walk this way while we talk. I found a dime in the gutter last week, and I've been saving it for a special occasion. I'll treat you to a soda at the Parkside Grill, over on Columbus. I mean, it's not every day I make a new friend from China, who happens to be French."

Maddy looked at her watch. She'd used up half of her time. She imagined the "blistering" she'd receive if she were late. She could say that she'd been sick in the bathroom. She'd probably get a beating, but no one would suspect she'd escaped. She decided to take the chance.

"That would be lovely. Thank you."

Katherine tucked her pencil behind her ear. This reminded Madeline of the question she was about to ask before their sudden exit from the park.

"What were you writing? And what did you mean by an interview?"

"Well," Katherine explained, as they headed toward the soda shop, "I'm a reporter. At least, I will be, someday. A journalist. A foreign correspondent. I'll travel all over the world, and write about wars, and people like Amelia Earhart. Now I only write stories for school. Sister Anne keeps telling me to make 'em up, but I think the real world is much more interesting. Like the newsreels at the movies. That's where I found out about Hitler."

"Hitler?" asked Maddy, more lost than ever. The word had a vague ring to it, like the name of someone she'd met a long time ago, but could not place.

"You know, the guy in Germany."

Maddy looked embarrassed. "I don't know anything about that. The sisters don't let us listen to the radio, except for the services on Sunday."

"Wait, you mean, you're at school on the weekends? You live there?"

Maddy only nodded, afraid that this fact, and her ignorance of world events, would mean she was no longer acceptable as a friend to a future foreign correspondent.

"Gosh. What did you do to get put in boarding school? Or are you just rich? I've heard of some kids who have to go to boarding school because they're rich. But mostly just the troublemakers have to go, from what *I've* heard. Are you a troublemaker?" Katherine's eyes shone with admiration.

"I suppose so," replied Maddy slowly, thinking again of the trouble she'd caused. She was responsible for her mother's death. That must be the worst kind of trouble anyone could get into.

But she decided not to talk about that, nor confess that she had, in the past, been rich. Being rich was not something one talked about. It was just something one was, and one knew it because one need only compare one's life to the Chinese to see what it was like not to be rich.

Katherine continued talking. "Well, I go to St. Agnes, up on Ninety-first. It's just a day school. Sometimes I go on reporting investigations, and tell Ma I had to serve detention, which she never doubts, on account of I really do have to, pretty often. So today I was lucky enough to get wind of this rally, and there I was, ready to scoop the story. And meeting you was gravy. What a great day."

By this time they'd reached the soda shop. Katherine strolled in, completely at home, and hoisted herself up on one of the round stools positioned at the counter.

"Hiya, Tim. A float for me and for my new friend here, Maddy. She's from China. What kind of float do you want, Maddy?"

Maddy paused. She didn't want to make a mistake. "Same as yours," she finally answered.

"But you don't even know what that is."

"Don't worry, miss. I'll give you the house special," said the soda jerk. His apron displayed the colorful remains of a day's work scooping ice cream.

"Good idea," agreed Katherine. "Tim here will take care of you. The best floats in Manhattan, right Tim?"

"You betcha." The grin Tim flashed revealed a tooth outlined in silver. Maddy was fascinated, but lowered her eyes when she caught herself staring.

Tim chattered away, dipping into the ice cream bin with professional ease. "So you're with Miss Pulitzer here, eh? From China? That's a ways to come for a soda, even the house special."

Maddy did not know what to say. She looked at Katherine for help. Misunderstanding her confusion, Katherine explained, "That's just what Tim calls me. Miss Pulitzer, on account of I'm gonna win the Pulitzer Prize some day. He probably doesn't even believe you're from China; he's always accusing me of making stuff up. But, I tell him, a reporter deals in facts, facts, facts, facts. Right, Tim?"

"Ab-sa-lootly," Tim placed two tall Coca-Cola ice cream floats in front of the girls with a flourish. "Betcha never had a float so good in China, eh Maddy?"

Maddy took a small sip of the drink. "*Sheh-sheh*. That's Chinese for thank you."

Katherine grinned with satisfaction and looked back at Tim. "See? What did I tell you?"

"You're one of a kind, kid," he said, and then turned to his next customer.

"So, where do you go to school?" Katherine quizzed Maddy, after taking a big swig of her own float.

"St. Mary's."

"Ouch. That's the worst. So you're one of Gabby's girls."

"What?" Maddy was both dumbfounded and delighted at the disrespect that Katherine's nickname for the Mother Superior conveyed.

"Sister Gabriella. One of her boarders. You know, word gets around. How did you get out today?"

"I snuck out."

"No kidding? You really are amazing. What grade are you in?"

"Fifth."

"Me too. Are you nine?"

"No. I'm still eight."

"Oh. Well, I'm already nine. But I won't hold that against you. So where are your parents? How come you're one of Gabby's girls?"

Maddy thought of all the lies she'd told the girls at St. Mary's. *My parents are traveling. My mother died in a plane crash coming to get me. My father is in Hawaii, growing sugar cane.* No. Something about Katherine made her want to tell the truth.

"My mother died over a year ago. She got killed in the war. A bomb. My father sent me to New York to live with my step—his new wife. She put me in St. Mary's."

"Holy cow. That's lousy. Can't you get your dad to come get you?"

"He doesn't want me."

Katherine looked astounded. She came from a big Irish family. Her own father died when she was only two years old, but surrounded by older siblings, cousins, aunts and uncles, she never much noticed the loss. Her mother was the matriarch of the family, keeper of a boarding house that sheltered as many family and near-family members as it could hold, as they made their way in from the old country and up the economic ladder in the new. The idea that someone in your own family could exile you to a strange country with a stranger was the most appalling thing she had ever heard. Her heart went out to her new friend.

"Well, my dad died. So we're both half-orphans. How did you manage to get out from under old Gabby's nose today?"

Maddy told the story of her escape from the convent, punctuated by frequent questions from Katherine.

"So how're you gonna get back in?" asked Katherine, finishing her soda and her question with a loud slurp.

Maddy, who had never in her life been able to make such a noise without being reprimanded, slurped the last of her own drink before answering. "I left the door unlocked, so I could sneak back in. I think I'll just tell them I was in the bathroom."

"Are you late?"

"I guess so."

"Me too. We better go." Bending over, she fished a dime out of her sock and laid it on the counter.

"That should cover it, Tim. Until next time," she called out, like a regular bar fly.

"Anytime, Miss P," Tim hollered back over the noise of the milk-shake blender.

"Hey," Katherine added, "can you spare a couple of extra napkins?"

"Anything for you, doll."

"Thanks." After grabbing a small stack of paper, she hopped off her stool. "C'mon, Maddy, I'll walk you back."

As they walked along, Katherine kept an eye on the curb, hoping, Maddy assumed, to find another wayward coin. When they were about a block away from the convent, Katherine halted.

"That oughta do."

To Maddy's astonishment, Katherine squatted down, and carefully, with the assistance of Tim's napkins, picked up a largish piece of dog excrement.

"What are you staring at?" she asked Maddy with a trace of pique. "I'm doing this to help you out, you know."

Maddy could not take her eyes off Katherine's meticulously wrapped bundle. "You must be joking."

"Geez, you act like you never saw a turd before. Look, this turd is your friend. When you go back in the convent, sneak into the bathroom, smear a little of this on the inside of the toilet, where the water doesn't really reach, then stick the whole little bundle behind the commode so you can't see it, but you can still smell it. This is fresh, so it'll stink up the place great in a minute or two. Then sit on the pot and howl. Be sure to flush it before anyone comes in. No one will doubt you've been in there, sick as a dog—ha, ha—for an hour."

"I can't carry that," Maddy protested. "I'll be sick."

"So much the better. If you puke, too, you'll definitely be in the clear. Maddy, if they catch you now, you'll never get out again, and I'll never see you again. The bathroom plan you were hatching was a good one, but take it from me, what you need is some evidence to back you up. This works. It even fooled Ma one time. It's not my idea, you know. It's been handed down, kid to kid, in my family, like a special family recipe. Remember," she offered Maddy the small bundle, "facts, facts, facts. Nobody can argue with the facts."

Maddy gingerly accepted the gift. "Well, if I do make it out next week, how will I find you?

"I'm usually home after school, at least for a while. I'll make sure to be home next Thursday." She gave Maddy the address. "It's not far. Just hop on over."

"Okay."

"Great. Well, good luck."

"Thank you. And thank you again for the soda."

"Ah, don't mention it."

Maddy watched for a moment as her new friend scampered off down the street. She looked at the napkin in her hand. Then she crept back in the convent, and followed Katherine's instructions to the letter. The plan worked perfectly, just as an old family recipe should.

FOURTEEN
NEW YORK, 1939

It was late in the afternoon, and Mrs. Margaret O'Connor was in the process of making bread for the evening meal. She peeled one swollen, yeasty mound of dough from the tin bowl where it had rested and risen for a second time, then plopped it down on the floured board set out on her kitchen table almost every day, at this same time, for the same purpose. Firmly and methodically, she pressed the air out of the dough with the heels of her matronly hands, stretching and pressing, stretching and pressing, until the dough was smooth and soft, ready to be shaped into two long loaves.

"Ma?"

Katherine's mother did not pause, not even for an instant. One could not raise a family of five children, make food for the family and boarders, see to the chores, and manage the house if one stopped what one was doing every time one was spoken to.

"Mary Kate, if you've come to help with the linens, we'll be usin' the rose set today. The gravy Mr. O'Leary sloshed off his plate yesterday stained the floral, so I had to change it. Not that I need more washin' this week. But people payin' good money for room and board are entitled to a clean table."

Katherine edged closer. "Ma?" she said again, ignoring her mother's instructions. "I have a problem."

"Well, we'll discuss it after dinner. At the moment I've too many—"

"Ma," insisted Katherine, her voice growing softer, not louder, "I have a real problem, and I think we'd better talk about it now."

Margaret finished forming the loaf, and laid it in a pan to rise. Without a word she emptied the second tin bowl and began the process again. A soft hiss of air escaped the dough as she began to knead the bread.

"So tell me. But dry the dishes while you're talkin'."

Katherine picked up a white ceramic plate, and started rubbing it with the dish towel over and over again. She had no idea what her hands were doing as she talked.

"You know my friend Maddy, Maddy Hoffman."

"Aye, the little one with such nice manners, who comes over on Thursdays. She's a lovely girl. Did she come today?"

"Well, she has a problem."

"I thought it 'twas you with the problem?"

"Well, Maddy is my problem. You see, her mother was killed by a bomb in China, and her father sent her away to live with Amelia, this woman he married, who Maddy didn't even know. And Amelia sent her to—"

"Mary Katherine Anne O'Connor," Margaret exploded, her plump fist hitting the bread dough in exasperation, "I will not have these stories. I don't care what kind've imagination yer teacher says you've got—"

"No, really, it's true," Katherine pleaded, rubbing the dish cloth on the now bone-dry plate in faster and faster circles. "I swear by almighty God—"

"AND DO NOT BLASPHEME IN THIS HOUSE," her mother roared, picking up the bread dough and slapping it back down on the table for emphasis.

Katherine winced, but did not back down. She shoved the plate and towel in the sink and ran to her mother, flinging her arms around the short, stout woman's waist, tears ready to pour from her eyes.

This took her mother by surprise. Mary Kate was not a crier. She was the youngest, and the smartest, of Margaret's brood. She had the sort of self-reliant strength that made her a blessing to a busy woman who was mother, father, and landlord to a household of hot-headed Irish. Wise as she was to her daughter's tricks and stories, Margaret was not immune to the seldom-seen sight of tears on her youngest's face. She relented, the anger gone from her voice.

"Sit down, Mary Kate, while I finish the bread. Then we can talk while we shell the peas."

Sniffing up her tears, Katherine sat silent in one of the big wooden chairs next to the worktable while her mother rounded up two more loaves, washed her hands, cleaned the flour board, and retrieved a bag of English peas and two bowls from the pantry. She handed one bowl to Katherine, who placed it in her lap and began to split the pods and dump the fresh, sweet peas into the bowl while she talked.

"It's true, Ma. Maddy was living in Shanghai with her parents, and then there was a war, and her mother was killed by a bomb. But then her dad didn't want her anymore, after that, so he sent her here, to New York, with this woman, Amelia, who didn't want her either, and she sent her to live with Gabby's girls, ah, I mean, made her live at the convent school at St. Mary's. And she's never had any friends here until me, Ma, and I think she's the best friend I've ever had. She's so smart, and friendly, and she knows so many interesting things. She can speak England English, and French, and she's seen so much. But you see, she sort of . . . well, she found a way to get out on Thursdays, and that's how we met. But now the door's locked, and she can't get back into the convent, and she's afraid that Sister Gabriella will make sure that she never gets out again, or that her stepmother will send her somewhere else, and we'll never see each other again. So I thought, maybe, you could talk to the sisters, or to her stepmother, because I know Maddy will get a beating, which she and I both deserve, but I just don't want them to send her away, and I'm her only friend in the whole world," she finished breathlessly, then fell silent, waiting for her mother to respond.

"Where is she now?"

Katherine leapt up, nearly dumping over her bowl of peas. She righted the bowl as it slid off her lap, and set it on the table.

"She's right outside, on the steps. Please come talk to her. I knew you would."

"Now just hold yer horses, Mary Katherine. I'm not makin' any promises, and 'tis none of me business. But Maddy seems a sweet girl, and if she's really been through all ya say, then, maybe a word on her behalf . . . but I'm ashamed of ya, for letting her come over here every week without the sisters knowin' about it. That's the cause of the trouble. Dishonesty always is, Mary Kate. I'll deal with *you* later."

"Yes, Ma," Katherine replied, all meekness, willing to accept any punishment meted out as long as there was some hope for Maddy.

They found her sitting on the front steps, forlorn as a lost puppy. Margaret could not help but be moved by the look of desolation on Maddy's face. *This is a child who has seen too much, and not had nearly enough love to make up for it.*

She sat on the step beside Maddy, and pushed a strand of her silvery-red hair back up into the bun she always wore while cooking. "I don't approve of how the two of ya have been carryin' on, Maddy. You'd never have been welcome in this house if I'd known you were sneakin' out of the convent."

Maddy's chin dipped even closer to her chest. She studied her fingers through half-closed eyes, unable to speak.

"Is it true what Mary Kate tells me, that you lost yer mother and yer father sent ya here with yer stepmother?"

Maddy nodded in silent reply.

"Ya probably won't believe me, Maddy, but yer father was just tryin' to protect you. Not that anyone could make you understand that, at yer age. So you're afraid you'll be sent away again, is that it?"

Another barely perceptible nod.

"Would ya like for me to go with ya to speak to yer stepmother? I'm not sayin' I'll have much to tell, but at least she'll know the truth about where ya been."

"Okay," Maddy whispered.

"Well, we best call the good sisters first. They'll be upset. And we'll have to make it over there quick. I have a full house to feed tonight. Mary Kate, run inside and get a sweater for Maddy here. It might be springtime, but it's not warm enough to be wandering about without proper clothes on. Then go dash around the corner and see if yer cousin

Michael's cab is still there. He could give us a lift before he starts his shift. You and Maureen will have to see to dinner. No, don't even open yer mouth. You're *not* comin'. Now scoot."

Forty minutes later Margaret and Maddy were at the entrance to Amelia's Fifth Avenue apartment. The doorman did not recognize Maddy, so infrequent were her visits, and he was not about to let the plainly dressed Irishwoman up unannounced. He rang Amelia.

"Sorry to disturb you, Mrs. Hoffman. There's a woman here with a little girl who claims to be your stepdaughter. Yes? Very well." He hung up the phone and pointed to the elevator in a patronizing manner. "You can go up."

Maddy started to bite at a nail as they rode in silence up to the penthouse. Margaret's heart went out to the girl. Such a small and dainty thing, and so lost.

Margaret O'Connor was not sentimental. She'd come from Ireland at the age of fourteen, with two older female cousins, and had worked as a housemaid for six years in several homes on New York's affluent Upper East Side before settling down with her Patrick, a plumber. She lost him when Mary Kate was barely two. Luckily for the family, her Patrick had always been a soft-hearted soul, and when his second cousin asked him to buy some life insurance, he'd done so, just to help the poor boy along.

Margaret, who at the time had berated her husband for wasting his money on such nonsense, took the proceeds of the policy and put it toward the mortgage, so when the Depression hit they were one of the few families in the neighborhood to keep their home. She packed the children and herself into three rooms and took in boarders. Some were relatives, some were not, but they all had to pay their way in cash or services to stay. Her two eldest boys were now in the merchant marines, sending home money and letters from around the world. Her third son was a policeman, and still lived at home. Her eldest daughter was engaged to a butcher. At a time when many families did not have enough to eat, Margaret kept her brood clothed, educated, and fed. She did so by using her God-given intelligence and common sense, and putting her own family's well-being ahead of everything else.

But Maddy, now, here was a child who needed help. Margaret could see in the girl's eyes the suffering she'd seen in the faces of young brothers and sisters left behind, in Ireland, before the war. It had been hunger in the stomach that had caused their pain. Maddy's starvation was of a different kind, but she was starving, just the same. Margaret could feel herself wavering in her resolve not to get involved.

When Amelia opened the door to her apartment Margaret looked beyond her. She noticed the fashionable, coldly sophisticated decor, the quality of the silk hanging from the windows, and the satin perfection in which Amelia dressed herself. There were no hints that the apartment was the home, even the temporary home, of a young girl. She made her decision.

"Will you please tell me who you are, and what you're doing with Madeleine?" Amelia demanded.

"I imagine we have quite a few things to discuss, Mrs. Hoffman, if you'd be so kind as to have us in."

Amelia gave Margaret a look of blunt appraisal. She took in the stout figure, the blue cotton dress, the graying hair tucked into a simple bun. She decided twenty dollars would reward the woman nicely, both for bringing Madeleine home, and for minding her own business. Now if only she could get the nuns to take the brat back. From the tone of Sister

Gabriella's voice over the phone, that might be difficult. Running away was not a small offense. Amelia was livid. The whole business was so damn inconvenient. She was about ready to put Madeleine on the first ship back to Shanghai.

"By all means, come in." Amelia stepped away from the door and into the living room. She did not ask them to sit down.

Margaret, who after years in household service was completely undaunted by the capricious moods of the rich and selfish, walked in and sat on the sofa. She held out her hand to Maddy, who moved, zombie-like, to her side.

The older woman's composure made Amelia rethink her own approach. Intimidation might not be the best tactic. Smiling at Maddy, Amelia took a seat across from the two of them.

"You must forgive my rudeness, Miss—"

"O'Connor. *Mrs.* Margaret O'Connor."

"Mrs. O'Connor. But you can imagine how worried I've been during the past two hours, ever since Sister Gabriella called to say that Madeleine was missing from the convent. Why, we had no earthly idea—"

"Oh, I can well imagine." Margaret noticed that during their whole exchange Amelia had scarcely looked at Maddy, much less inquired after her well-being. She tried to keep the scorn out of her voice.

"Mrs. Hoffman, Maddy has been comin' to our house almost every Thursday for the past six months or so. She and me own Mary Kate, who's just a wee bit older, have become great friends. They met at the park. Seein' her every week, I thought Maddy lived near us. Mind you, I would've put a stop to it right away if I'd known she was sneakin' out of the convent, but she must've been pretty clever about it all to go along this far without gettin' caught.

"I think it's fair to say that Maddy hasn't been happy with the nuns, God bless them and keep them, but St. Mary's isn't a proper boarding school, we both know that. And I think you're honest enough to admit that you'd prefer Maddy not be underfoot. I'm sure ya have yer reasons, but I don't think they've anything to do with her, for she's a lovely child.

"I'm sure the good sisters are quite upset about what's happened, but if she found the guts to get out once, she'll find a way to get out no matter where ya send her, as long as she's unhappy. I've five kids of me own, so I know a bit about children. I run a boarding house. It's a healthy, clean place. No drinking, no night visitors. The boarders are all fine, upright people, for I've me own family to think of. Maddy would be welcome. I'll charge you less than that school does, of that I'm sure, and Maddy will be happy with us. She won't leave. She'll be safe."

Amelia reached for the silver cigarette case that lay on the glass coffee table in front of her. "I don't think," she said as she lit her cigarette, "that an Irish boarding house is exactly what her father had in mind for her."

"From what Maddy's told me her father hasn't laid eyes on the child for well over a year. If it's her happiness he cares about, he'll not object. She can go to school with Mary Kate. She's a bright one, and got herself a scholarship to St. Agnes. You'll have no complaints about the child's education."

Amelia blew out a cloud of smoke as she considered the proposal.

"I suppose you have some references?"

"Aye. I worked for some of the finest families in Manhattan before I married. I'll give ya a list of names and numbers, and you're welcome to talk to the sisters at St. Agnes as well."

"That won't be necessary," decided Amelia aloud. "I'll ring up the convent and give my permission for you to pick up Maddy's belongings. But I want one thing clear: she's to come back here if and when her father shows up. And all mail goes through me. Am I understood?"

"As you wish." Margaret stood up, took Maddy's hand, and headed toward the door. "Well, we'll be goin' then. Good evening, Mrs. Hoffman. We'll be in touch."

"Don't make it too often." Amelia slammed the door behind them.

Maddy did not say a word until they were back in the elevator. Then she looked up at Mrs. O'Connor. "Is it true? Am I going to live with you and Katherine?"

"Aye, little lass. It's true," said Mrs. Margaret O'Connor, reaching out a calloused hand to stroke Maddy's silken black curls. "You'll have a home with us."

The happiness on Maddy's face was all the thanks she needed.

FIFTEEN
SHANGHAI, 1939

"The Chinese are an inherently dishonorable race, Mr. Hoffman," said the general, just before lifting another piece of delicately fried tempura from its lacquer box. He dropped the shrimp from the tips of his chopsticks into his wide mouth. When he chewed, his eyes closed slightly, displaying the sensual pleasure he received from each morsel of food.

Leo watched in silence. He'd seen the general slice off a man's head with ruthless fury, yet the man ate his meals with the elegance of a royal courtier. The officers of the Imperial Army presented a study in contradiction.

"It's certainly true," he finally responded, after sampling the sweet, hot sake set before him, "that the Chinese live by a different moral code. But one likes to think that there is the potential for greatness in at least some members of the Chinese nation."

"You sound like a Catholic priest, Mr. Hoffman. I had not yet seen the optimistic side of your nature. But I disagree. The Chinese lack the physical, intellectual, and moral qualities necessary to succeed."

"Their weakness before the Japanese has certainly been demonstrated."

The general took a swallow of his sake. His hand dwarfed the fragile porcelain cup, yet he held it as delicately as a flower. "If the Japanese had suffered such a defeat—which would, of course, have been impossible—but had their efforts to protect their homeland failed, as did those of the pathetic Chinese army in their defense of the Shanghai territory, then all of the officers would have killed themselves. Such dishonor would never have been tolerated."

"Now that's an interesting point," Leo commented, his brow darkening. "In my culture, suicide is considered an act of cowardice. It's seen as a way of escape. A selfish act, if you will, rather than one of atonement."

"Ridiculous. If one has failed to live up to one's duties, there is no honorable alternative."

"Perhaps. I suppose it depends on whether one considers it more difficult to die, or more difficult to go on living. Perhaps one who has betrayed one's honor must continue to live. He does not deserve to die, for only by living can he be assured of the punishment he deserves. Death may be a release."

"Not a very Christian perspective, Mr. Hoffman. For surely your Christian God would ensure the suffering necessary for atonement after one's death? Continued existence in this world offers the possibility for personal redemption. So is it more selfish to live, and get a second chance, or to die, and take the punishment that God avails? I find the Christian perspective on suicide distressingly contradictory."

"I suppose it is." Leo said no more. His private struggles would remain private.

His dinner companion was not ready to cease his criticism of the Chinese, and he returned to the original subject.

"Take, for example, the stupidity of the Great Wall. It stretches for thousands of miles, unassailable. And do the Mongols breach it? Yes. Not by force, but by exploiting flaws in the Chinese character. They merely bribe the guards to open the gates. This would never have happened in Japan."

"Surely not."

"And then there is this business of Chiang Kai-shek's relationship with this gangster, Liu Tue-Sheng. No Japanese officer would stoop so low. Our loyalty is to the Emperor, not some rich maggot. He strips the wealth of the peasants by selling them opium, prostitutes their daughters, then shares the proceeds with the incompetent General Chiang. Disgusting."

Leo was startled to hear the general discuss Liu with such candor, although he was careful not to show it. "A most unfortunate situation," he agreed diplomatically. "I'm sure there are many who would be pleased to see Liu eliminated. He's been a thorn in the side of the Japanese for too long."

"And now he hides behind the British throne in Hong Kong, sitting in the Peninsula Hotel like a pet dog," the other man hissed. "We will soon eliminate that problem."

Although Leo would've loved to know what plans, if any, the Japanese had to assassinate the man, he changed the subject, lest he seem too interested in the fate of Liu Tue-Sheng.

"I'm sure the British will be busy with other things, now that they've declared war on Germany."

"Hitler is a genius. He understands the value of the lightning attack. And his armies are loyal; he realizes that this type of loyalty is achieved only through racial purity and rigid indoctrination. Honor comes through breeding and heritage. That is why mongrel races like the Chinese are doomed."

"And the Americans?"

"The Americans will also fail. But they are not at war."

"No, not yet. But once this war in Europe gets going, they'll jump in again. The Americans won't let Hitler take France and England."

"You are German, are you not, Mr. Hoffman? Why do you not return and assist the Führer in his conquest? Surely a man of your talents would be useful."

"You're too kind, sir. My business interests have long rested in Shanghai. Given that the Japanese Emperor has generously allowed the international community here to continue its normal activities, there's no place I would rather be."

There was no where else Leo could be. He was alive but dead inside, living in a dying city that pretended to be alive. For there was no question that Shanghai was dying; the people of Shanghai woke in the morning and saw death in their mirrors. Yet they got dressed, and went to work, and drank and danced and played cards until the wee hours of the morning, just as if they had not seen the evil apparition. Silt began to fill the harbor, and trade with the interior of China gradually dried up, but the trickle of commerce that remained allowed those Shanghailanders who were unwilling or unable to leave to continue to hope that death would come tomorrow, not today.

And in this dying city Leo had an even bigger role to play. Liu's flight to Hong Kong gave Leo more leeway. He paid off a gambling debt there, arranged a mortgage here, and then tore up the note, later, after he and his debtor reached a convenient arrangement. By putting his debtors comfortably at ease and getting them out of embarrassing situations, he made many new friends.

The arrival of the sing-song girls steered the evening toward more sensual pursuits. Leo was not sure yet whether the general trusted him, but he knew that the cultured man enjoyed his company, and that was a good start.

Wading through the frigid silence of the early November morning, Leo pondered the general's comments regarding Liu Tue-Sheng. Would the Japanese try to eliminate his nemesis? What would that mean for him? Would he actually be able to join Maddy in America? Would he have the courage to do so?

He sent money, and wrote, and received reports back from the nuns, and from Amelia, telling him that Maddy was doing well. He understood that her refusal to answer his letters was the sign of a deep, unrelenting anger, and he could not blame her. His only comfort was the fact that she was alive. Maddy was alive, and he would be better off dead. Yet death always seemed to escape him.

When he'd promised to stay and work for Liu he had no clear notion of how long that would be, for he had no idea how much longer he would be alive. After no bombs blew him apart and he refused himself the luxury of suicide, he focused on retrieving evermore sensitive information, sure that he would be shot in the back by someone who'd realized that Leo had betrayed him. But no one seemed to catch on. Martha was gone, and it was his fault. Yet punishment continued to elude him.

What if Liu was assassinated? Would he dare go to New York? How could he face his daughter? He had killed her mother, then sent her away with a stranger. What if Maddy looked even more like Martha, now that she was older? How could he stand the pain of looking at that familiar face?

How could he bear to stay away?

Several blocks away, in the plush home of the American consul, three men were finishing up a totally different sort of evening. Charts and papers, magnifying glasses, and black-and-white pictures covered two tables in the library. The air was heavy with cigarette smoke, and the unemptied ashtrays testified to the lateness of the hour.

"There's just no getting around it," said the first man, a naval officer with leathery skin and a tobacco-and-whiskey voice. "Hitler won't be satisfied with Poland, and unless France and the Brits find some way to stop him, the Nazis will have the whole of Europe. The Japanese will rule the Pacific, and Hitler will rule the Continent. I don't like the looks of that picture."

"But the president's hands are tied. How can we go to war when we've got nothing at stake?" asked the youngest of the group, a blond gentleman in his late twenties.

"Nothing at stake?" barked the naval officer who'd made the first remark. "What kind of rot do they feed you at the State Department, Paul? What about freedom? What about the freedom of all of our trading partners?"

The consul intervened. "We know how you military men view the issue, Gerry. The problem is that no one's proven that Nazis are bad businessmen. With the antiwar sentiment as strong as it is back home, we're not at liberty to step in. For the time being, we have to find other ways to assist our European allies."

"And I suppose you're ready with a suggestion?" remarked Commodore Gerald Ballard as he reached for another whiskey, not bothering to keep the sarcasm out of his voice.

"Just look at what Paul has brought us tonight," the consul said, gesturing to the document-laden tables. "Look at how the Nazis attacked in Poland. Their strategy involves a tremendous amount of preparation, on-the-field communications, and, by some reports, a fifth-column network of great magnitude. We may not be able to get weapons to the British in the near future, but we can start giving them something vital. Information."

The commodore snorted. "I see," he said. "We're to find and loan them another Mata Hari. Only this time, instead of working for the Germans, she'll fight to save the free world, is that it?"

The consul took no offense. He'd not been in Shanghai long, but he knew that behind Ballard's bluster lay a sharp mind. He would catch on quickly, and his help could prove very valuable. "Paul has dispatched his responsibility quite well. He's carried the details of the Nazi invasion to every major diplomatic post in Asia. But the reports upon which his facts are based come from a myriad of sources, mostly foreign. And the State Department does not necessarily know what the Office of Naval Intelligence knows, or what the Army's Military Intelligence Division knows. The United States has no systematic way of gathering and disseminating strategic information. Gerry, you were asked to this briefing because you are the highest-ranking military officer posted to Shanghai at the moment. But I asked you here for more than just the opportunity to enlighten you. I need your help."

A raised eyebrow was the only response he received, but it was all he needed. The consul knew the commodore well enough to know that if the man stopped talking, he was intrigued.

Now the consul reached for the whiskey. He poured himself two fingers, looked at the glass for a moment, then set it down without tasting it.

"You've both heard of Colonel William Donovan, of course."

"Of course, sir. Wild Bill Donovan, the most decorated soldier of the Great War. Except for MacArthur, that is," replied the attaché. Ballard merely shot the consul a look of annoyance.

"Yes. Bill and I have known each other since we were boys. He's already putting a bug in Roosevelt's ear about creating a centralized agency for the coordination and use of secret intelligence. An organization that could assist us in the kind of covert operations and propaganda that will enable us to help Britain and the rest of Europe beat back the Nazis.

"It's precisely because we are *not* at war that Americans have more mobility, not only in Europe, but around the globe. That's helpful, especially for recruitment purposes. For if the president does give a green light to Donovan's idea of a coordinated central intelligence agency, the start-up time will be crucial."

"You mean, you're asking us to recruit spies?" asked Paul, delighted at the prospect of getting involved in some cloak-and-dagger intrigue.

"Not recruitment, really. More just the identification of possible recruits. And we aren't necessarily looking for Americans. We want to take advantage of our current neutrality to get into enemy territory and lay the groundwork. We need German nationals who understand the evil that Hitler stands for; we need French nationals willing to risk their lives to preserve their freedom. And, if the Japanese keep cozying up to the Nazis the way they seem to be doing, we'll need Asians as well. We need to identify people who can be our eyes and ears now, who can engage in more concrete activities later, should America actually enter the war."

"You're serious?"

"Dead serious, Paul. You and Commodore Ballard here both have a good deal of freedom of movement around the Far East. You're to identify potential candidates and advise me. I'll do the rest. You'll never get any confirmation of the outcome of any interviews, for obvious reasons. We're still at the blueprint stage, gentlemen, but the need for secrecy is absolute."

The commodore no longer wore a sarcastic expression. He spoke thoughtfully, as if he'd already sorted through a thousand different possibilities in his mind and discarded all but one.

"I think I know someone you might like to meet."

Leo stood by the floor-to-ceiling windows in the bar on top of the Cathay Hotel, staring out at what had once been the Chinese district of Hongkew. Now the whole area was called "Little Vienna," having been rebuilt by the 20,000 Jewish refugees who'd settled there since 1938. Most had traveled first to Japan, admitted to the country for reasons that remained a mystery to all but the Japanese. Then they were shipped out of Japan *en masse* and dumped into the burned-out rubble of Hongkew.

Worried that Shanghai would soon be inundated with poor Jews fleeing the Nazi regime, the Municipal Council, for the first time in Shanghai's history, instituted entry requirements. One must have $500 cash or proof of employment before the magic portals of Shanghai would open. The change marked the end of an era.

In the middle of the harbor sat an American destroyer, making a stop on its way back to Hawaii. Under the ship's lights Leo could see signs of the busy activity that meant the ship would sail out with the morning tide. It was the only military ship in port at the moment, but there seemed to be many there these days. Mostly Japanese.

"Always a striking view, isn't it?"

Leo turned to find the American consul standing beside him. He offered Leo his hand. "Nice to see you again, Mr. Hoffman. I believe we met at Victor Sassoon's event last fall."

As they shook hands Leo thought it unlikely that the diplomat actually remembered him. The event he referred to had been thrown in the consul's honor, shortly after he took up his post, by the richest man in Shanghai. There'd been hundreds of people there, and Leo said no more than a few obligatory pleasantries to the man while going through the receiving line. Something was up.

"How gracious of you to remember me, sir."

"Well, to be honest, you've come to my attention since then. Do you have a moment? Very good. Let's take this table. Allow me to refresh your drink." He signaled to a waiter, who whisked away Leo's half-empty gin and tonic. In an instant the two men were seated next to the plate glass window, and Leo possessed a fresh drink.

"Cheers," said the consul. Leo lifted his glass, waiting for the other man to start the conversation.

"Tell me, Mr. Hoffman, did you fight in the last war, or were you too young?"

"Both."

"Clever enough. Which side?"

"The losing side."

"And you chose not to stay in Germany. What brought you to Shanghai?"

"What brings anyone here? Money. Opportunity. Fate."

"Yet you've stayed, when many in your position would have left. Why?"

"I had nothing to go back to."

"In Germany, you mean?"

"Anywhere in Europe."

"I see."

"No, you probably don't. For one thing, I'm not German. I'm Hungarian. After the Communist Revolution in 1919, it was impossible to get a visa to go anywhere. The whole world saw Hungary as a sort of virus-laden body politic, capable of spreading Bolshevism across the globe. Those of us who did get out were not always welcome back."

"Ah, so you're a closet communist."

"Hardly," Leo snapped, more bitterly than he'd intended. "Though I knew some people who were, and things ended badly for them. No, I'm an apolitical beast. I came to Shanghai to make a large fortune out of a small one. I did, and I stayed."

"It's that simple?"

"It's that simple."

The consul took another sip of his drink and leaned back in his chair. "I know several people who think very highly of you."

"I'm flattered."

"They say you're a man of unusual talent, and very trustworthy. I'm looking for those kind of men."

"I'm not interested."

"You haven't even heard what I have to say."

"Sir, if you'll forgive my bluntness, there's a war in Europe and a war in Asia. War will soon engulf the world. The United States will not stay neutral forever. I know many people, and I speak several languages.

There's only one type of work I could do for you, and I'm not interested in doing it. But thank you for asking."

"Good. I would have been suspicious if you'd been too keen on the idea. Now please listen to my proposal. There are times in a man's life when he is asked to do something for reasons that go beyond his own happiness—"

"Someone made me a similar offer many years ago. It did not turn out well."

"You worked for the Hungarian government?"

"No. I was a pawn in the hands of men who wanted to overthrow it. At any rate, politics does not interest me, in covert, overt, or any other form."

"What do you do?"

"I stay alive."

"Why?"

"Inertia."

"I've heard many things about you, Mr. Hoffman, but no one told me that that you were a cynic. We're all going to die. The question is why go on living. For money? For your country? For your daughter?"

Leo's expression did not change. "What about my daughter?"

"I know your daughter is in America. I know you entered into a paper marriage with an American citizen days after your wife was killed to get your child out of Shanghai. And I know you didn't go with her, even though legally you could have. Why not?"

"I have my reasons."

"I'm sure. And I suspect they have something to do with honor, and loyalty."

"Don't be too sure of anything."

"Good advice. Mr. Hoffman, you've lived for years without a country. I'm prepared to offer you one. In September, President Roosevelt signed a special executive order making any foreign national of good moral character who joined the American military eligible for U.S. citizenship. The United States Navy could use you. Specifically, the Office of Naval Intelligence."

"Did Commodore Ballard have anything to do with this?"

"A little. He mentioned that he'd had some personal dealings with you. Said you're the kind of person people confide in, that a Father Confessor would come to you to clear his conscience, and he thinks you speak at least five languages. He was impressed."

"Too easily."

"I think not."

"What makes you think that I wouldn't just become a double agent? Sell secrets to the highest bidder?"

"Well for one thing, we know your first wife was Jewish. At least she would be according to Hitler with a maiden name like 'Levy,' even if she were Catholic when you married her, as it indicates on your marriage certificate. No one who knew you then doubts how much you loved her. I'd count on that to keep you from helping the Germans this time."

"And the Soviets?"

"We have to fight one war at a time, Mr. Hoffman."

"You do. I don't. I've fought all the battles I'm going to fight."

The consul tipped his glass toward Leo in a silent salute. "Very well. It's seems you really aren't interested. That's a disappointment."

"Thanks for the drink." Leo shoved his chair away from the table. Outside he could see the lights blinking on the American ship. *America. Maddy.*

Why was he walking away from this? If Liu found out and sabotaged this plan, then Leo would only suffer the fate he'd long deserved. He leaned back toward the consul.

"I'll need a passport. Mine was lost in '37, during the bombings."

The other man smiled. "I believe that can be arranged."

"And I want to leave tomorrow. On that ship. If I take my time getting ready to go, questions will be asked. People disappear in Shanghai all the time. Just let everyone assume the worst."

"Ah, there, you're in luck. I know the captain. I'm sure we can make arrangements for you to travel as my private guest. And if he thinks I've made a mistake, he'll just drop you off somewhere in the middle of the Pacific."

"That's all right. I know how to swim."

Leo's interviews, or "debriefings" as Captain Herbert Lewis called them, started soon after the ship reached the China Sea. He told the truth about himself, editing out only the two facts he thought worked against him: that he had taken the Cartier necklace with him to Shanghai, and that he was on Liu Tue-Sheng's payroll. But he told his interrogators everything else: that he came from a peasant family in Hungary, and had been adopted by a wealthy Jewish family in Budapest. He told them that his family had been killed in the Great War, in which he had fought for two years; that his foster mother had been assassinated during the terror following the communist coup; but that he had no connection to the Communist Party. He told them that he'd worked as a concierge at the Hotel Bristol until he was recruited by a Hungarian nationalist group. He told them that he'd killed one of their members in Paris, in self-defense, after he'd discovered that he'd unwittingly played a part in their counterfeiting scheme. And, he explained, it was that murder that caused him to flee to Shanghai.

"What happened to the necklace?" asked the lieutenant in charge of his interrogation.

"I don't know. I left it in the hotel room with Károly's body. I imagine Janos Bacso retrieved it, or the maid stole it. I'd left the country by nightfall."

"How did you get to Shanghai?"

"I took the money Károly had in his wallet. It was a considerable sum, in English pounds. Probably received in exchange for counterfeit francs, but at the time I didn't give the matter much thought. I had to get out of Paris, and I couldn't go home."

"And in Shanghai?"

"I was lucky. I invested what little capital I had and made a mint in the rubber boom of '26. So I sent for Martha. All went well until '29. Then I had to start over, so I got a job at the bank."

"And then you lost your wife in '37."

Lost my wife. "A rather stupid euphemism. Yes. My wife died."

"Is there anyone who might be able to corroborate any of your story?"

"In Shanghai, no. It's a very private place, and most of the people who were there in '26 left in '37. I suppose you might try to get hold of a man by the name of Lawrence Cosgrove, if he's still around, in London. He worked for an architectural firm: Leeds and Gates, I believe."

"And your second wife?"

"A casual acquaintance. She did me a tremendous favor, getting Maddy out. No one knew how bad it would get, you see, and Martha—"

"I'm sorry, Mr. Hoffman. I know this is painful for you, but we need complete information."

"Of course."

"And why haven't you tried to get to the United States before now? After all, you're technically the spouse of a citizen, and your child is there."

"I was afraid that if I applied for a visa, something about my past might surface. The possibility of being sent back to France for murder does something to chill one's mobility."

"I see. Is there anyone in Budapest we could contact who could verify any of this information?"

"I have no idea. Well, I suppose there may be someone left at the Bristol who remembers me. And there was a family friend. A Countess. Julia Podmaniczky. If she's still alive."

Later, in the captain's private quarters, the lieutenant presented his findings. "We'll know more if we can locate these people he's mentioned. But what if he's not telling the whole truth about the counterfeiting mess? What if he was in on the whole scheme from the beginning, and just bailed out to Shanghai?"

"What if he was, lieutenant? We're not looking for Boy Scouts. We're looking for spies. I'm sure we can trace newspaper stories about that counterfeiting incident. And that was a long time ago. He was twenty-five then; he's forty now. The fact he came clean about it says a lot."

"I hope so, sir. There's one more detail. He would like to go to New York and visit his daughter before going into training."

"Sounds fair. Did he say how long?"

"A week."

"You mean he hasn't seen his child in over two years, and he only wants a week?"

"Yes."

"Did he say why?"

"He said if he were you, he'd have him followed during that time to make sure that he wasn't making any enemy contacts, and he didn't want to put you to more than a week's worth of trouble."

"Good Lord. Well, he's either perfect, or a perfect fake. I'll wire ahead to have his sources checked before we reach San Francisco, but I have a good feeling about this Mr. Leopold Hoffman. I think he's okay."

"I hope you're right."

SIXTEEN
NEW YORK, 1939

On an unseasonably warm day in mid-December, Katherine and Maddy emerged from St. Agnes Catholic School, in the company of fifty other girls equally impatient to make their escape. Above the gaggle of voices and the busy sounds of a New York afternoon, the two heard a familiar voice call:

"Mary Kate! Maddy! Over here, girls."

Katherine stood still, squinting with suspicion. "Ma's come for us. I wonder what for? She never comes to get us at school."

"We'll soon find out," answered Maddy, with more trepidation. "Come on, Katherine. She's waiting."

A few quick steps brought them together. Katherine immediately noticed that her mother was dressed up: as well dressed as she had ever seen her, short of a wedding.

"Ma, what are you doing with your Sunday coat on? And a hat? And gloves? And those shoes? Has someone died?"

"Hold yer tongue, ya rascal," was Mrs. O'Connor's sharp reply. "Ya

have to see yourself home today, Mary Kate. Maddy and I have somewhere to go."

A pit full of dread opened in the bottom of Maddy's stomach. "Me?
Where? What's happened?"

"Here, dear, take me brush and run it through yer hair. That's it.
Lucky yer not one to make a mess of yerself, like my Maureen was. 'Til
she was thirteen she could find a way to get her face dirty in church, the
Lord knows how. You look fine," she observed, more to reassure herself
than Maddy. "Now let's be off."

Katherine refused to be ignored. "Where are you taking Maddy?"

"I'll thank ya not to be speakin' to yer mother in that tone of voice,
Mary Katherine Anne O'Connor," Margaret snapped back. She grabbed
Maddy's hand. "We're goin' over to Mrs. Hoffman's. Her father's sent
for her."

"My father?" Maddy squeaked.

"Her father?" Katherine asked at the same time.

"Aye, her father. She has one, ya know. And he's here, in New York,
and wants to see her. And don't go asking me any more questions, for
that's all I know. So we're off. I'll be home for dinner. And Mary Kate,
you help with dinner when ya get home or they'll be no dinner for you
'til Sunday."

"IS SHE COMING BACK?" Katherine shouted at her mother as she
and Maddy crossed the street.

"I SHOULD THINK SO," she shouted back, with a good deal more
conviction than she felt.

Margaret walked to the corner and hailed a cab. "Yer stepmother
sent a boy 'round with cab fare, and said I was to get ya to her place
lickety-split. Said yer father is in town and wants to see ya. That's all I

know, little one, but don't ya be scared, now. Maggie O'Connor won't let anything bad happen to ya."

Mrs. O'Connor kept up a steady stream of conversation, commenting on anything she saw out the window: hats, dogs, other cars. Maddy tried to listen. All she really heard was the pounding of her heart.

As they rode the elevator up to Amelia's suite, Mrs. O'Connor gave her another critical look, then patted her shoulder. "He'll be proud of ya, Maddy. Don't worry," she said one last time. In a moment they were knocking on the door.

It flew open.

"Madeleine, darling." Amelia dropped to her knees and hugged the dazed child. "Thank you, Mrs. O'Connor, for bringing her so promptly." Then she stood up and made the necessary introductions.

"This is Mrs. Margaret O'Connor. She helps me with Madeleine from time to time. In fact, she has a daughter who goes to school with Maddy. Mrs. O'Connor is a treasure. A sweeter woman there never was. Isn't that right, Maddy?" she finished, searching for confirmation. Maddy stayed silent, her gaze fixed on the man standing behind Amelia.

"*Bonjour, ma princesse,*" said Leo.

"*Bonjour, Papa.*" She did not move away from the door.

Amelia pulled Maddy into the room. "Thank you, Mrs. O'Connor. We won't be needing you until next week. My husband will be staying for seven whole days. Isn't it marvelous?"

"Quite wonderful." Margaret didn't know what to do. She didn't want to cross Amelia and then have the woman take it out on Maddy;

she'd have to leave the child there. "Don't ya fret none, lass," she whispered to Maddy as she bent down to kiss her goodbye. "I'll see ya on Monday, sure as there's a sun and a moon in the sky."

"Well then, ta-ta," Amelia chirped, practically shoving Margaret out the door.

Leo had not taken his eyes off his daughter. She was so beautiful. So perfect. And the spitting image of Martha, with his own black hair. At that moment he understood that he'd found the courage to come see her only because he had a commitment that would make it impossible for him to stay. He was afraid of this child: afraid of what she might make him feel. Afraid of what it would do to him to lose her, too. It was easier to pretend that she was already lost. It was easier to disappoint her before she could make her expectations known.

"Well," said Amelia, her voice dripping with feigned enthusiasm. "Here we are. All back together. What do you say we go out and celebrate? Come, Maddy, let's change your clothes." She grabbed Maddy's arm and headed down the hall and into one of the bedrooms.

To Maddy's astonishment the room actually looked like it might belong to a young girl. There was a soft pink quilt on the bed, and a collection of white teddy bears sitting on a small white vanity. Several new-looking dresses and a pretty coat hung in the open closet.

"Okay kid, here's the deal," said Amelia brusquely as she yanked Maddy's coat off and then pulled her school uniform over the top of her head. "You make believe you live here, and we'll get along just fine. You pull any tricks, and when your dad leaves, I'll send you to a convent in Wyoming. Clear?"

Maddy wasn't even sure where Wyoming was. She was still hypnotized by the sight of her father. He looked the same, except nothing was the same. He no longer loved her.

Amelia was still talking. "So this is your room. Don't offer to show it to your father, but if he peeks in, it's acceptable. Thank God he called me from the Port Authority, so I had a chance to pick up a few things. Enough to get us through a week, anyway. But a lot of decisions about your future may well be made in the next few days, depending on how things go for me. Do you understand?"

Maddy nodded. She understood nothing, except that she desperately wanted her father to hold her in his arms, and at the same time wanted to be somewhere, anywhere, other than where she was right now.

"All right then. Now, remember, good children do not speak until they are spoken to, and then they give simple answers. You live here, and you go to school at St. Agnes. That's enough."

"Don't you look lovely," Leo remarked as Maddy and Amelia reentered the room. "Where's a nice place to go, Amelia?"

"Why, the Rainbow Room. Top of Rockefeller Center. You'll love it, Leo. And Maddy will, too. We've talked about going there when your father got here, haven't we, Maddy dear?"

"Yes, Amelia."

"Well then. To the Rainbow Room it is." His genial tone sounded forced, even to his own ears. "Tell me, Maddy, have you ever tasted a Shirley Temple?"

Hours later, after cocktails and dinner and a long carriage ride in Central Park, Leo and Amelia tucked Maddy into bed, as if she really lived there, as if the two adults with her were really mother and father to her.

Amelia could not wait to be alone with Leo. She, unlike Maddy, knew her role in the farce they were playing, and had memorized her lines.

"It's so good to see you again, to know you're safe," she cooed once she and Leo were back in her living room. "We've been so worried about you."

"I can't tell you how much I appreciate what you've done for Maddy. I know you never expected things to go on this long. Neither did I. But it proved more difficult to get out of Shanghai than I had imagined."

Amelia drew closer to him. "You don't owe me any explanation, Madeleine is a delightful child, and I would do it all again in a second . . . for you."

"Amelia, I'm sorry. I've had our marriage annulled."

"What?"

"It was a simple enough procedure. We were only married a few hours before you sailed. Non-consummation and desertion."

The tenderness evaporated from her voice. "But that's a lie. You deserted me."

"You have every reason to hate me, I know. I took advantage of your generous offer, and it took me much longer to get here than I thought it would."

"Hate you? No," she hastened, recovering her composure. "Of course, I only suggested a paper marriage to help get you—and Madeleine—out of Shanghai alive. Of course, I had no right to expect anything more. It's just that Madeleine and I have grown so close. I really feel as if she's my daughter. I know she'll be so disappointed, if she thinks . . . of course, I would never want to separate you from your daughter, but if you're going away again, well, can't we just leave things as they are for now? Can't we just," she moved closer to him, putting her hands on his shoulders, "can't we just stay married for a few . . . more . . . days?"

She pressed her body into his, and captured his mouth with her own. Elation mingled with her desire as she felt Leo begin to respond to her kiss.

"NO," Maddy screamed from the doorway. "It's all lies! She hates me. She never even let me live here. Not that I would want to! But she shut me up with the nuns, and they put me in a closet, and it wasn't until I ran away, and Mrs. O'Connor let me come live with them that I was happy, Papa. I was happy there. Please let me go back. Please let me go back—" The rest of her words were swallowed by her tears as she collapsed onto the floor.

Leo pushed Amelia away from him, started toward Maddy, then looked back. Amelia averted her eyes, but it was already too late. Leo had seen all he needed to see. Her hatred for Maddy had surfaced long enough for him to know that his daughter was telling the truth.

"Leo," Amelia implored, as he bent to pick up Maddy, "she's jealous, that's all. She doesn't want to share you."

"She won't have to." Then they were gone.

Amelia stood alone in the room, stunned into silence. Over two years of waiting. Over two years of planning, fretting, and longing, all for nothing. She'd had him, she could feel it. But the brat couldn't leave well enough alone.

With shaking hands she lit a cigarette and walked into what had briefly been Maddy's room. She yanked one docile white bear off the vanity and threw it savagely against the wall. She hammered her fist into the face of another, hitting it until both china eyes were crushed and the seams had split. Then she took her cigarette and buried it in the bear's nose.

After she'd cried, and was well on her way to becoming quite drunk, she propped the burned and broken bear up in front of her and made herself a promise. Madeleine Hoffman would pay for this. Somehow, someday. The little bitch would pay.

Mrs. O'Connor was startled by the knock on her front door. The boarders came and went as they pleased until ten o'clock. Surely it wasn't that late. She checked the old clock on the kitchen wall. It was just past nine. Her youngest son was a policeman; any unexpected nighttime visitor sent an instant alert throughout her maternal nervous system. She wrapped her shawl around her housecoat and said a silent prayer as she hustled to the door.

To her bewilderment she found Leo standing there in his shirt-sleeves. He was carrying Maddy, asleep in his arms, wrapped in the jacket of his suit.

"May I please come in?"

Mrs. O'Connor recovered from the brief paralysis caused by the split reactions of surprise and relief. "Of course, sir. You must be freezing. Come lay the little lass in bed. 'Tis this way."

Leo followed the rumpled figure down a narrow hallway to the left, and then to a small room at the rear of the house. Katherine was already asleep, a warm woolen blanket pulled right up under her chin.

"Put her here," Mrs. O'Connor whispered, pulling down the covers next to Katherine. Leo did as he was told, bending low to lay his daughter down carefully, then covering her with the blanket. She mumbled something but did not wake. Brushing his child's tangled hair away from her face, Leo planted a gentle kiss on her forehead.

"This way," whispered his hostess. She was impressed by his way with Maddy. And, she had to admit, by how uncommonly good-looking the man was, with all that black hair and those eyes. Why, she didn't think she'd ever seen such a handsome man in all her life: not in this country, or in Ireland, either. He didn't seem like the cold, uncaring parent she'd imagined him to be. There was a story here, and she was determined to hear it.

"Now please," Margaret said as they sat down in the kitchen, no longer whispering but still speaking softly, "tell me why it is that Maddy's back here, and not at Mrs. Hoffman's . . . I mean, yer apartment."

Leo sat down in what he hoped was a sturdy chair. He looked at Mrs. O'Connor's face, and realized he could do nothing but tell her the truth.

"To begin with, Amelia is not my wife."

"Not yer wife? But Maddy said—"

"She was my wife, but only on paper. It was the only way I could get Maddy out of Shanghai. The marriage has since been annulled. We never lived together as man and wife."

"The good Lord spared ya something there, sir, if ya don't mind my sayin' so."

Leo gave her a sardonic smile, then continued. "You see, during the summer of '37, Shanghai was caught in the middle of the war between China and Japan. There were bombs dropped on the city. My wife, Maddy's mother, was killed."

"So that much is true."

"Yes. And I couldn't get a visa to get out of China, so Amelia offered to take Maddy to New York, to keep her safe. I kept thinking there would be a way I could join them, but nothing worked out until now."

As a member of a large immigrant Irish clan, Margaret was no stranger to the obstacles posed by visas and travel restrictions. That part of his story, also, made sense.

"I've written to Maddy often, but I've never received any letters from her."

"Since she's been with us, she's not gotten one of them. I can swear to it."

"After what I heard tonight, that doesn't surprise me. You see, I only received word about Maddy from Amelia and Sister Gabriella. They told me she was doing well. But tonight Maddy told me the truth. All of it. And I want to thank you for saving my daughter. For giving her a home."

Margaret acknowledged his thanks with a wave of her hand. "Maddy's an easy child to love. She has a good heart, once she lets it out of the box. I know she's not really one of us, 'tis to say she's not from the workin' class people. But she tries hard to fit right in, and we all love her for it. I've done her no favors, Mr. Hoffman. She's paid her way, and worked besides. We've been glad to have her."

"I know how lucky she is to have you." The irony of the situation did not escape him. As a child, he'd been introduced to a new life by a foster family. Now his daughter was having the same experience, by traveling in the other direction: down the social ladder. But maybe Maddy was getting what she needed.

"I suppose, then, that you'll be takin' her away from us?"

Leo stood up and walked over to study a faded botanical print hanging on the wall, his discomfort apparent. "That had been my original thought. I was going to send Maddy away, perhaps to Switzerland, to a really fine boarding school. You see, I'm only here in the States temporarily. My business will take me in many different directions over the next few months. It may be years before I can actually settle down. And that can't be helped. There are certain circumstances beyond my control."

Rubbish, thought Mrs. O'Connor. But she said nothing. Leo was not finished.

"The one thing that became clear to me, listening to Maddy tonight, was that she wants very much to stay here. I think I'll probably be in Europe. With the Americans. So it will be difficult, perhaps impossible, for me to visit."

He turned to face the plump Irishwoman. "You see, Mrs. O'Connor, I loved my wife. And when she died . . . I'm not sure I have anything left to give Maddy, except money, and I can do that from a distance. I think perhaps she should stay here with you."

Margaret stared hard at him, a mixture of reproach and sympathy coloring her scowl. "You're nothin' but a coward if ya leave that poor girl. I lost my Patrick ten years ago. Ya can't run away from yer pain, Mr. Leo Hoffman. So just stop running."

It was a moment before Leo answered. "I could give you some excuse. Something close to the truth: that before I can come back, I have to fulfill another commitment. But the real truth is that you and I are made differently, Mrs. O'Connor. I'm no good, take my word for it. And please, take care of her for me." He started for the door.

"But wait," she called after him. "Ya can't just leave. Ya have to say goodbye to the child. Good Lord, how will we find ya?"

"I'll be in touch." He closed the door behind him.

"Holy Mother of God," whispered Margaret O'Connor, her eyes still on the door. "The man has the devil in him, worse than I've ever seen it. If that's what lovin' a woman does to a man, I want no part of it for me boys. Saints preserve them."

SEVENTEEN

"Where's my father?"

Margaret looked up from the mass of eggs she was scrambling to see Maddy in the doorway. The child wore the dress she'd slept in, its elegance now diminished by many wrinkles and several splashes of mud.

Margaret thought about all the ruses she could use to put off answering Maddy's question. Breakfast. Laundry. The butcher had to be paid before noon today or she'd lose her good credit.

Maddy did not move. She didn't even blink.

Margaret turned off the gas. The eggs could be reheated. Small hearts broke quickly.

"Come and sit down, Maddy. Do ya fancy some tea?"

Maddy shook her head. She padded over to the table in stocking feet and sat down, with all the dignity of a princess royal. Then she asked her question again.

"Where's my father?"

"And is Katherine still sleeping then?"

"Yes."

"That one could sleep through an earthquake, wouldn't ya say, Maddy? And she may do it someday, if ya listen to her. She'll be travelin' to far-off lands." She fixed herself a cup of tea as she spoke, and threw in an extra lump of sugar. Damn the budget. Today she needed it.

Maddy sat, hands folded in front of her, as patient as a stone.

Margaret took a place across from her, adultlike. The truth would hurt, but it best be out. Let her get used to it while she had other things to do. Tears were best saved for the pillow.

"Well, Maddy, I'm afraid he's left." She saw Maddy's nostrils quiver, but other than that, she showed no reaction. *How much suffering can such a small soul take?*

"It's not that he doesn't love ya, Maddy. He does. These things are hard to explain, and even harder to understand. I know I've told ya this before, but he sent ya here to try and save ya from being killed, same as yer mum. He didn't know what a wicked thing that Amelia was. And ya know, people can't just jump from country to country when they want to. It's not like catchin' the bus uptown, darlin'. A person has to have special permissions to come in and out of another country. If you sneak in, and they catch ya, why, they ship ya out and never let ya back in. Or send ya to jail. Or worse. Believe me, we know about these things, we Irish. Your dad couldn't just come along." *So he says.*

Maddy still stared at her, immobile. *Please, Lord, help me make sense of the thing to this child. Help me find the words*, Margaret prayed. She'd spent the better part of the night awake, thinking about everything Leo Hoffman had said to her, trying to come up with some explanation to offer his daughter as to why he'd abandoned her again. A reason other than the fact that her father was a brokenhearted coward, too caught up in his own suffering to face his pain for the sake of his daughter.

"We had a good talk last night, yer dad and me. He told me all about how he had to ship ya off to America to keep you safe, expectin' to be able to join ya any day. And ya know dear, he did write. Lots and lots. 'Twas that awful woman kept yer father's letters away from ya."

That made an impression. "He wrote to me? He said that?"

"Aye, and it broke his heart you never wrote back. 'Not that I could blame her, Mrs. O'Connor,' he told me. 'Maddy had every reason to be angry at me. But every day away from her was an eternity.' "

Maddy leaned forward. "He said that?"

God forgive me. "That he did. And he said he'd thought he'd take ya to Switzerland, in Europe, but he could tell from talkin' to ya last night that you wanted to be here with us. So that's what's going to happen, while he's away."

"But where is he, Mrs. O'Connor?" Now the tears appeared, quickly filling her eyes and then trickling down her face. "Where did he go? Why did he leave?"

Margaret steeled herself. From what she could piece together, after sifting through every word Leo had said, the story she was about to tell Maddy could be something like the truth.

"It's a complicated business. Ya see, America is a marvelous place. And all over the world, people dream about comin' here to live. But if they let everyone in who wanted to be here, why, soon we'd be living like chickens in a hen house, one on top of the other, scratchin' around for food and water and nobody happy about it.

"But knowin' that so many people do want to come to America, sometimes the men runnin' this country will put out a sort of 'help wanted' sign. That's what happened back in the 1860s, when America was fightin' the Civil War. You've studied about that, haven't ya? In school?"

Transfixed, Maddy nodded.

"Well, back then, an able-bodied Irishman could come to America, and become a citizen Maddy, meaning he could vote and bring in family and really make a life here, if he just agreed to fight for a couple of years in the Union Army, to beat the Confederates. So, many did." *And they mostly died. She'll figure that part out soon enough.*

"But we aren't at war now. There's no Civil War. We're not even fighting Hitler. Why would the government want my father to do that? Anything like that?"

Margaret could hear the panic in the child's voice. She reached across the table and patted her hand. "Well, we're not fighting Hitler yet. But in sneaky ways, we're tryin' to help our friends in Europe. Yer dad's going to Europe with the Americans who are already there. Same thing happened last time, you know. Americans joined up with Canadian troops and jumped in early to fight the Kaiser."

Maddy appeared to be sorting all of this information out in her mind. "And that's the only way he'll be allowed to stay here with us? If he goes to fight in the war first?"

"Aye, lass. That's the situation. Now, there, don't be cryin'. Yer father is a brave man. To think, he's willin' to be a soldier if it means he can come home to you."

She got up and moved around to where Maddy now lay, arms crossed, head down, her shoulders shaking with sobs. "But what if he dies?" she managed to wail. "What good will it have done then, Mrs. O'Connor?"

Margaret stroked her back. "He won't die, lass. He might not even be in the real fightin', a man as smart as yer dad. He'll likely have one of them desk jobs, helping soldiers keep track of their shoe laces and such."

"What about soldiers and shoe laces?" Katherine stormed into the kitchen. "What happened last night? Maddy, why are you crying? What's going on?"

For once Margaret O'Connor was glad her daughter acted like a bulldog with a bone when it came to getting an answer to a question. "Maddy will tell ya all about it, Mary Kate. Now, go wash yer face, dear. That's a love. I've a house full of people who'll be wakin' up and expectin' a meal in less time than I care to think about. And you two need to be gettin' ready for school."

Leo stared up at the gilt and paneled ceiling, his head supported by the generous volume of several goose-down pillows, and tried to remember where he was. *Oh yes. The suite at the Waldorf. New York. Amelia.*

Maddy.

He sat up. The gin he'd consumed the night before began to exact its punishment. What time was it? He squinted through bloodshot eyes, trying to focus on the clock sitting on the mantelpiece across the room. Only eleven. He still had a few hours.

First he had to make a phone call.

The girls of St. Agnes piled out the double oak doors of the school's main entrance at precisely three o'clock, cascading like a blue-and-white waterfall down the stone steps and out into the street. Maddy and Katherine walked down the stairs together, both lost in thought, both sure they were thinking about the same thing. Neither looked up until a slightly older girl stopped in her tracks near the bottom of the stairs, forcing Maddy and Katherine to pull up short.

The girl pointed at a man waiting on the sidewalk a few feet from where the parade of girls began to fan out in different directions.

"Who's that?" she asked loudly, her question aimed at no one in particular. "He looks like Gary Cooper."

"Maddy, it's him." Katherine whispered, not taking her eyes off Leo.

The older girl turned and faced them. "It's who?"

"That's my father," Maddy answered.

"It is?" The older girl looked skeptical. "I didn't think you even had a father. Everyone says—"

"JUST SHUT UP." Katherine shoved her red head up into the taller girl's startled face. "Don't go repeating stupid stories when you don't even know the FACTS."

"Okay, okay. Calm down, you little heathen."

Maddy ignored them. She just stared at her father. He looked back at her. They both seemed afraid to move.

"Go on." Katherine bumped Maddy with a shoulder. "He's not here to see me. I'll take your books."

Leo watched as Maddy handed her books to her friend then walked toward him, every step laden with uncertainty. She looked so much like Martha. The resemblance was killing him.

She stopped when she was still a few feet away, eyes wary, and Leo had the sense that if he moved too suddenly she might flee. Not that he would blame her if she did.

"*Bonjour, ma princesse.*"

He thought he saw something like joy flicker through her eyes before they filled again with suspicion. "Mrs. O'Connor said you were gone."

"Well, I was able to get a little more time before I have to leave. I thought we might go for a walk now, if you like."

Maddy glanced back at Katherine, who gave her a look clearly communicating, *what are you waiting for?* She turned back to Leo.

"I have a lot of homework"

"We'll make sure you have time to do it all."

"I usually help Mrs. O'Connor with dinner on Tuesdays."

"I asked her permission to take you out this afternoon."

"You did?"

He knelt down, as close as he dared get to her. "Yes, Maddy, I did. And I'd like to spend time with you every day, if you like, until after Christmas. We can go to for a walk in the park, or to the zoo, or even shopping at one of the department stores."

She flinched. "No shopping."

How could he be so stupid? Martha died the last time they went shopping. "Right you are. No shopping. How about I help you and Mrs. O'Connor make dinner?"

To his relief, Maddy laughed. "You can't cook."

He stood up. "Oh yes, I can. I can make Chinese chicken and rice. And roast beef."

"Biscuits?"

"Maybe you'll have to show me how to make biscuits."

She gave him another look of amused skepticism, then popped out with, "Can we go to the movies?"

"Sure. Do you go to the movies a lot?"

"No. Only sometimes. But I love to go."

"Then let's go. We can go to a movie now, if you want."

"Can Katherine come?"

"Today?"

Maddy hesitated. "Well, maybe tomorrow. Maybe we could be together, just the two of us, today."

Leo smiled down at his daughter. He held out his hand. She looked at it for a fraction of a moment. It was the longest moment of Leo's entire life.

Then she put her little gloved hand in his.

He began to walk, keeping his stride short to keep pace with hers. "What movie would you like to see?"

"Not a war movie." She looked up at him. "Mrs. O'Connor said that you left last night because you have to go and fight in the war. She said that even though the Americans aren't in the war, that they're trying to help the British people, so that some soldiers are going over to Europe, and that the only way that you'd be allowed to stay here in America with us is if you first go help out in the war. She said it was just like when some of the people in her family first came to this country in the American Civil War. When they first came, she said, right off their boats, they had to leave to go fight in the Union Army if they wanted to come back and live in New York. Is that true? Do you have to go fight?"

Thank you, Mrs. O'Connor. "Yes, that's all true. I do have to go help out in the war before I can come back to live in New York with you."

Her voice dropped to a whisper. "But what if you die?"

Leo knelt down again and cupped her small face in his hands. His love for his child surged within him, like a lion roaring a challenge to the sun.

"Maddy, my little love, I'm not going to die. I'm going to help the British and the French beat the Nazis. And in two years, I will come home, and we will live together. And I'll make sure that you are never, never alone again."

Her frightened eyes searched his, looking for the reassurance she needed. She must have seen something there that helped, for at last she whispered, "Okay."

"Okay." He wrapped his arms around her. "I love you, Maddy."

He heard her sniffle. "And I love you, Papa."

Leo closed his eyes and held her close. He would get through the next two years alive. He would get back to his daughter. And then love would give them a second chance.

DISCUSSION QUESTIONS FOR READERS' GROUPS

1. In many ways Leo is a flawed person. Did this affect how you related to him? Can you think of other literary figures who were similarly "morally challenged"?

2. Martha and Leo both survive very tragic events early in their lives. Do you think this had an effect on their attraction to each other?

3. Leo denies his Jewish heritage in an attempt to protect his family. What do you think of this decision?

4. Were the consequences of Leo's choices predictable?

5. Why do you think Leo sent Maddy off with Amelia? Did you feel that his decision was the correct one, given the information he had at the time?

6. Do you think you would have liked living in Shanghai during the 1920s?

7. Do you think Maddy was better off staying with the O'Connor family than going to a European boarding school to be closer to her father?

8. The author relies extensively on historical facts to help build the plot. Do you think she did so effectively?

9. What role does the ability to forgive play in the relationships between the main characters?

10. What parallels do you see between the political situation in China in the 1920s and 1930s, and some global trouble spots today? Is there anything to be learned from the experience of the European powers in Shanghai?

CONVERSATION WITH M. L. MALCOLM

The historical context for Heart of Lies *bridges two world wars and takes us from Hungary to France to Shanghai to America. How did you go about conducting your research?*

Well, I did my research the old-fashioned way: in the library. For the most part, the information available on the internet is pretty shallow, but what the internet can do is point you in the right direction. I read a lot of out-of-print books, eyewitness accounts from the era, and hunted down old newspaper articles stored on microfiche in the bowels of several academic institutions. The public relations department at Cartier's was also very helpful, even though I kept telling them it was a *stolen* necklace.

In addition to being historically accurate with respect to details of time and place, I wanted the turbulent history of the era to help drive the plot. All of the events in *Heart of Lies*, from the chaos after World War I, the Hungarian counterfeiting scandal in December of

1925, the manipulation of the rubber market in 1926, to the bombing of Shanghai in 1937, all actually occurred, pretty much the way I describe them. I just added a few fictional characters. And I did change the name of the police chief of Budapest, because in real life he sort of got away with the counterfeiting scheme, but in my book, he needed to die.

Where did you get the idea for Heart of Lies?

This book was very much inspired by my husband's family. My husband's maternal grandfather was born in Budapest, into an affluent, highly assimilated Austrian-Hungarian Jewish family. He lived there through World War I and its horrendous aftermath: total economic meltdown, invasion by the Romanians, and the massacre of thousands of Hungarian Jews. Leo's story reflects some of the struggles Dr. Gulton faced, although he was a successful industrialist, *not* a diamond thief.

Dr. Gulton, his wife, and their daughter (my mother-in-law) were living in Germany when Hitler became chancellor in 1933. That winter the family went on an alleged "ski vacation" to France and never went back. Although he passed away before I met my husband, I believe that one of the reasons Dr. Gulton left Germany so soon after Hitler came to power was because of the deadly anti-Semitic backlash in Hungary after World War I. He'd lived through that, and wasn't about to stick around to see what life would be like in Germany with the Nazis in charge.

While living in France, her parents had my mother-in-law baptized and enrolled her in a Catholic school to try and protect her.

They left France in 1938, again just one step ahead of Hitler, and came to the United States. My mother-in-law had to stay with a foster family in Chicago while her parents traveled to various cities and tried to figure out how they could build a new life in America. She was nine years old and couldn't even speak English. Although she was without her parents for only a month or so it was pretty terrifying for her, and that inspired some of what Maddy goes through in New York.

Another character that inspired the story was my mother-in-law's aunt, Melitta Braun. In 1941 she used her skill as an artist to forge a Siamese (Thai) transit visa for herself, her husband, and their child. She figured no one would know what it was supposed to look like. On the strength of this forged document they were able to board the Trans-Siberian Express, and then escape to Shanghai. Melitta and her family were even able to evade confinement in the Jewish ghetto created by the Japanese in 1941; they lived rather luxuriously in the French Concession for the duration of the war because, like Leo, they invented new identities for themselves. In fact, it's my understanding that Melitta's daughter was an adult before she discovered she had Jewish heritage. And I never did find out how Melitta's husband made his fortune in Shanghai: "import/export" was the only explanation I ever got out of him.

Eventually Melitta's family also made it to the United States because their daughter was a piano prodigy. They were invited to come to the U.S. so that she could study music after the American ambassador in Shanghai heard her give a concert at the *Cercle Sportif Français*, when she was just eight years old.

So I'd collected all this amazing family history, but I didn't really want to write a book about World War II. The pieces all came together when my husband and I visited Shanghai on a pleasure trip. The idea that for years it was literally the only place in the civilized world where you could just show up and start over really captivated me, as did all the colorful stories of the people who made—and lost—fortunes there. It was a wild place.

I wanted to write about the heyday of Shanghai, the way it existed in the twenties and thirties, before the Japanese took over. At some point I came across a story about this notorious Shanghai gangster, Du Yue-sheng, the head of one of the Chinese Triads, which were like the mafia families, only worse. He supported Chiang Kai-shek in rather nefarious ways, and that was the genesis for another part of Leo's story. I changed his name slightly (to Liu Tu-Sheng) only because Du did not speak English well, and his nickname was "Big Ears," which I didn't think was very villainous. But everything else I wrote about him is dead accurate, down to and including the description of his house.

How would you summarize the theme of Heart of Lies?

Well, I didn't intend to write a morality tale, I just wanted to tell a good story. But if there's any underlying theme I guess it would be that perseverance and forgiveness are both essential to living a decent life. Life is all about getting smacked down and getting back up again. There were these toys around when my little sister was a toddler, the Weebles. They were these little wooden dolls that had a round base, and they were weighted somehow so that they just couldn't fall over. Their slogan was, "Weebles wobble but they don't fall down!" That's been like a personal mantra to me. To live means always getting back up.

As for forgiveness, I believe we've all done things for which we need to be forgiven, and that the ability to forgive is really love's foundation. Not being forgiven is like carrying a large stone on your back; not being able to forgive is like carrying a small stone in your heart. Martha has to forgive Leo if they are to move forward with their lives. Leo has to forgive himself before he's capable of loving his daughter again. But forgiveness, both giving and receiving it, can be very tough.

Did you intend for Leo to be an admirable character?

I wanted him to be a human character. Sometimes decent people do rotten things, especially when it's a question of survival. When Leo is still relatively young, he loses the people he loves most, and he doesn't have a lot of moral guidance. Most of what he does thereafter is really just an attempt to create a life he can control. If I'm successful as a writer, people will connect emotionally with Leo, and, at least at the end, be rooting for him.

Do you think there are any lessons to be learned from the historical events you write about?

The opportunities to learn from history are always there, we just rarely do. For example, there are very interesting parallels between what's happening now, in the Middle East and with terrorism, and what was happening in China at the beginning of the last century.

In both cases Western countries took advantage of a power vacuum to stake out territorial claims; in China, after the collapse of the Manchu Dynasty, and in Arabia, after the collapse of the Ottoman Empire. Those decisions triggered a tremendous amount of resentment, which created long-term consequences. We're still paying the price today.

You've worked as an attorney, a journalist, and a fiction writer. Does one type of writing help or hinder the others?

Well, it's hard to say because I've done all three for so long. I wrote my first short story when I was six. I've written stories all my life. In high school I was editor of the school newspaper, and worked briefly for the *St. Petersburg Times*. As a lawyer, I was a litigator, or trial attorney. In some ways that was similar to being a journalist, because you have to be able to marshal facts quickly, verify information, and, perhaps most importantly, learn to accept criticism of your writing. Then I started working as a freelance journalist. Both those career moves also taught me the importance of meeting a deadline. I'd say good writing is good writing, so learning how to do it better in any context helps.

Heart of Lies seems designed to have a sequel. What will that book be about?

The sequel deals with Leo's career as a spy, but it's more Maddy's story, about how she handles the challenges she faces once all of her father's lies are revealed. It's also about the jazz scene in New York in the fifties, Robert Kennedy's efforts to confront the Mafia, and passion, adventure, and intrigue. All the good stuff.